Praise for the
MIRABELLE BEVAN MYSTERIES

BRIGHTON BELLE

"An entertaining series launch . . . Plucky, resourceful
Mirabelle Bevan is off on an adventure that calls on all
of her considerable skills as a linguist, arms specialist,
and connoisseur of fashion. This is a wonderful book
for those who like to take a peek at life in the 1950s,
including the mores, manners, and clothes."
—*Publishers Weekly*

"An entertaining mystery read—light, intriguing,
and ideal for a weekend escape. Bits of history
enhance the plot without overwhelming it, and a
handful of unexpected twists keep the reader guessing.
The main character brings to mind Nancy Drew
and Maisie Dobbs."
—*RT Book Reviews*

"Great fun. The world needs Mirabelle's feistiness,
intelligence, and charm. A real tonic."
—**James Runcie**, author of the
Grantchester mysteries

"Early 1950s England is effectively portrayed in this
intriguing mystery story . . . An excellent read for the
beach or a long flight."
—*Historical Novel Review*

"After many twists and turns, she finally unravels the mystery in an entertaining romp pitting her wits against underworld characters and scheming impostors."
—*Bookseller*

"Mirabelle has a dogged tenacity that rivals Poirot's."
—*Sunday Herald*

"I was gripped from start to finish."
—*Newbooks* magazine

"Unfailingly stylish, undeniably smart."
—*Daily Record*

"Plenty of color and action . . . will engage the reader from the first page to the last. Highly recommended."
—*Bookbag*

"Fresh, exciting, and darkly plotted, this sharp historical mystery plunges the reader into a shadowy and forgotten past."
—*The Good Book Review*

LONDON CALLING

"The story grows progressively darker as Sheridan delves into issues of race and class—not to mention loyalty and abuse of power—in this extraordinarily rich historical."
—*Publishers Weekly*

"Mirabelle Bevan continues to do very little debt collecting, but as that would make for rather boring novels, this works to the reader's advantage. Her second case takes her into the divided worlds of underground jazz clubs and missing debutantes, and the social and racial perspectives of the era are compellingly woven throughout the story. As a British historical mystery, this fits the bill."
—*RT Book Reviews*

"A gripping, stylish narrative that helps reclaim the 'cozy' murder mystery by consciously including the more uncomfortable aspects of society that it has always embodied under the surface."
—*Dundee University Review of the Arts*

"We loved the first in this post–World War II series, *Brighton Belle,* and the second adventure is even better."
—*Lovereading*

"A beguiling page-turner."
—*Good Book Guide*

"A thoroughly readable mystery with an interesting backdrop."
—*The Rocker BlogSpot*

LONDON CALLING

A Mirabelle Bevan Mystery

SARA SHERIDAN

KENSINGTON PUBLISHING CORP.
www.kensingtonbooks.com

KENSINGTON BOOKS are published by

Kensington Publishing Corp.
119 West 40th Street
New York, NY 10018

First published in the UK by Polygon. Published in arrangement with Polygon, an imprint of Birlinn Ltd, West Newington House, 10 Newington Road, Edinburgh EH9 1QS, Scotland.

All Kensington titles, imprints, and distributed lines are available at special quantity discounts for bulk purchases for sales promotions, premiums, fund-raising, educational, or institutional use. Special book excerpts or customized printings can also be created to fit specific needs. For details, write or phone the office of the Kensington sales manager: Kensington Publishing Corp., 119 West 40th Street, New York, NY 10018, attn: Sales Department; phone 1-800-221-2647.

KENSINGTON BOOKS and the K logo are Reg. U.S. Pat. & TM Off.

ISBN-13: 978-1-4967-0124-4
ISBN-10: 1-4967-0124-0

First Kensington hardcover printing: April 2017
First trade paperback printing: February 2018

10   9   8   7   6   5   4   3   2   1

Printed in the United States of America

First electronic edition: April 2017

ISBN-13: 978-1-4967-0123-7
ISBN-10: 1-4967-0123-2

For Molly

Every murderer is probably somebody's old friend.
—*Agatha Christie*

PROLOGUE

Society has the teenagers it deserves.

11:15 p.m., Thursday, January 31, 1952
Upper Belgrave Street, Belgravia, London

The kitchen smelled of roasting pans and spilled wine. The servants were in bed, and the family's plump ginger cat lay dozing in front of the black range. Rose Bellamy Gore tiptoed across the flagstones. With her parents' bedroom above the hall and a distinctly squeaky door handle, using the front entrance was far too risky. Rose slid the bolt across and eased open the door. Thank heavens it wasn't raining or worse—the smog made the whole city seem oppressive. She pulled her fox fur around her shoulders and with perfect deportment crept up the stone stairs, before cutting smoothly through the long shadows cast by the railings. The street was deserted. The white stucco porticos at every front entrance framed a line of rectangular black caves. Perfect for the wolves that lived here, Rose thought. The neighbors were ghastly—every one.

The gas lamps glowed hazily in the smog. Rose's breath clouded in her wake. Harry was waiting farther along the street in his racing-green Aston Martin, an eighteenth birthday present from his parents. Her gloved hand moved to her throat to check the pearls—her birthday present only a month after Harry's big day last autumn. The cousins were close. Their parents had hosted a lavish joint eighteenth party, which both Rose and Harry agreed had been insufferably dull—champagne and canapés and some dreary band Harry's mother had heard was fashionable.

"Chop chop!" Harry grinned, holding the door open and beckoning her into the tan leather interior. "We're going to be late."

Rose smiled. She slipped elegantly into the front seat exactly as she had been tutored, sitting first then pulling in her long legs before tucking the skirts of her yellow dress out of the way.

"I'm going to die of boredom if we don't have some fun soon," she said.

Harry started the car as Rose lit two cigarettes from her brushed-gold case, engraved with the first notes of her favorite number from last year—"Too Young" by Nat King Cole. Her father had peered at it the other day but the old man couldn't read music. He'd never even heard of the hit parade and probably thought the notes were written by Benjamin Britten or, worse, Mozart. Rose had already tired of Nat King Cole; these days she much preferred Chet Baker. She handed Harry one of the cigarettes. He took a deep draw, savoring the combined taste of lipstick and tobacco. Rose always smelled good, of L'Air du Temps, Earl Grey tea and hair lacquer.

"I'm dying for a cocktail," she announced, tossing her hair. "Something bitter with gin."

Harry was about to pull away from the curb and into the night when a female figure emerged from the thin smog—one with a familiar clumsy gait.

"Damn!" Rose snapped. "Do you think she's seen us?"

The girl was wearing an ankle-length blue cape. Her mousy hair was pinned up with a diamanté clasp. She gave a little wave as she homed in on the Aston. They had no choice but to speak to her.

Harry wound down his window. "Vinny!"

Lavinia Blyth leaned in. Grinning broadly, her lips were chaotically painted with orange lipstick. "Gosh," she said, "I was hoping I might catch you. I saw Rose's bedroom light and thought you must be going to some club or other. You two are always out on the town! The parentals would be livid if they caught us out this late and off somewhere, well, mysterious, wouldn't they? What fun!"

There was a moment's hesitation that would have indicated reluctance in the car's occupants to anyone more sensitive than Lavinia Blyth. Harry rolled his eyes and glanced at Rose. There was nothing to be done—they'd have to bring her along. Quite apart from the rudeness of leaving her, now that she'd seen them Lavinia could blow the whistle. Next time they'd be more careful. He jumped out of the car and held open the door.

"In you get."

Rose did not offer Lavinia a cigarette as they bundled together.

"Top hole!" Lavinia cooed, oblivious. "Are we off to Greek Street? Dougal McKenzie told me they dance all night in Soho! It sounds thrilling! I can't wait!"

She licked her lips, smearing the orange lipstick.

Harry eased into the driver's seat and flicked his cigarette out of the window. The orange embers sparked on the pavement. They might as well have a good time with Vinny, now that she was here. She'd probably be shocked, but there was nothing for it. Soho at night was a labyrinth of unsuitable delights. He expected Vinny might quite like to be shocked and, for his part, the idea of enlightening one of the famously straitlaced Blyth girls about what really went on in London's nightclubs gave him a thrill. Harry loved pushing the boundaries. He dedicated a good deal of his time to it.

"Right, ladies," he said, "there's somewhere I've been meaning to try. Hold on tight!"

And with that, the Aston pulled into the chilly January night. The youngsters were so self-involved they didn't notice the black Ford Zephyr with two passengers following them at a distance.

1

A scout is never taken by surprise.

8:25 a.m., Friday, February 1, 1952
Brighton, England

Mirabelle Bevan turned up East Street from the front, the wind forcing her round the corner so she almost lost her footing. Her hand went up to check if her hat was still pinned in place, which she achieved miraculously without losing the morning newspaper tucked under her arm. From behind the long Georgian windows of her flat on The Lawns, the winter sunshine had appeared deceptively warm that morning, though now she came to consider it the waves had looked choppy as they broke on the pebble beach. Mirabelle had had a turbulent night. She struggled to recall the detail of the disturbing dreams that had forced her awake, shivering and achingly alone, at two o'clock and then again at four. She didn't like to think too much about the war, or Jack, or even the events of last year when she and Vesta had gone on the trail of a missing Hungarian girl. So, instead of going back to sleep, she had huddled under a quilt by the window, distractedly wondering why there were no seagulls. Perhaps they sheltered under the pier. Checking her watch, Mirabelle noted she could scarcely feel the tips of her fingers through her green calf-skin gloves. She had walked in to work in record time. There was no point in dillydallying. It was time for a cup of tea.

It was set to be a busy day at McGuigan & McGuigan Debt Recovery. Five weeks after Christmas and the wages of Yuletide borrowing were about to be visited on Brighton's debtors. There had been a queue of new clients snaking out of the beige office and along the dingy hallway for at least some of the day on Wednesday and Thursday. Each client clutched unpaid invoices from the festive period. The agency's reputation was growing. Mirabelle sat at one desk, her sidekick and office clerk, Vesta, at the other as they methodically took down everyone's details. For two days there had been so much paperwork they hadn't had time to chase a single payment.

"At this rate," Mirabelle commented dryly when they left work the evening before, "we're going to need extra staff."

The thought of having someone to boss around clearly appealed to Vesta. "Fresh meat!" she declared happily. "Well, I'd like a handsome black man. Not just a debt collector—someone who could take me out dancing." She winked. "Wouldn't it be nice to have a fella round the office? We could extend our portfolio, Mirabelle."

Ever since the two women had taken over the agency a year ago Vesta had been trying to expand the business. She wanted McGuigan & McGuigan to take on commissions that were not strictly debt collection and more in the line of private investigation. Steadily Mirabelle had knocked back the ideas, one by one, and refused two cases, which although ostensibly about debt clearly concerned one family member looking for information on another or a husband trying to find out what his wife was up to during the day.

"It's not our business," she insisted.

"But we'd be good at it." Vesta was adamant.

Mirabelle, however, did not want to get involved. Cases fired by emotion rather than money were dangerous. For three months last year she hadn't been sure if she would end up in prison because she'd fired a shot that had killed a young man—a young man who was trying to escape and who would have killed her given the chance, but still. In the end she had been exonerated but it remained one of the horrors Mirabelle still dreamed about. Not last night, but sometimes. She was determined to lead a quiet life now. If the firm took on another member of staff she'd need to make sure that Vesta was still fully employed on the company ledgers or the girl would inevitably find something more interesting to do; something that would land them, no doubt, testifying in the divorce courts. Mirabelle smiled indulgently; Vesta was a honey and she was great with people, but she had to be kept in check.

Mirabelle crossed the street opposite Brills Lane and entered the office building. Her heels clicked smartly up the stairs to the first floor, but there she stopped in her tracks. A drenched young black man crouched in the office doorway. A small puddle of rainwater had collected on the faded linoleum around him. As Mirabelle came into view he jumped to his feet. Mirabelle noticed he was wearing extraordinary black-and-white shoes with red laces. He was holding a battered saxophone case.

"Miss Bevan?" he asked, his accent a cross between the broad vowels of London and the even more expansive vowels of Jamaica.

Mirabelle nodded briskly. This chap wasn't the kind of customer who usually turned up at McGuigan & McGuigan—he looked far too interesting. She was intrigued.

"And you are?"

"Lindon. I'm looking for Vesta."

"I'm afraid we're not quite ready to take on a new

member of staff. I don't know what Vesta has told you, Mr. . . ." Mirabelle's voice trailed off.

"Claremont."

Heaven alone knew what Vesta had organized overnight. Mr. Claremont, like Vesta, was only in his early twenties. If they did take on someone new, it would be far better to find an experienced man, perhaps one with a military background, someone tough who was used to getting the job done. Lindon Claremont smiled. He had nice eyes, and Mirabelle wondered how large a part Lindon's appearance had played in Vesta's recruitment criteria. *I bet he can dance,* she thought. Sometimes the girl could be impossible! This chap would never do—his whole demeanor was far too accommodating, and though his clothes were smart he was dressed like a spiv. Collecting debts was an intractable business. As Big Ben McGuigan used to say, no one wants to hand over the money. You have to be firm.

"Do you mind if I wait for her?" Lindon asked. "I mean, if I'm in the right place? This is where she works, isn't it?"

"Yes. Vesta won't be in till nine. I'm afraid we're very busy, there's a lot of work to do today. There really isn't anything for you, Mr. Claremont."

"I wasn't sure when you opened. Been waiting a while," Lindon continued. "I got wet, see. It was stormy around half five."

"You've been sitting here for three hours, soaked to the skin?"

Lindon shrugged.

Mirabelle pulled the office key from her clutch purse, and the young man moved obediently out of her way.

"Well," she said, "we can't have you catching your death. There's a towel in the cupboard and I'll boil the kettle. I want to be clear though. There isn't a job."

Lindon grinned gratefully. "Vesta said you were a kind woman, Miss Bevan. I'd love a brew."

Lindon sat by the electric fire warming up and sipping tea. As he dried, Mirabelle peered periodically over the pile of papers—debts she was putting into geographical order so she could visit to collect payments later in the day.

"Morning," Vesta called as she came through the doorway amidst a jumble of bags and brandishing an umbrella so battered Mirabelle doubted it would be of any use. "Double deckers are off in the high winds. The service is still running though—it's just slow. Sorry I'm late." She turned, clutching two greasy-looking paper bags, which it was immediately apparent from the smell contained pies she had picked up from The Pie Shop on St. James Street on her way in. "Beanos," she said delightedly and then, noticing Lindon, let out a high-pitched scream.

"Lindon, boy!" She launched herself into his arms. "Sweet Lord Almighty!"

Lindon rose to his feet and wrapped himself around her.

Mirabelle glanced toward the door. It was fortunate, she noted, that there were no clients in the office. All this hugging was not entirely professional.

Lindon and Vesta, however, showed little restraint and were clearly delighted to see each other. They launched into a conversation so fast, and containing so much slang, that Mirabelle couldn't understand a word they were saying. The sounds were almost musical.

After a minute or two of catching up Vesta turned Lindon around as if he were a child. "Mirabelle, this is Lindon Claremont."

"Yes, we've met. Vesta, I know we talked about hiring someone but really we need to chat about it. . . ."

Vesta looked nonplussed. "This one? This one? Pardon me, Lindon, but this one would be hopeless—completely hopeless! He'd end up lending people his own money! Oh, Mirabelle!" She began to laugh.

"But . . ." Mirabelle started. "Well, in that case, what is Mr. Claremont doing here?"

"No idea," Vesta grinned. "I ain't seen you, Lindon, since last summer."

Lindon nodded. "Must be about that."

"Would you like a pie? They're hot," Vesta offered. "They make these wonderful pies down here—beanos. They're a taste of the seaside. I haven't seen them in London but they'd go a bomb. Delicious!"

"I'm starving," he admitted.

Vesta handed him a beano before scrambling around on the floor and picking up her possessions. "I'll make more tea and then you can tell me what you've been up to. We got a lot of catching up to do."

Mirabelle glanced at the sea of paperwork strewn over Vesta's desk. "I'll need to go out and get started on the collections. Can I leave all this with you?"

"Sure." Vesta gestured, as if the mountain of paperwork could simply be dispersed by a wave of the hand.

Mirabelle reached for her coat and hat. She had done up the buttons and was considering whether, given the wind, it was worth even taking an umbrella, when for the second time that day Lindon Claremont made her stop in her tracks. His voice changed to a low register, and he had the demeanor of a naughty child, one who clearly couldn't wait any longer before blurting what was on his mind. He leaned over Vesta's desk.

"Thing is," he hissed, the pie uneaten in his hand, "I had to come. The police are probably looking for me. It's not my fault—I didn't hurt anyone. They was too fancy—I said that to the others. The police have found out I talked to the girl, I think, and now they'll assume what they always assume." He drew a long finger across his neck in a macabre motion. "I didn't do nothing. I didn't hurt her. I swear it."

Vesta froze. "Shit," she said. "What are you talking about? Who didn't you hurt, Lindon?"

Lindon's eyes sank to the drab linoleum floor. He

shrugged his shoulders. The boy's expression suddenly became difficult to read. "They didn't give no names. I just spoke to them. Young white kids. The girl, she was laughing, you know, chatting. Glossy they was, well turned out. Liked music. Liked dancing. She gave me this." He held out a gold cigarette case with musical script engraved on its face and laid it on Vesta's desk. His hand was trembling slightly.

She picked it up. "That is fancy merchandise," she said.

" 'Too Young,' " Lindon replied wistfully.

"Oh no," Vesta groaned. "I should have known! Too young for what?"

"Nothing like that, girl. 'Too Young' by Nat King Cole. The music on it. See." He gave an engaging smile and began to sing the tune, pointing to the notes. "She said she was sick of it and didn't want it no more. She thinks she's cutting edge, whatever. Hep."

"And then what?"

"She went off. I went back inside for a drink. Next thing I know, Barney tells me the police have been around the clubs asking about her. The girl's in trouble. She's hurt. Last place she'd been was with me, and now the pigs are working their way round, trying to figure out where she's been and who's responsible. I didn't do nothing, I swear, Vesta. They left. I never laid a finger. But you know what it's like. I panicked."

"You said she was hurt?" Mirabelle stepped in. "What do you mean hurt?"

"I dunno. Barney didn't say. But I got some white chick's cigarette case, and they're trying to figure out what happened to her. I didn't touch no one, but things don't go so well for a brother, not that kind of thing. Vesta will know what to do, I said. I walked to Victoria straight and got on the milk train. I mean, you solve mysteries, right? You're cozy with the law? You caught all them Nazis last year. You'll be able to tell them it wasn't me."

Mirabelle ignored the inaccuracies—the less said about last year, the better.

"It was really Mirabelle who worked everything out," Vesta started, "with the Nazis."

Mirabelle waved her off and focused her attention on Lindon. "Was it this girl?" she asked smoothly as she turned over the paper. The headline read MISSING HEIRESS and there was a photograph taken the previous year of a girl in a white ball gown and pearl earrings. The police were appealing for information.

"That's her!" Lindon's finger hovered over the picture. "Rose Bellamy Gore," he read, clearly sounding out the words for the first time. "Some name!"

"But it says she's missing," Mirabelle pointed out. She scanned the paper. "They don't know what happened to her. She's not necessarily hurt, Lindon, they just don't know where she is."

"That's not what they was saying last night," Lindon insisted. "Barney said someone hurt her. I thought she was dead!" He bit into the pie and chewed slowly, looking slightly sheepish. Perhaps he'd jumped the gun by making a dash for help.

"Well, she might be hurt, of course," Mirabelle mused, removing her coat and sitting down at the desk. "And that's the assumption, I suppose. Tell me your story one more time, Lindon. Tell me everything all over again."

Twenty minutes later, Lindon Claremont was beginning to wonder if showing up at McGuigan & McGuigan wasn't more trouble than turning himself in to the police. He had gone over the story several times, but Vesta's boss wasn't giving up. He'd told her about the damp bedsit in a run-down Georgian tenement off London Spa where he'd lodged for the last four months and the clubs where he played his saxophone. He'd explained how sometimes the gigs paid and sometimes they didn't. If the company was right, he drawled, he played free, just for the experience. He'd told her about everything he'd done the day before, how long he'd known Barney the doorman (ever since he started booking proper gigs in Soho—eighteen months) and exactly what had happened when Rose and two of her friends arrived at Mac's Rehearsal Rooms where he'd been jamming. Then he'd explained jamming and revisited the conversation he'd had with Rose about her favorite musicians—Tony Crombie, Ronnie Ball, Leon Calvert—some of whom Lindon had played alongside. It was difficult to break into the scene, he said, but his persistence had started to pay off.

"The girl—Rose—had seen me on the horn, but she didn't say where. Then she ranted on about Ronnie Scott, how he was only in it for the money, and then she said, 'And money's just too dreary, darling. Too dreary for words.' She called me darling but she didn't mean anything by it. Cut glass she was."

Vesta perched on her desk, listening intently as Mirabelle asked question after question. Occasionally she nodded but she let her boss get on with it.

"So Rose knew about music?" Mirabelle confirmed.

"Oh yeah. She knew what was what."

"But she didn't play an instrument herself?"

"Nah. She was audience but she'd been around every swing joint in town, even the trade ones—bare lightbulb and a bad bottle of whisky if you're lucky. She'd spent time. Asked me about Charlie Parker. Johnny Dankworth. We had a laugh, really. The other two was dancing but she wanted to talk."

"And she was drunk?"

"Yeah. She'd had some. That time of night all of London is drunk as a fiddler's, innit? She liked my shoes," Lindon said proudly.

Mirabelle considered a moment. Rose was missing, and, at the least, Lindon was a key witness. The boy was no saint, but the police would certainly need to speak to him. Until he'd turned in a statement, there was no other way to establish his innocence, unless the girl turned up in the meantime.

"Vesta," she said, "we need to speak to Detective Superintendent McGregor."

Lindon sat up straight. "You're turning me in?"

Vesta put out her hand to calm him. "Don't be silly, Lindon. It's not like that. Mirabelle's right. If they're looking for you, you'll have to speak to them in the end. And you'll be better off if you volunteer the information than if they catch you halfway across the country on the run."

Lindon bent forward in the chair and moaned. "Mama's gonna kill me if I get nicked again."

"Any trouble from your mother and I'll speak to her," Vesta snapped.

"Again?" Mirabelle enquired.

"Last year." Lindon kept his eyes fixed on the floor. "Drunk and disorderly. Happens to all the jazz boys now and then. It's like they got a room reserved for us at Savile Row nick—the jokers even call it the dressing room. Seems there's always one of us in there. I've been more careful since. It's easy to get carried away. I was stupid, but I was unlucky, too. They don't catch a brother every time."

"I see," Mirabelle nodded. "Well, it's time to see what we can do at Brighton police station, I'm afraid."

She gestured toward the coat rack. Whether she liked it or not she was involved now. Lindon's eyes met Vesta's. Should he comply? She nodded. "You got to sort it out properly, boy," she said. "Official."

Lindon let out a heavy sigh and got to his feet like an unwilling five-year-old. "Will you look after my sax, sister?"

Vesta nodded.

As Mirabelle waited she turned over the newspaper in her hand. She scanned the front page. Police corruption was so common in the Brighton and Hove forces she almost didn't bother to read the tiny item right at the bottom: BRIGHTON COP ADMITS VIOLENCE. When she did she turned hurriedly to page five to get the whole story.

"Perhaps McGregor can help us with more than one issue on our plate today," she murmured.

"What?" Vesta asked as she helped a reluctant Lindon into his mackintosh. The fabric was so thin she couldn't help worrying it would never keep him warm enough in this weather. Nowhere near it. She felt anxious but reassured herself that Mirabelle knew best.

"Aren't you coming with me, Vesta girl?" he moaned.

"One of us has to stay in the office, Lindon, and you're better off with Mirabelle. Think about it. Apart from anything else, two black kids turning up at the station isn't going to go down as well as you arriving with a lady. Mirabelle knows the detective superintendent. She'll take care of you."

If anything, Lindon did up his buttons even more reluctantly. He watched Mirabelle from beneath hooded lids.

"Go on then," Vesta shooed him.

As they left the office, she decided not to worry too much about Lindon. He'd been in and out of scrapes as long as she'd known him—since they were kids—but nothing as serious as a missing person. The police, she was sure, would take one look at him and realize he wasn't a criminal. She distracted herself from the niggling concern by fiddling with her typewriter. It was well past its best. They'd been talking about getting a new one. A fancy IBM Model A with a green case. So far it had been difficult to track down. Vesta sighed. She sat back a moment and peered at the newspaper Mirabelle had left behind. There was some ridiculous story about a policeman who had got into a fight over his dog. Surely that wasn't what she had been looking at.

2

I'm not against the police; I'm just afraid of them.

Brighton police station was a three-minute walk up the hill to Bartholomew Square. Emerging into the biting cold, Lindon stared longingly at the bright shaft of sea at the bottom of East Street as if he was thinking of making a run for it. Then with his eyes on the pavement he turned to the right and fell obediently into step. The wind almost blew them up to the station.

"They gonna lock me up?"

"Yes," Mirabelle answered honestly, glad the wind was at her back. "They'll probably take you up to London. The police who are dealing with the case will want to interview you. You're a witness, Lindon."

The pair continued in silence until the imposing station came into view and they climbed the steps and entered. The hallway stank of bleach. The floor had just been mopped, and puddles of water pooled on the linoleum. In the background, the clattering of a typewriter suddenly stopped. There was a burst of raucous male laughter.

At the front desk a potbellied gray-haired sergeant folded his newspaper and stood straighter at the sight of Mirabelle. She hadn't been inside the station since last year, but he never forgot a face.

"Miss Bevan," he greeted her.

"Simmons, isn't it?" Neither did she.

"What do we have here then, miss?"

"This is Lindon Claremont, Sergeant. He is coming in voluntarily to help with a London inquiry. He noticed this item in the paper this morning"—she unfolded the sergeant's edition on the high wooden desk and pointed at the headline—"and as he spoke to Miss Bellamy Gore last night before he departed for Brighton, he's coming forward to see if anything he recollects might help to locate her."

Sergeant Simmons slid a pencil behind his ear. "That right?" he said. "Take a seat."

"I wondered if Detective Superintendent McGregor might be around?" Mirabelle found herself hopping from foot to foot. It was only a small movement but it wouldn't go—like a nervous tic. She cursed herself inwardly and tried to stand still.

"Give me a second, miss."

Simmons disappeared into the back room though they could still hear his voice.

"Sid," he said, "there's a . . . darkie out there wants to give a statement."

So noteworthy was this occurrence that Sid popped his head around the doorframe to verify it and then hastily withdrew.

Mirabelle smiled apologetically at Lindon. "McGregor will see us," she promised.

They didn't have long to wait.

The superintendent had moved into a larger office upstairs with a view over the small square at the front of the station. The case last year had not bagged him a promotion but it had settled his men into a more or less coherent team underneath him and put paid to the initial disquiet at his transfer from Lothian and Borders. It would be a long trail to weed out the deep-seated corruption in the Brighton and Hove forces but McGregor had established where he stood and at least made a start on changing things.

Mirabelle noted that his brown tweed jacket was missing a button. A sign, she thought, that he remained a bachelor. When he rose to shake her hand his smile was genuine.

"I'm surprised not to have seen you in such a long time, Miss Bevan," he said.

This wasn't entirely true. Quite apart from his testimony at the inquiry into the shot Mirabelle had fired the year before, McGregor had seen Mirabelle several times from a distance in the street. Her slender frame stood out in a crowd and it perturbed him that his eyes were drawn toward her. The truth was he'd found himself unexpectedly shy. Although he'd wanted to, he couldn't seem to pluck up the courage to speak to her. She'd done a remarkable job when the investigation had come her way last year and though at the time he'd considered her nothing but a nuisance, on reflection he'd had to acknowledge that without her they would never have solved it. What impressed him most was that Miss Bevan hadn't dwelled on this fact. As a result of both her actions and her humility, both during the case and at the tribunal afterward, he now held her in awe. Last summer while she was in the newsagent's at the end of the Twittens he'd spotted her through the window. His fingers had gone weak and he'd avoided going in, instead retreating at speed to the Sussex Bar where he spent some time trying to figure out why he'd run away. After a soothing half-pint he'd realized it wasn't only because Miss Bevan was beautiful, it was that she was unnerving. It was as if she could see right through people. The last time they had spoken was at one of the funerals after the Nazi case. He'd noticed Mirabelle weeping behind the veil of her pillbox hat and he had wanted to put a comforting arm around her elegant shoulders, but he'd found it impossible.

Seated opposite him now she sat straight and businesslike.

For her, what had happened last year and its aftermath had been devastating. She had lost an old friend for which she still blamed herself. If only she had realized earlier what was going on she would at least have been able to save Father Sandor. The sight of McGregor was a reminder of everything that had happened and she most emphatically did not want to think about it. Instead she gathered her courage, introduced Lindon and explained why he was there.

"Sounds like London will be happy we've found you, Mr. Claremont."

"Mr. Claremont is volunteering his information, Detective Superintendent," Mirabelle pointed out. "I'd like that to be perfectly clear when you hand him over. He came down to visit Vesta for the weekend and then saw Miss Bellamy Gore's picture in the paper." Mirabelle decided to fudge the truth.

McGregor stared at Lindon thoughtfully. "So Miss Bellamy Gore spoke to you?"

Lindon nodded. "Yes."

"Had you met her before?"

Lindon shrugged his shoulders. "Might've."

"Well, had you or hadn't you?" McGregor pushed him.

Mirabelle shifted in her seat. Lindon had become monosyllabic. He couldn't do a better job of seeming guilty if he tried. "You need to be honest with the police today, Lindon. You don't have anything to hide. Just tell the detective superintendent what you told me. Answer his questions."

"I might've seen her. She'd been around. But I'd never spoken to her before. She came up to me, see. She was interested in the music. She asked a couple of questions. Wanted to talk about saxophone players—the legends, that kind of thing."

McGregor pressed one of the buttons on the telecom on his desk. He didn't want Mirabelle coaching the boy. Her intentions were good but she wouldn't help matters. The lad was reacting to her being there, and they'd get a lot more out of the kid if they spoke to him alone.

"Robinson, will you interview a witness?"

McGregor's second in command, though initially resentful of his appointment, had become a friend. It had taken a while to earn each other's respect but the men worked well together now. Sometimes they played a round of golf. McGregor invariably won.

"Mr. Claremont, we need to get your statement down on paper," he said.

Lindon squirmed. "Miss Bevan got me covered," he said. "Police stations always make me jumpy. 'S only natural."

McGregor ignored the implication. "Well, you'll need to tell the story in your own words. Then the Met will want to interview you. Robinson will take a statement and then one of our officers will accompany you back up to town to make sure you get there safe and sound."

Robinson knocked on the door and stuck his head into the office. "All right, come on then, son," he said.

Lindon looked frightened now.

Mirabelle forced herself to smile. "Don't worry," she said. "The police are just trying to find Rose. You'll be able to help them."

Lindon looked beseechingly at her and then nodded before following Robinson into the corridor.

"Do you think he was involved?" McGregor asked.

"He seems so immature, I doubt it." Mirabelle smiled. "He just panicked and assumed he'd be blamed, that's all. I don't think Lindon hurt Rose. Sometimes a story that isn't completely consistent is a mark of the truth. Liars are too careful. If I were investigating I'd be interested in the club where he was playing more than anything else. He was warned, you see, before the police arrived. Would you let me know what happens? He's a friend of Vesta's—their families have known each other for a long time."

McGregor nodded. "I could pop in later if you like?"

Mirabelle shrugged.

McGregor couldn't help but notice that her eyes were even more hazel than he remembered. He liked that the tip of her nose had gone pink in the cold and that her green scarf was knotted symmetrically over the collar of her tweed coat.

Mirabelle got up, making to leave, and then turned at the last minute. "There was just one other thing I wanted to ask you, Detective Superintendent. I noticed an item in the paper this morning and wondered if you might help me to locate the person it mentions?"

"Of course. If I can I will," McGregor volunteered. "Who is it?"

3

Dogs are my favorite people.

The force hadn't let Constable Turpin keep Buster after
the fight, and that had been the worst thing about the
whole bloody business—far worse than losing his job.
Constable Turpin loved dogs, and running the police
kennels had been the perfect way for him to earn a living. Perhaps in a week or two he'd see about getting a
puppy—a cross of one kind or another. A pedigree would
be too expensive. Buster had been a pure-bred Alsatian—a
first-class working dog with a lovely nature. Poor sod
couldn't help being German. Bill Turpin was convinced
he'd done the right thing in defending the animal. Even
now.

Bill had spent his time helping round the house in the
weeks since his suspension. Now that he'd actually been
fired he'd need to sign on, roll up his sleeves and go looking for work. He'd joined the force fresh from the army
when he came home in '46 and had expected to be set till
retirement. He'd trusted the police force and it had let him
down. Now he found the array of possibilities spread before him on Civvy Street bewildering. Bill Turpin liked rules,
discipline and routine. It was important to him to know

where he stood—like one of the well-trained police dogs he'd spent the last six years looking after.

In the kitchen Mrs. Turpin banged her baking tins as she cleared up the remains of a morning spent making bread for the week. The oven had been fired since early and now the whole house smelled deliciously yeasty. The produce of her morning's labor was airing on racks over the pale yellow kitchen surfaces—rolls, bite-sized biscuits and tiny scones. Mrs. Turpin and her side of the family pooled their rations and she worked her magic on them. Bill knew there was a stew in the oven—tripe and carrots in gravy. Two peeled potatoes sat in a pot ready to be boiled and mashed. When he'd asked what time it would be ready, Julie got sniffy.

"It's not a stew, it's a casserole," she insisted. "And I won't be serving it till five so you can forget any nonsense. You should be out looking for work, Bill Turpin."

Bill had decided to leave the business of job hunting until Monday, so instead he retreated to a comfortable chair by the tiled, green fireside. Normally he'd read the paper but he didn't have the nerve to pop down to the shop to pick up a copy. He felt uncomfortable with the attention. The very idea of being on the front page of the morning edition made his skin prickle. They hadn't heard yet about the *Argus* but whichever page the story ran on, one thing was sure: everyone knew. Actually everyone seemed to be on his side.

"Ridiculous nonsense. The bloke was a coward, Bill. Good on you," they said. "Harming a poor animal that way—a police dog, too."

Bill shrugged his shoulders. The scumbag had got ten years in Lewes for murder. It would only have been nine if the man hadn't stubbed out his cigarette on Buster. He would never have done it if the dog hadn't been muzzled.

"Bloody stupid Hun beast," he'd sneered.

Bill wondered, not for the first time, what might have happened if instead of lashing out in temper and breaking the guy's jaw, he'd simply loosened the muzzle and let Buster deal with the scumbag on his own. On balance, though, that would have been more risky—Buster might have been put down. Better that Bill simply lost his job. He'd find something else.

In the meantime, Bill stared out of the window and waited for the day's wireless programs to start. The street was quiet today. He was carefully adding coal to the embers of the fire when he noticed a lady who seemed vaguely familiar checking the numbers on the doors, hesitating, and then approaching their house. Bill knew everyone round Lynton Street but he couldn't place her. She was smartly dressed in a dark green coat and matching hat—a bit too expensive for a woman round this part of town. He wondered fleetingly if she might be from the newspaper. Surely they'd had enough of the story by now.

The knock on the front door was brisk.

"Bill!" Julie called from the kitchen.

She was probably elbow-deep in soap suds. Bill opened the front door.

Mirabelle Bevan smiled kindly. "Detective Superintendent McGregor gave me your address, Mr. Turpin," she said. "I hope you don't mind."

Bill Turpin looked promising, she thought. He stood square in the doorframe and didn't smile, as if he was considering things seriously. He was tidily dressed and of medium height with meticulously combed blond hair in which a few streaks of white added gravitas. He looked as if he could handle himself—just as she'd expected.

"I heard what happened . . ." she started.

Turpin cut in. "I don't want to say any more. What was in the paper today was quite enough, thanks."

"Well, yes, quite. It's not even that I'm particularly a dog lover . . ."

A thin woman came out of the kitchen in a floral overall on a waft of lemon scent and the smell of fresh bread.
Her hair was carefully pinned in a Victory roll. Now
Mirabelle came to think of it, the whole house seemed
rather old-fashioned.

"Please," Mirabelle started. "I don't mean to disturb
you. It's only that I wanted to offer you a job."

Bill Turpin hardly shifted. "What kind of job?" he said.

"Debt collection. McGuigan & McGuigan. Corner of
East Street and Brill Lane—the office is on the first floor.
We need you to start on Monday at nine. It'd be the same
salary you were on in the police force with a monthly
commission payment on top of that if you make the targets.
We're overcome with debts to collect on behalf of our
clients, Mr. Turpin. We need an enforcer. Someone to make
the rounds."

A flicker of concern passed across Mr. Turpin's face.

"Have you already taken another job?" Mirabelle said.

"He hasn't and he'll be there," the woman in the floral
overall interrupted. "Thank you, Miss . . ."

"Bevan."

Bill turned to his wife. "But, Julie," he implored, "whatever shall I wear?"

Julie looked at him as if he were a madman.

"A suit will be fine, Mr. Turpin," said Mirabelle. "This
weather, of course, you need to be warm so wear something heavy. And shoes you don't mind walking in. You'll
be out most of the day. There's a lot of legwork. The collections are all over Brighton and in some of the outlying
areas as well."

Mrs. Turpin's eyes dropped to admire Mirabelle's elegant high heels.

"I always wore a uniform before," Bill said.

"A suit is a uniform, in a way." Mirabelle's voice was
comforting. "When I saw your story, I knew you'd be perfect for the job. An ex-police officer knows how to deal

with people and Detective Superintendent McGregor has given you a glowing reference. We just need you to take no nonsense and get the payments in. After Christmas is one of our busiest times. You look like someone who can handle himself."

Bill nodded. Mirabelle could see that once he'd made up his mind, he'd be immovable. What she didn't know was that Bill Turpin was already considering the possibility of taking a dog with him on the job. Something with a touch of Doberman pinscher might be useful—a breed with a bit of backbone. It was another German dog, of course, but they were magnificent animals and could really stand their ground. This time he'd keep it on a lead but without a muzzle. Debt recovery, he knew, was a serious business. Still, it looked like he'd earn more than he had on the force—he'd hit whatever targets they liked.

"Rightio, Miss Bevan. Thank you." He reached out to shake Mirabelle's hand.

"Glad to have you on board, Mr. Turpin. See you on Monday, nine sharp."

4

Manners are love in a cool climate.

By the end of the afternoon the paperwork was whipped into shape and a route had been prepared for Bill Turpin to start on. Vesta regarded the line of figures.

"I added it all up. We've got more than five hundred quid to pick up next week. I hope this new bloke knows what he's doing."

She laid everything neatly in a pile next to the bank of pot plants that had incrementally built up over her time in the office. Vesta had decorated the place over Christmas— newspaper bunting and a jaunty sprig of mistletoe at the window. That was all gone now but the pot plants were in robust health and almost taking over the tops of the filing cabinets. One or two of them still had the vestiges of festive red ribbon taped to their pots. Things had changed since Mirabelle ran the office on her own—for a start the place smelled of Camp coffee and toast most of the time. It felt lived-in.

"Do you think Lindon will be all right?" Vesta asked.

Mirabelle smiled indulgently. "They'll look after him. McGregor said he'd keep us informed. Police business takes time. Well, we know that!" She tried to change the subject. "What are you getting up to this weekend?"

Vesta kept up an active social life and many of her clients from her last job at Halley Insurance were still in touch. Car fanatics to a man, they made sure her weekends were busy with rallies and day trips up and down the coast followed by late-night meals in Sussex's finest restaurants. This weekend, however, Vesta was staying in Brighton.

"They still got *Scrooge* running at the Regent," she replied, inspecting her perfect pillar-box-red nails. "I love the organ music there. Alastair Sim is a darling. And it's handy for dancing after. I might give ice-skating another go on Sunday—it's just down the road. What are you up to, Mirabelle?"

Mirabelle wasn't sure where her free time went. Saturdays and Sundays often seemed to disappear in one smooth movement that went from buying the *Argus* on her way home on Friday evening to taking a stroll along the Kingsway late on Sunday afternoon. Despite the occasional outing with Vesta to a concert or to a variety of, frankly, strange cafés of Vesta's choosing where they tucked into mugs of tea and sometimes bread and dripping for a penny, she spent most of her time alone. Fridays could be difficult—she missed Jack most on the cusp of the weekend when they would have cooked dinner together and listened to the radio, curled up on the sofa.

"I might do some reading," she said. "And if McGregor hasn't got back to us by tomorrow afternoon, I'll chase him up. I'll give you a ring."

Vesta gathered her things. "Thanks."

"Why don't you get off early? I'll finish up."

"Oh good," said Vesta. "If I catch the early bus there is this absolutely crazy old woman with a pink hat. She sings to herself! That always cheers me up." She scooped up her coat, checked her makeup in a tiny compact and disappeared out the door, waving good-bye.

Mirabelle raised a hand in a parting gesture and wondered what had driven the woman with the pink hat over the edge.

Brighton was full of characters. During the summer there were the men who sold ice cream from bicycles, the children's entertainers with strange bushy mustaches and beauty queens in polka-dot swimsuits. In the winter chimney sweeps carried their brushes from house to house along the front and there was a succession of tramps who sheltered near the railway station and were moved on periodically by the equally familiar figures of policemen on the beat. Grubby children played in the streets of the city center slums throughout the year. The well-known faces of Brighton locals were like rhythms in a song to Mirabelle. Lately she had reflected wistfully if people even noticed her—a smartly dressed woman who came and went along the Promenade. Always alone. Never wearing black because she couldn't bear to. Even when she smiled, her sadness was tangible. She felt a pang of regret and then pulled herself together. It didn't do to feel sorry for yourself. Lots of people were far worse off. Everyone had lost someone.

No sooner had Vesta left the office than Mirabelle began to turn off the lights and collect her things. She clicked off the electric bar on the fire and watched as the orange glow died down. She was straightening her hat when there was a brisk knock at the door. Detective Superintendent McGregor shambled round the doorframe with the air of an eager puppy.

"Finishing up? Fancy a drink? The Cricketers isn't too busy yet."

Mirabelle smiled gratefully. She liked it when people kept their word. In fact, she was glad to see him. "All right," she said. "A drink it is."

It was warm inside the bar, which smelled of stale smoke and beer. The Cricketers was always a popular pub, but at the end of the working week the bar was packed to the gunnels with men nipping in for a swift one on their way home. In the snug, three women, probably secretaries, Mirabelle thought, were being fawned over by a succession of men in suits. The drinks were stacked three-deep in front of them. Gins and tonics, by the look of it.

"Scotch?" McGregor checked, shouting over the din.

Mirabelle nodded and pointed to a tiny table by the fireplace that was free. There were no stools left. Still, she settled to wait, watching the secretaries in the snug bat off the men's advances with aplomb. McGregor returned with drinks, fighting his way through the crowd at the bar.

"They think it's him," he said, putting down the glasses. "Lindon. They've taken him into custody."

Mirabelle studied McGregor's face. When he said, "They think it's him," she realized he meant that he did, too. She swirled the whisky around her glass and tried to sound casual.

"Really? Do you know why? They must have evidence."

"Witness statements. More than just one or two from the sound of it. Turns out there was another girl with Miss Bellamy Gore and she's made a statement. According to her she last saw the girl in Lindon's company. They left the club together. These upmarket types! Lavinia Blyth! Rose Bellamy Gore! Very la-di-da! Anyway, I've met the investigating officer a couple of times—Chief Inspector Green. He's a good man. I can leave him a message and try to get some more information for you, though of course by now he might not get it till Monday. Looks like your boy wasn't being completely honest."

Mirabelle ran through this information before commenting.

"Lavinia Blyth?" she said.

McGregor grinned. That was what he liked so much about Mirabelle. She listened to everything—no detail was too small for her attention.

"Yes. Mayfair girl. Belgrave Terrace or Square or something. What these highly respectable girls were doing in Soho in the middle of the night . . . Well, at least that type makes a reliable witness."

"I think the Blyths live on Belgrave Street," said Mirabelle. "Not the Pimlico end, of course. They're up by the square. Unless they've moved."

McGregor nodded. Mirabelle was always surprising. That was one of the other things he liked. "I might have known. You're acquainted with her then?"

"Oh, I know her father. He worked with . . . I knew him during the war."

McGregor hesitated. It was a touchy subject but he wondered about Mirabelle. She gave so little away. "So how did you meet him? What did you do, Mirabelle, when the war was on?"

Mirabelle knew her standard response of "Land Girl" would not cut any mustard with McGregor. He knew her too well by now.

"Nothing much," she said, sipping her whisky. It would be easier, she thought, to deflect the attention back onto the superintendent. That generally worked with men. "What did you get up to?"

McGregor smiled shyly. Was he blushing?

"Well, actually, nothing much either. I was stuck in Edinburgh hoping they weren't going to bomb Leith Docks. That's where I was working. We didn't see much of the Blitz. Most of the planes were heading over to Clydeside and passed us by, thank God. But still they dropped a couple. There was one that blew the front off a grocer's shop one night and brought down a couple of tenements. A few people died. Terrible. I . . . wasn't conscripted for military service," he stuttered, feeling awkward. "I tried a couple of times but they wouldn't have me."

McGregor stopped. His gut was churning. It had been a while since he'd felt the need to explain what he'd done in wartime but something about Mirabelle kept making his thoughts return to those six years and how guilty he felt for not actually fighting. Now that he'd told her the army hadn't taken him she would know there was something wrong with him.

"I'm glad you didn't do something amazingly heroic," McGregor admitted. "I always feel like an idiot because I stayed at home. The Guard isn't the same. You can volunteer all you like but it's not a patch on what some men went through in action."

"Everyone did their bit," Mirabelle soothed.

"It's probably how I ended up in the police force." McGregor finished his whisky, glad to have got what felt like a confession off his chest. "At least these days I get to do people some real good now and then. . . . What are you up to this weekend? Fancy going to the Regent? Alastair Sim's in *Scrooge*."

Mirabelle breathed in the scent of the last drop of whisky in her glass. If Lindon was in police custody she had other plans. "I'm sorry, Detective Superintendent, I can't. I'm going to London."

5

Sometimes I miss the spirit of London,
but it's a very gray place.

Trains went up and down to London till late at night
but on a Friday most of the traffic came from the capital and consisted of weekenders looking for a break by
the seaside. Even in this weather there were plenty of people who wanted to escape the smog and spend a couple of
days in the brisk, clean air of the Sussex coast. Mirabelle
hovered in the main concourse of the station pulling her
coat around her to keep warm. It would do no harm to go
up to Victoria and have a look around. She owed that
much to Lindon at least. Despite what London's finest had
decided she was convinced that the young saxophonist
was not responsible for Rose's disappearance. She wasn't
even convinced that Lindon had been the last person to
speak to the girl. The intriguing thing was that no one appeared to have discovered what had happened to Rose.
Mirabelle wondered if McGregor's friend, Chief Inspector
Green, had charged Lindon and, if so, with what crime.

The six o'clock train was almost empty. Mirabelle settled into a seat in a first-class carriage, folded her gloved
hands on her lap and stared out of the window. It was difficult to discern anything in the dark as Brighton receded.
The glass reflected a mirror-bright image of the empty car-

riage and a woman who kept checking her slim gold wrist-watch. Mirabelle made herself stop looking at the time.

The prospect of London still made her jumpy. It had been a long time since she'd lived there, though the place abounded with wartime memories, many of them painful. She hadn't been back since the previous spring but some of her happiest reminiscences were of this time of year. It had been in the winter that her love affair with Jack had started. With a jolt she realized it was ten years since they first got together. It seemed a very long time. They met when she was taking notes at a War Office meeting. There had been heavy snow that January, and the secretary who usually took the minutes had been stranded somewhere out of town. Jack took Mirabelle for a drink afterward, and they had both immediately known they'd be together. It was like falling under a spell.

"I'm sorry. I don't want to lie about it," he had said. "I'm married."

Mirabelle hadn't panicked. "Oh, I see."

When he'd kissed her later, he'd tasted of Glenlivet. "I don't want to rush you," he whispered.

But Mirabelle hadn't felt rushed. Being with Jack had been right from the very beginning—the most natural thing in the world. It had surprised her.

"I hope your place isn't too far away," she had smiled.

She cherished the image of Hyde Park covered in white and those first chilly midnight trysts trying to keep warm in Jack's shabby flat during the blackout. For some reason, one frosty morning walking in to work not long after the affair started had particularly stuck in her memory. Jack's cheeks were pink and his eyes kept alighting on her face as they made their way up the Strand past the big white building with the clock.

"They're calling it Big Benzene," Jack quipped.

It was the headquarters of some oil company. The clock face was larger than Big Ben's. During the war it had seemed ridiculously flash and almost un-British, but the building had gone up well before the breakout of hostilities. The Strand was busy with silent commuters on their way to work. It was ten to eight and not yet properly light. Mirabelle and Jack had been up most of the night.

"I could do with some breakfast," he said.

They were out of coupons. That happened sometimes at the end of a run when they had to rely on the office canteen and stick to non-rationed items. When they got in, Jack fetched scalding chicory coffee with hot milk he'd managed to blag and some bread with margarine. They'd scoffed it secretly—no one could know about their fledgling romance. No one ever knew about it in the end—not one other soul over the whole eight years. It was mundane, but she'd give anything to eat bread and margarine with Jack. Just one more time.

At Victoria Mirabelle disembarked, her poignant daydreams still playing around the fringes of her mind. The smog curled between the streetlamps and the spokes of wrought-iron framework. It seeped through your body and into your bones. Mirabelle's heels clicked as she made her way onto the chilly concourse. One or two people waiting at the arrivals board were coughing. London was still here, in fact with the smog it looked as if it had hardly changed. Already there was something comforting about it despite the seeping spiteful cold.

Mirabelle decided to walk. It was still early and the jazz clubs wouldn't be open yet. She cut past Buckingham Palace where three off-duty guardsmen were heading into St. James's Park. The park was a notorious haunt. Churchill, when he was told about what went on among the bushes, said it made him proud to be British that men would go there in the dead of an English winter, no matter what they got up to. Mirabelle smiled. She and Jack had made love al fresco a couple of times. Air raids seemed to fire Jack's passion. They both hated the smelly overcrowded shelters and the crush to find a place to sleep on the Tube station floor or the basement of the department. Several times they'd opted to be out in the open air. The whole town was pitch in the blackout. Jack said it was the London way. Even now the thought gave Mirabelle a frisson.

She headed toward Piccadilly past Jermyn Street and then doubled back. It was almost like time traveling. It had been ages since she'd been in this part of town. Her pace increased as she sneaked down the alleyway behind St. James's and into the discreet hallway of Duke's Hotel, which although not decked out in the grand style of the nearby Ritz, was at least warm and comfortable. The flame-haired receptionist looked up and smiled.

"I'm just in for a drink."

The bar was situated down a corridor. A smart waiter in a crisp white jacket took Mirabelle's coat as she entered. There was generally only one kind of woman who frequented a hotel bar alone. Well, two, if you counted Americans. He sized her up and discounted both options. This woman was British through and through, and certainly didn't look like a prostitute—she possessed a different kind of glamour.

"Are you waiting for someone, madam?" he asked with a soft Italian accent.

Mirabelle shook her head. "I'll have a whisky sour," she said.

The waiter disappeared and she took in the surroundings. Effortlessly understated, Duke's Hotel catered for travelers, not tourists, and only those with money. The claret-colored walls were dotted with traditional paintings in gilded frames. The lighting was dim. Small electric lamps with yellowing linen shades lit every alcove and table. Jack used to meet Naval Command staff here in one of the back rooms. It was rumored the barmen at Duke's mixed the best cocktails in London. The Italian waiter served the whisky sour with a flourish and left a small bowl filled with tiny crackers. Mirabelle lifted the glass to her lips. The rumors were true. It was the best whisky sour she'd ever tasted. She settled into her seat and contemplated smoking a cigarette. There was something about London that brought out the devil in her. In Brighton she would have been sitting at the window of her flat on The Lawns reading the *Argus* with *Friday Night Is Music Night* on the wireless in the background and contemplating a fish paste sandwich before bedtime. This was better.

Taking another sip of her drink, Mirabelle turned her mind to Rose. The girl came from this world, and Duke's or at least its surroundings were no doubt familiar to her. The Bellamy Gores were established—old money. Rose had come out at court last season. The photograph in the paper had clearly been taken at her debutante presentation. This meant a round of parties and a flurry of privilege. Even during wartime debutantes donned white dresses, pearls and diamonds, though many of them, not least Princess Elizabeth, took up worthwhile wartime occupations. They became secretaries, nurses or drivers in addition to the role they undertook at court, much of which was centered on bagging a prestigious husband.

One of Jack's friends had romanced his driver only to discover she was titled and the heir to a huge fortune. Jack said it had entirely put off the poor fellow. Still, it took a certain kind of person to come from such luxury and seek out danger. Unlike the secretaries, nurses and drivers, Rose had not sought danger in a good cause. The girl was self-assured, clearly, and there was no harm in that. However, the way Lindon had described her suggested that she was perhaps overconfident—even superior. The girl didn't seem to have made any attempt to put Lindon at his ease. Perhaps Rose wanted to be the fish out of water. She'd been happy to stand out, dispense her opinion (which she no doubt considered expert) and flash her gold cigarette case. Why had she given the case to Lindon? There was something indiscreet about that and she'd disappeared immediately afterward. Had the girl's brashness simply upset someone, Mirabelle wondered. Perhaps she didn't realize that if they felt humiliated some men might lash out. Or perhaps the girl wasn't missing at all. Perhaps she'd taken off voluntarily. It would be unusual for someone in her social position but there was nothing to say Rose didn't have a lover. After all there was still no news of how she'd actually gone missing, or indeed if she'd come to any harm. Lindon had said, "They left." Did he mean Lavinia Blyth and the other, as yet unidentified "glossy" young person? She wished he'd been clearer or that she'd pressed him on the point. In any case, in whatever company Rose had departed, she had left only the mystery of where she had gone. There was the possibility, of course, that Lindon had lied and he had accompanied Rose, but if that was the case why had he come to Brighton? There was no question in Mirabelle's mind that whatever time Lindon left the club, he'd certainly returned later. His account of getting the news of the police looking for him rang true.

So deeply was she pondering this that Mirabelle didn't notice the man approaching her table.

"Mirabelle? Mirabelle Bevan! Well, I'll be blowed!"

Mirabelle started, almost spilling her drink. It took her a moment to realize who the handsome man was, now that his hair was graying at the edges and he was out of uniform. Puffing laconically on a cigarette, martini in hand, he wore a lounge suit and an understated silk tie with a discreet regimental insignia woven into the fabric.

"Eddie." She smiled. "What are you doing here?"

"Well, I could ask you the same thing. You look radiant, of course. Always do. Can I get you another?"

Mirabelle considered the offer for a moment and then nodded. This place was redolent with Jack's memory and she had a little time on her hands. Eddie waved at the Italian waiter and motioned for a round. Then he sat on the dark velvet chair opposite her, wafting a tiny wave of spicy aftershave her way.

"I haven't seen you in a long time, Mirabelle. Did you hear about Jack Duggan? Dreadful business. He died in Brighton, I heard. After all he'd been through it seems ironic it was Civvy Street did for him. Heart attack, wasn't it?"

Mirabelle nodded and managed to bite her tongue. Like all her wartime friends and acquaintances, Eddie had no idea about her relationship with Jack.

"I keep meaning to go down and pay my respects. Gravestone flowers and a visit to his widow. I expect she's getting over it now and probably wouldn't welcome the reminder."

Mirabelle had last seen Mrs. Duggan brazenly inviting Detective Superintendent McGregor for dinner the year before. They had been standing only yards away from Jack's grave. The woman hadn't appeared the slightest bit bereaved.

"I expect so," she snapped.

"So, for whom are you waiting in Duke's bar? Lucky bugger! Come on—confess! What have you been up to? I haven't seen you since things wound up at Nuremberg. Pretty grim, wasn't it?"

"I'm not waiting for anyone—I just fancied some jazz, Eddie. I've heard there are some smashing clubs up here around Soho."

Eddie took a slug of his martini. "Oh God! You're in absolutely the right place. Actually there's no need to go as far as Soho. It's splendid! There are a couple just round the corner. There's even one on Jermyn Street opposite my old man's tailor. It's on the left in a basement and there's another up on Piccadilly. Have you ever been? It's marvelous! You sit in the dark, smoking. The drink is variable, of course—some places better than others. Anyway, you sit in the dark, in a very small space in the smoke, and the music is incredible. It's different every time—that's what gets me. It's not like going to a dreary old-fashioned concert. The musicians just take off! These black guys come over from the States and what they can't do with a horn or a set of drums!"

"Is it dangerous, Eddie? I mean, for a woman on her own?"

"I'll take you! I insist!"

"So it is dangerous?"

"Well, not for you, Mirabelle. I mean, you're fully trained."

"I only worked in the office," Mirabelle cut in. "I never went on operations."

"Yes, but even so. I'm sure you picked up a thing or two. You always knew what was what, and people who know what's what don't land themselves in trouble. Or at least they don't land themselves in trouble they can't get out of. Mostly the jazz clubs are not half as bad as people say. They only say those things because they don't know. I've seen a couple of fights breaking out but no worse than you'd find in a pub. They say a lot of the musicians use cocaine—you know, the stuff the dentist gives you for toothache. Creative types, of course."

"It's only that I heard about a deb who went missing a couple of days ago. She was in a jazz club somewhere in Soho?"

"Rose something or other? Yes, I read about that. The *Standard* ran a whole shock-horror about it. Terrible business. Can you imagine young girls out late at night like that? I mean to say, that's the scandal. I couldn't make out if the kid had a chaperone or not. I'd hate to think of my little nieces . . . Well, they're probably on the young side for that kind of thing, but still. Who lets their daughter out to a jazz club, green as grass? Those places might not be the dens of iniquity everyone says they are but they're definitely dives. No wonder the girl got into trouble."

"Actually, she wasn't alone. She was with Commander Blyth's daughter, I think."

"Paul Blyth? Oh God, I hadn't heard that. Poor chap will be frantic." Eddie flipped open his cigarette case and offered Mirabelle a smoke. She leaned toward him as he gave her a light. She scarcely ever smoked these days but Eddie had American cigarettes. The musky taste emboldened her.

"So what are you really doing here?" she whispered.

Eddie's eyes twinkled. He lowered his voice. "Thing is, the palace staff come in when they get off duty. Officers, mostly. There's nothing like a military man, even out of uniform. And apart from anything else, it's so convenient for the park."

"Oh, Eddie!" Mirabelle laughed. "You haven't changed a bit!" He always sailed close to the wind—and got away with it.

6

The best thing for a case of nerves is a case of Scotch.

The whisky sours were stronger than expected and as Mirabelle checked her appearance in the mirror of the ladies' room she realized that she was rather flushed and swaying slightly. The small crackers had not provided adequate ballast. Despite his promises, Eddie had taken off with a naval lieutenant for a "baccarat game." Mirabelle decided it was time to eat something and then get going. It was well after nine o'clock and surely a respectable enough time to get to a jazz club—dive or not. Carefully checking her hat was in place, she exited Duke's and made her way to Piccadilly Circus to pick up some chips. In the doorway of Fortnum & Mason a young couple was kissing, oblivious to the world. The neon signs mounted on the buildings cast a glossy veneer over the streetscape, glowing through the smog. Around the statue of Eros there were crowds of youngsters. The girls were a mass of bobby pins and ribbons, hardly dressed for the cold weather. The boys wore suits with thin ties. They were bantering on their way from the cinemas and theaters to the bars, dance halls and music clubs farther along.

"I fancy you, Kitty Dawson," a lone boy shouted.

This provoked a cascade of giggles from a group of girls

who then, as one, turned and walked away smartly along Regent Street. To one side a busker strummed a guitar and sang a Bing Crosby number with clouding icy breath. No wonder he sounded forlorn. Mirabelle followed her nose to a street stall and ordered chips with salt and vinegar. The newspaper poke was satisfyingly warm. She removed one glove and ate the contents with her fingers. It tasted good. Feeling fortified and a good deal less wobbly, she went back down to Jermyn Street to take a look at the jazz club Eddie had recommended. She wanted to find out as much as she could about Lindon Claremont and see if any-one knew Rose.

"Information gathering," she murmured.

From the pavement there wasn't much to see or hear. The lights in most of the windows on Jermyn Street were out for the night and not many of the buildings had base-ment premises. Only the presence of a bouncer loitering by the railings and a single orange streetlight over the entrance below announced the club to the world. As the door opened a girl burst out pulling a pink mohair wrap around her shoulders. A snatch of music escaped into the night air. It was a saxophone solo.

"Is that Lindon Claremont playing?" Mirabelle asked the bouncer.

The man shrugged. His face divulged nothing and if he knew Lindon was in custody he did not show it.

"Tone deaf, me," he admitted. "Can't tell one from the other." He stepped back and gestured downstairs. Mirabelle paid at the desk where she was given a grimy ticket and waved into the club. Inside it was warm, dark and the music hit her in a wave. The saxophonist alone was loud, never mind what it might be like when the rest of the band started playing. Near the stage there were a few tables, mostly taken by couples drinking bottles of cheap plonk from shiny bucket stands. The ice had melted and the half-empty bottles bobbed in little black pools. By the bar a crowd of men stood with all eyes on the platform, which was lit by a bare lightbulb with such low wattage it looked yellow. Apart from that and a single bulb over the bar there was no light in the room. If anything the club was even darker than the street outside.

Mirabelle waited until her eyes became accustomed to it. The atmosphere felt unexpectedly intense and the music was frantic. The beat made it both difficult to think straight and pleasant to move—like swimming almost. No one was dancing but one or two of the women were swinging in time. Mirabelle felt her fingers twitch as the saxophone player continued his solo. Everyone had such serious expressions. To one side four other musicians were listening, sitting intently by their instruments—a set of drums, a guitar, a bass and a piano. Then the drummer picked up the syncopated rhythm and they joined in one by one. The feeling in the room changed instantly. The audience burst into chattering life, waves of laughter cut through the music and people lit cigarettes in a flurry of tiny flames, briefly illuminating their faces in an orange glow.

Mirabelle moved to the bar. A man with a thin mustache smiled grimly and drained the last of his pint. He straightened his tie before leaning in to shout over the music, asking if he could buy her a drink.

"I was hoping to hear Lindon Claremont," Mirabelle shouted back, cupping her hand against her cheek.

"Lindon Claremont? Plays saxophone? He's usually over in Soho. I've never heard of him playing in here." The man's face was shiny with sweat and he was trying to speak clearly over the music so that he sounded aggressive, punctuating his words by jabbing his finger toward the stage. "These guys are good," he shouted drunkenly. "The one on guitar is Len Williams. He's only just back from Australia. He's why I came tonight. I heard he'd be on. He's amazing! If anything he's got better since I last saw him, which must have been during the war. It was the

Bouillabaisse in those days. There was just a crazy West Indian, some crates of booze and not much else. The music though! Christ! It feels like a hundred years ago!"

He motioned to see if she'd like a drink, leaning in too close. Mirabelle shook her head. "I'm fine, thanks." She stepped back.

Mirabelle moved away and shifting out of his line of sight, she motioned to the bartender. Someone here must know something about Lindon. The jazz world, she guessed, was tiny, and one in which Lindon's arrest would be big news; if only she could find someone to talk about it.

"Is Lindon Claremont on tonight?"

The man's fingers clenched uncomfortably. "Lindon doesn't play up this end of town. If he's on he'll be over in one of the Soho clubs."

"Is he playing over there then, do you think?" Mirabelle pushed.

The bartender's eyebrows rose almost imperceptibly. "Lindon's not regular anywhere, is he?" he shouted.

"I hadn't heard of him on the circuit for a couple of days. I wanted to find him, you see. I was wondering where he'd got to."

The bartender weighed things up. "He got nicked, miss," he admitted and then hurriedly added, "but I don't know nothing about it."

He turned away as a burly fellow pushed in and ordered two gin and tonics. Mirabelle loitered but the bartender studiously avoided catching her eye. When the gin and tonics were paid for, he deliberately moved to the other end of the servery and started polishing glasses.

"Excuse me!" She waved her hand, but he turned away clearly not willing to discuss the matter any further. How frustrating! Mirabelle tapped her foot to the rhythm. The music was infectious. She moved slightly toward the stage and hung around. A man beside her nudged her arm and proffered a cigarette straight from the packet. There weren't

many black men in Jermyn Street. Apart from the saxophonist and the bass player on stage, he was the only
black bloke in the whole club. He was smoking Chesterfields. Mirabelle let him light her one.

"Thanks," she mouthed. "The barmen aren't very friendly
in here, are they?"

The man nodded. He was dressed in a tight tan-colored
suit. The material had an unusual sheen. His hair was so
short it was practically shaved and was slicked over with
some kind of hair oil. Mirabelle could smell it—a tannin
note on the smoky air.

The man gestured toward the stage and shouted in a
deep American drawl. "Benny got the beat. He's one bad
brother. You like music, lady?"

"You're a musician?" Mirabelle guessed.

"Yeah. I came to hear Len, and he's good but he's not
good, you know? Benny's the one holding it together up
there."

Mirabelle took a deep draw on her cigarette. "I was
hoping to hear Lindon Claremont play."

The man looked at her quizzically. "Here? You don't
know one joint from another, lady. Lindon got banged up.
Not much loss—he's more a shape in a drape than a hep
cat. He don't make love to that sax of his, know what I
mean? They say he plugged some solid chick. That's what
I heard."

"Excuse me?"

"He plugged a chick. Over in Soho. You want to ask at
Mac's Rehearsal Rooms."

"Where's that?"

"Windmill Street, lady. I wonder sometimes if you English people really speak English at all!"

"Do you think he did it? Lindon?"

"What kind of question is that? Are you with the Baby-
lon, lady, or you just crazy?"

And with that he turned away.

Mirabelle scanned the room. There was no one she could make out who was likely to know any more about Lindon, apart from the band. She attracted the attention of a man to her right and motioned to the stage. "What time do they finish playing?"

"They only just started, love," he said, swinging his hips. "That's Len Williams. With any luck we'll be here well beyond midnight."

He slid his eyes down Mirabelle's body and took a step closer. Mirabelle moved smoothly to one side before heading determinedly toward the barman. She'd give it one last try. The man didn't move away quickly enough and she collared him.

"I don't think Lindon did anything," she shouted over the music. "I don't care what people say. And I'm going to try to prove it."

The guy put down the glass he was cleaning. His skin was pockmarked and even in light this low Mirabelle could make out the brown stains on his teeth. When he shouted, he practically growled. "I wouldn't get involved, myself," he said, his eyes hard. "God knows what happened to that girl."

"Did you know her?"

"She'd been in here. She'd been everywhere. Danced like a snake! I didn't know her name till I read it in the paper. I'd keep out of it," he shouted. "You'll get into trouble, asking questions about that darkie. You best be careful. Lots of the boys are jumpy."

"Why's that?"

"Stands to reason." He leaned over the bar to make his point. "Young boy gets into trouble and the police are looking for any reason to shut down jazz clubs. The law don't like jazz clubs. No one wants anything to do with that kind of trouble, see. We ain't had a raid here since 1947 and that's the way we want to keep it—not like the boys in Soho. Nice lady like you ought to be heading over to Feldman's, if anywhere. Come here when you're meeting a fella you can't take home to your mother. Now, I suggest you leave it alone."

Mirabelle decided to push him a little further—after all, this man knew Lindon. Why didn't he seem to care? Did no one feel responsible for the people around them anymore? "I don't think Claremont did anything. I think he's innocent. That's why I'm asking," she tried to explain.

"Guilt and innocence is one for the judge and jury, innit? He didn't play here. Nice enough lad, but he's none of our business. If you want to pursue it you need to go to Soho."

Mirabelle shook her head. She wasn't going to get any more here tonight. "All right." She squeezed her way back to the door.

The air outside was refreshing after the smoky atmosphere. Her ears rang from the music, and she shook her head.

The doorman stared at her. "You all right, miss?" Jazz occasionally overcame the ladies.

"I'm fine," Mirabelle snapped. She could do without his solicitude.

Soho was about a mile away. The walk would do her good.

7

It's not always the cold girls who get the mink coats.

As she headed up Shaftesbury Avenue, Mirabelle couldn't help thinking it would never have been like that during the war. People would stick their necks out for justice and, more than that, they shared an empathy with anyone who found themselves in a fix. During the Blitz people risked their lives for complete strangers. They took in waifs and strays. They stood up for what they thought was right. During the war anyone who knew Lindon Claremont and believed him innocent would have been on his side.

She was amazed at how busy the city was and how many cars there were. At the traffic lights a queue of four identical Morris Minors sat revving their engines waiting for the signal to change. Rolls Royces and Bentleys with chauffeurs waited outside the theaters. Paperboys were stationed on the street corners selling the last of the evening editions. Buses you could scarcely see into because of the thick fog of cigarette smoke flashed past, like clouds encased in red metal. The walk took less than fifteen minutes. The streets of Soho were packed with people. Windmill Street housed several pubs, restaurants and coffee shops in its narrow ramshackle buildings, most of which had survived the Blitz intact. London had rebuilt faster than Brighton, and Mirabelle noticed there were hardly any gap sites in this part of town. The city seemed to have healed itself, yet it had lost some of its wartime camaraderie.

There was no sign of Mac's Rehearsal Rooms—not a notice or a light. Mirabelle checked the basements and the shadowy doorways, remembering that the Jermyn Street club had hardly advertised its existence and that Mac's was an underground place and might be even harder to find. Most of the basement lights were out and the lower floors appeared to be restaurant kitchens or storerooms. There was no sign of a jazz club anywhere.

Mirabelle walked up one side of the street and down the other, listening. Windmill Street was relatively quiet, and the people going in and out of doors didn't look like jazz types—not judging by what she'd seen at the Jermyn Street club. There was nothing for it but to ask. She sized up the premises that were open and made a decision, going into a café where three bored girls sat smoking cigarettes. Cups and saucers and a solitary gray teapot sat on the table. They turned hopefully but seeing Mirabelle went straight back to their conversation.

"Excuse me, I'm looking for a jazz club along here—Mac's Rehearsal Rooms?"

The youngest girl eyed Mirabelle's outfit carefully. Mirabelle was aware that the dark green coat and the flash of tweed they could see underneath it must make her look like a governess. By contrast the girls were wearing an array of brightly colored tops in shades of orange and pink. They sported jaunty matching scarves tied at an angle and vivid matte lipstick. In the dark foggy night and the down-at-heel café they practically glowed.

"You're not exactly dressed for jazz," one of them said.

She had a point. Mirabelle sighed. "No," she admitted, "I didn't change."

"Well, it's not on tonight anyway, love. You'll need to go to Feldman's. Feldman's is better for you in any case."

"What do you mean?"

The girl stared at Mirabelle. "It's smarter, you know. More proper. For the older crowd."

The girl's candor made Mirabelle smile. The other two looked away, trying not to laugh as their friend dug herself into potential trouble.

"I see." Mirabelle sank into one of the bench seats and out of nowhere a thin waiter with a crumpled white apron came to take her order.

"A strong coffee, please, with milk. And whatever these ladies would like."

The waiter didn't need to ask. The girls shifted in their seats to face Mirabelle, all smiles. She had known they were working girls from the minute they opened their mouths. Their reaction to simply being bought a cup of tea confirmed it.

"He'll bring biscuits, you know. If he's got any."

Mirabelle nodded. "Good. Tell me, do you know a sax player by the name of Lindon Claremont?"

The girls oohed and aahed.

"The nigger what killed the deb, you mean?"

The waiter put a plate of raspberry wafers on the table, a fresh pot of tea and a frothy coffee made with copious amounts of milk. He did not loiter.

"Yes," Mirabelle said, "that's exactly who I mean though I wouldn't use the word *nigger*. It isn't kind. This is your patch, isn't it? I'm trying to find out what happened that night. I don't suppose you know?"

One of the girls picked up a biscuit and another started pouring the fresh tea.

"You ain't a copper, is you, missus?"

"Friend of a friend, that's all."

"You're the friend of a colored fella who used to play at Mac's?"

"Nah," one of them corrected the other, "she's a friend of the deb, ain't you?"

Mirabelle took a sip of coffee to give her strength. It

was scalded but it helped. She fervently wished she hadn't let Eddie buy her another whisky sour. It was only just after ten o'clock.

"So," she ignored the question, "did you ever meet him? Lindon Claremont?"

"Love," said the girl in orange, "I done more than that. He's a customer, he is."

Mirabelle grinned. The girl had probably been trying to shock her but that was all to the good. "So I've come to the right person."

"Oh no." The scarf around the girl's neck fluttered as she shook her head. "I never talk about me fellas. Not even to my aunties or nothing. Not even to my mum."

Mirabelle reached into her purse, pulled out a ten-bob note and laid it on the table. "Give it a try," she said. "I'd like to hear anything. Small details can be very important. Do you think he did it?"

"Are you press?"

Mirabelle shook her head as the girl sized up the money and then picked up the note slowly before deftly popping it into her purse.

"I was a bit surprised when I heard they nicked him," she said as she bit into one of the biscuits. "He didn't seem the type. Bit useless, really."

"That's exactly what I thought, too," Mirabelle said, brushing some crumbs from her lap.

The girls gawped.

"Oh, I'm not a . . ."

They started laughing.

"Thank gawd for that," the youngest girl said.

"He doesn't have a temper, Lindon. That much I do know," the older one continued. "He ain't a beater or a slasher or nothing like that. No temper."

"How long have you known him?"

"A few months. Most of them nig nogs . . . Is nig nogs okay?"

Mirabelle shook her head solemnly. Above the table a picture of the king smiled down and from farther up the café another one of Winston Churchill smoking a cigar and making the famous "V" symbol was fixed to the wall with pins. Both had been roughly cut out of magazines and mounted on card.

"Well," the girl continued, "whatever you call them, mostly they don't use white girls. There's plenty of our blokes like a bit of chocolate. Best of both, you know. But Lindon was unusual for a darkie. He liked white skin. I charged him a bit extra to be honest, 'cause it's kinky, ain't it? He liked the contrast, he said. He liked the *idea*." She rolled her eyes.

"So he might have been attracted to Rose, then?"

"I'm sure! Did you see the picture in the paper? She was pretty enough. But, Lindon, he's shy that way. Sweet. I don't reckon he's got a bad bone in his body—not really. He'd eat you out of house and home, let you buy him a drink—he's a talker. With talkers it's all going on in their head. But I can't see him kidnapping someone or hurting them. He's not that way. Once when he saw a bruise on me he got proper upset. That's what I mean—he was sweet. Said he didn't like to think of me getting bashed around and that. And he never laid a hand on me. If anything, he was too gentle."

Mirabelle noticed that the only other customer in the café—a scruffy, very elderly man in a worn coat—was listening intently. She tried not to catch his eye.

"You know the papers haven't said that Rose was hurt? They just say she's missing."

"Stands to reason though, dunnit? That girl's most likely done for. Face it."

"Yeah," the younger girl chipped in. "I mean, what else could it be? She's out in a club, goes missing and doesn't turn up for, well, it's been a whole day now. Her mama and papa must be beside themselves. Them girls are like pearls, ain't they? When did a deb ever go missing for a day, let alone overnight? She's got to be hurt. Makes you shudder just thinking of it."

Mirabelle nodded. The girl continued. "Well, there you go. And as soon as a darkie's involved the Bill assume it's him. Who knows, they might be right. Stranger things have happened, ain't they? Maybe he was different from what he seemed. Maybe he had a brainstorm and went mad. Just 'cause we ain't seen his temper don't mean he ain't got one."

"Nah." The other girls shook their heads.

"Well, I want to find out," Mirabelle said firmly. "I want to find out what happened to the girl, of course, and I want to make sure they don't fit Lindon up for it. I'm just not sure how to track things down. I'll get there but I'm not sure yet."

"But the Bill got him, don't they? I mean they must know what's happened. Why'd they be out looking in the first place if something hadn't happened? It'll all come out."

"The thing is, the police don't always think enough," Mirabelle said. "They don't see through things." The girls nodded in agreement, as if this was a sage point that they had previously never considered.

"And another thing," the older girl leaned in conspiratorially, "it happened fast. I'll say that for them. I mean, how long does someone have to go missing before the Bill get involved? Longer than an hour, usually. Jesus, when Mary Grady got knifed in Peckham they took more time than that to turn up. No, something's happened. They just ain't saying what."

It didn't take long for the tea to run out and the biscuits to be finished.

"I might try Feldman's, after all," said Mirabelle.

The girls insisted on donating powder and thick red lipstick to help a reluctant Mirabelle paint her face.

"I'm not sure I need this," Mirabelle tried.

"You gotta look your best for Feldman's," the girls insisted, and she let them apply the makeup. "You want to be turned out proper."

When she checked in the mirror the transformation was marked and she had to admit that she looked a good deal more suitable for Soho at night. She seemed younger, she thought, like when Jack used to take her out.

"You brush up nice. What you need is a frock, really. Evening wear."

"I didn't bring anything to change into. It's a good thing it's dark," she said.

Outside it was getting colder and the smog hung in little clouds around the streetlights. Heartened by the conversation, Mirabelle cut down Rathbone Street and onto the main road. Feldman's was only round the corner. Its entrance was less discreet than the club in Jermyn Street. It was definitely not the doorway to anything remotely underground or controversial. In fact, there was a red canopy with the club's name scrawled in white script. A solid-looking bouncer was hovering outside.

"Evening, ma'am," he said solemnly as he opened the door.

It cost twice as much as Jermyn Street to get in but Mirabelle didn't quibble. The interior was more luxurious than anything she'd seen in a long time and the place was crowded. Red leather banquettes were fitted around one side of the stage and the walls were covered with shimmering black material. As well as the stage lighting there were tiny spotlights set into the ceiling. They glowed blue. On stage, six musicians in stiff-looking suits played a frenzied tune, though they were, Mirabelle noted, less frenzied than the four barmen, two of whom seemed permanently employed in shaking cocktails and pouring them into chilled glasses set up in a row. Waiters buzzed efficiently around the tables.

Mirabelle pushed her way to the rear and found a high stool on which to perch. Couples had taken to the small dance floor and there were even some single girls dancing alone or twirling their friends.

Mirabelle decided to try a different tack. She flagged down a waiter. "Never been here before. My niece told me about it." She raised her voice over the music.

"Yes, ma'am. Can I get you something? A club cocktail perhaps?"

"I wondered if you knew her. My niece. She's the girl who's missing. Rose. Rose Bellamy Gore."

The waiter twitched. "I think she used to come here sometimes. Eh, yes, I'm sure she did," he stammered.

"We had no idea she liked this kind of thing, of course. Still, I can see the attraction. Rose loves music, and it certainly is lively. Do you know if she was in yesterday night? Were you on duty?"

"No. She wasn't here. I wasn't working, but, well . . ."

"Oh, I'm sure everybody knows about what happened. Everyone has been very kind. Sometimes one needs to find things out for oneself though. I'd like a whisky, please. Islay if you have it. Glenlivet if not. No ice."

The waiter disappeared. At the end of the number the crowd clapped. A boy at one of the tables stood up and whistled. Then the band started again, this time a gentler number. Three couples stayed on the floor but most of the dancers returned to their tables. Mirabelle watched. A few minutes later a man in a dinner suit pushed his way through the crowd. He was bulky, but there was nothing soft about his body. Completely bald, he looked extraordinarily clean and in the low light his pale skin gleamed. "You are Mrs.?"

"Miss," Mirabelle insisted, "Miss Bellamy Gore."

"Can I help you in some way?" he offered.

"Do you work here?" Mirabelle asked unnecessarily.

The man nodded abruptly. "We're all very sorry about your niece. It's a dreadful thing."

"I just felt the need to see what it was like." Mirabelle

waved her hand airily. "It's a different world. I can see why Rose was attracted to it. She's still missing, you see, and I wanted to see for myself where she sneaked off to. Naturally we had no idea she enjoyed jazz music quite so much. To be frank, it's nowhere near as, well, seedy as I expected."

"Feldman's isn't that kind of jazz club, madam. Your niece didn't go missing here."

"Oh yes. But she had been here, hadn't she? By all accounts she's a regular."

The man bowed his head. Mirabelle noticed he was fiddling with something in his pocket. It was good he was nervous, she thought. It usually meant you were on the right track.

"She is such a charming girl," she pushed on. "I'm terribly fond of her. And it's a worry not knowing where she is. Or for that matter where she'd been."

The man drew a little object from his pocket. His huge fingers moved across it, rubbing it almost desperately, like an old woman with a set of prayer beads. He clearly wanted her to leave but he didn't know how to say it. This was the aunt of the missing girl, after all.

"Oh, I say, is that a fumsup? Haven't seen one of those for years," said Mirabelle, hoping to break the ice.

"Yes. I've had it since the trenches. It's been everywhere with me." He held out the tiny metal figurine.

"Who gave it to you?"

The man flinched almost imperceptibly—no more than a blink. "My dad. It got him through the Great War. He said it'd see me through whatever the fighting threw my way."

"Well, I wish Rose had had one of those with her last night. Her father was at the Somme, you know. He served in the last war as well, though not cavalry of course—too old for that. And now this."

The man looked around. Did he want to get away or was he simply checking to see if he was being observed?

He was anxious, that much was certain. Mirabelle stared wide-eyed and didn't falter. "Are you a family man?" she enunciated clearly over the music.

It took a moment or two for this to sink in. The man didn't respond but he made a decision. "Come with me." He jerked his head toward the banquette seating. "We can talk in the back. It'll be quieter."

The door to the office was concealed next to the final row of seating. Behind it there was a brick-lined passage. Two spotlights were mounted on the ceiling. After the subdued lighting of the club Mirabelle's eyes smarted in the brightness. The big man's skin seemed too smooth, somehow, now she could see him properly. He reminded her of an overgrown baby. A big, hard baby. He wore a heavy yellow-gold signet ring on his left pinkie finger and his suit was ill-fitting and stiffly starched. He had a very slight limp.

The music faded as they moved down the corridor. When they entered the office at the end and closed the door everything fell almost silent. Inside, it was utilitarian— two chairs, a black metal filing cabinet and a telephone on an otherwise bare desk. It reeked of stale alcohol, and away from the crowd and with no heating the air was chilly. The man directed Mirabelle to one of the chairs and pulled out a bottle of brandy from the desk drawer along with two tiny balloon glasses.

"Would you like one?"

"Thanks. I don't know your name."

"You can call me Barney."

Mirabelle's heart skipped a beat. She smiled. Lindon had mentioned a Barney.

"You were there, weren't you, Barney? You saw Rose last night."

Barney's eyes narrowed as he took a second or two to process what Mirabelle said. "Is it that obvious?"

"Were you working at Mac's?"

He poured them two generous measures of brandy, finishing the bottle. "I hate it on the door at Mac's," he said, "but sometimes needs must. I used to be handy with my fists, but these days any trouble breaks out I just block the way." He slapped his stomach. "I help out a few places."

"So you saw Rose?"

"Yeah. I seen her before. Your niece was an enthusiast, if you don't mind my saying. She knew her stuff. Last night she got talking to Lindon Claremont the sax player when he came off. Mac's ain't a proper show. Just musicians playing. They start, they stop, different combinations and that. Jamming, they call it. Lindon and your girl was talking a long time. Thick as thieves. They had a dance. Then they left together. I'm sorry. It's not something that a lady, such as yourself . . . The Bill got the lad though. They caught up with him in Brighton, I heard."

"So last night Rose left with Lindon?"

"Yeah."

"And they were alone? You saw them?"

"Yeah."

"But I thought she was at the club with a friend."

"She arrived with two of them—the fella I'd seen before but the girl I hadn't. Anyway, your niece left with Lindon. Her friends weren't too chuffed but she'd made up her mind. Wish I'd tried to stop her now."

"And neither of them came back later? Neither Rose nor Lindon? They didn't return?"

"No. I didn't see either of them again. They hailed a cab outside. I don't know where they went to."

"And her friends?"

"Well, they tried to stop her but then they came back in. They was slow-dancing for a while. After that they left. We get them, you know, young kids from the upper end. Jazz is an adventure. They like the music and sometimes, if you don't mind me saying so, madam, they like the mix-up. You know, the black fellas. I don't know about your niece. I don't mean to be disrespectful."

"Barney, I simply want to know what happened. I'm not worried about any judgments. So the other two were dancing after Rose left?"

"Yeah, they saw Rose out, then they stayed but not long. Things was winding up by then."

"And what time did Rose leave?"

Barney's stare was even. He was humoring her but he didn't like it. "Half three? Four? I don't wear a watch, Miss Bellamy Gore, so it's difficult to be exact. I told the police that, too. But it was late. After hours. Mac's starts late and goes on till dawn easy, till the last player runs out of juice. See, audience turns up there but it ain't really for the audience. Mac's is for the players. It ain't a show or nothing. Audience covers the cost of the booze, that's all."

Mirabelle downed her brandy. "Thank you," she said, "I feel better knowing. Tell me, this Lindon chap, what do you know about him?"

Barney shifted in his seat. He pulled out a hip flask and topped up his drink, motioning to see if Mirabelle might want the same. She laid her hand on top of the glass. She'd had more than enough.

Barney took another sip. "The Bill got him, miss. You don't need to worry."

"I want to know about the young man. Please, Barney."

"He's a sax player. A darkie. He's young, I suppose. They're all the same. There's a lot of drink in these places, miss, and other things, although I'm not suggesting that your niece liked any of that."

"Thank you. I suppose that is a relief," she said. "Had you ever known Lindon to take up with ladies before?"

Barney froze with his eyes so wide open they were like little pink circles. "I dunno. Begging your pardon, but not many men aren't into the ladies. Especially a girl like your niece. The police got him, miss, and that's the main thing."

"Yes, but no one has found Rose, have they?"

This left the big man, Mirabelle noticed, looking quite bereft. He didn't answer.

"Had you known Lindon for long?" Mirabelle persisted.

"These guys come in. They play. They leave. I dunno much. He's a good musician—not a genius or nothing. What they call a session musician."

"But had you ever seen him leave the club with a woman before?"

Barney thought for a moment. "Nah. Can't say as I have."

"But you'd seen Rose in the past, hadn't you? It wasn't her first time out. I do wish I'd known."

"Yeah. I seen her before in lots of places. Miss, I got to ask you to leave now. I gotta get back." He downed his drink and scraped the chair across the floor as he got to his feet.

"That's all right, Barney. I appreciate your talking to me."

They walked in silence down the corridor. The icy night air seeped in as Barney held open the backstage door.

When Mirabelle passed through, she turned and said, "I'd just like to check about the other two. Lavinia Blyth and her friend."

"The boy?"

"Yes. They saw Rose out, you said."

"Yes."

"But they came back in again?"

"Yes, miss."

"How long did that take, Barney—all of them outside like that?"

"A couple of minutes, I suppose."

"I see."

"Did you watch?"

"I was on the door."

"Did you see it all?"

"She gave Lindon her cigarette case."

"Outside?"

"Yes." Barney pulled back and opened the door a little wider.

Mirabelle decided she'd got enough out of him for now. "Thanks," she said. "It's a comfort, you know." She was aware of his eyes still on her as she made her way down Berniers Place into the foggy night.

When she was sure she could no longer be seen she slowed her pace. She needed to think. It was intriguing; there was no doubt about it. The story kept shifting. Somewhere in all the detail there must be a path to follow—the path of what actually happened—but identifying it would be difficult. Perhaps Lindon had left with Rose but she doubted that. Something was wrong. Mirabelle's mind was buzzing as she ran over everything Barney had said, the words the girl had used about Lindon in the café and the tense air around the barman in the Jermyn Street jazz club. And the one thing they had all seemingly agreed on—Lindon hadn't been in trouble before. He wasn't a womanizer. He was a nice lad, a competent musician, gentle—too gentle—and a bit useless. Barney might be right about where Rose had handed over her gold case. Maybe they'd walked out together—all of them—but Lindon had definitely gone back inside. The gift of the cigarette case was surely a parting gift. You don't give a man your cigarette case when you're about to get into a taxi with him. It had been a grand gesture of farewell. Yes. That was a start. Poor Barney, Mirabelle mused, if he had any feathers they would be well and truly ruffled. She smiled as she imagined him as a huge fat bird, feathers on end. Who, if anyone, would he tell about her visit? Had he told them about her already? She checked her watch. It was well past midnight and the last train to Brighton was long departed. She was almost back at the park. There was nothing else for it. She'd have to stay in London overnight.

8

*Be careful going in search of adventure—
it's ridiculously easy to find.*

Breakfast in Duke's Hotel was served in the Dining Room, which was reached by a series of passages that would have been impossible to navigate were it not for a succession of small signs on wooden stands. However, once you got there, Mirabelle thought, it was certainly worth the trip. You'd almost think rationing had been abandoned. Admittedly she felt slightly the worse for wear this morning on account of the whisky sours and Barney's rough brandy. As a result she was one of the last of the patrons to take a table at half past nine. And, uncharacteristically for this time of the morning, Mirabelle was ravenous. Her late-night forays appeared to have done wonders for her appetite, if not her head.

Most of the guests were reading the *Telegraph*, although at one table she noticed a French paper propped up against the toast rack. At another table a young couple mooned at each other as they sipped the last of their tea. The window looked out over a small courtyard where wisps of smog swirled around two statues.

A waiter arrived to take her order. "Madam?"

"Do you have sausages?" she asked.

The waiter looked slightly surprised at the question. "Of course, madam. Beef or pork?"

"Pork, please, with mushrooms and toast."

"No eggs?"

Fresh eggs were a rationed treat. The taste of the powdered substitute the Ministry of Food inflicted on the British public made Mirabelle feel queasy. Vesta seemed to have mastered baking with them. In fact, she had made excellent pancakes a few times and, once, a kind of Madeira cake. However, in Mirabelle's view powdered eggs certainly couldn't be stomached alone, even if whisked with water or milk and scrambled.

"Do you have real eggs?" she checked. "Fresh ones?"

"Of course, madam. How many would you like?"

"One, please. And a pot of tea."

Before she checked the top stories of the day, Mirabelle stared in wonder at the generous pat of butter the waiter brought on a porcelain plate and the small bowl containing what looked like strawberry jam. She breathed in the sweet fragrance—yes, it was strawberry. No one was roughing it at Duke's.

Well, I might as well enjoy it, she thought. This *is* a treat.

As the waiter fetched her breakfast she scanned the *Telegraph* for any more information about Rose, but there was nothing. Perhaps another paper might be better— something more sensational. A down-market rag more likely to pick up rumors or actively search for a story rather than simply printing police statements. To all intents and purposes Mirabelle was looking for gossip.

"Excuse me," she asked a waiter, "do you have anything other than the *Telegraph*?"

"The London *Times*?" the man offered. "I can fetch it from the reading room, madam."

"No thanks, that's not what I'm after. How about the *Express*? Or the *Daily Herald*? Both if possible. Oh, and the *Mirror* and the *Mail* if you have them."

The waiter didn't pause though his disapproval was clear. "I shall send out," he said coldly.

Ten minutes later, a selection of newspapers, warm from having been ironed, was delivered to her table. The breakfast was excellent, and as the Dining Room emptied of guests Mirabelle perused the news while finishing her toast and the last drops of tea. Sure enough, there was an article in the *Mirror* entitled ROSE OF ENGLAND. It detailed several arrests that had taken place over the last year in London's jazz clubs and then culminated with the story of Rose going missing and Lindon being taken into custody. It did not mention that he had volunteered his witness statement, and referred to him as a "dark jazz fiend." "When will this evil music stop?" the *Mirror* asked, as if the syncopated rhythm of the music itself had been responsible for Rose's disappearance. In another paper there was a photograph of Rose, this time in school uniform. She had studied at Cheltenham Ladies' College and the school had refused to comment on the girl's disappearance.

Mirabelle folded the papers and got up from the table. Today, she thought, she'd pop along to Belgravia. It was the best lead she had, though she would need to be a good deal more careful with her inquiries there. No one in Jermyn Street or Feldman's had loved Rose or was related to her.

Mirabelle settled her bill and then set out briskly through the quiet streets. She stared at the upper floors of the buildings, many of which were familiar. Working for Jack had taken her into inner sanctum after inner sanctum, not least to 10 Downing Street on more than one occasion and the War Rooms—both of which were nearby.

It was strange that Rose had been with one of Paul Blyth's daughters. Blyth, Mirabelle recalled, had two daughters, the younger of whom, Lavinia, must be more or less the same age as Rose. She knew Paul Blyth well—an authoritarian who ran his department with terrifying efficiency. He was infamous for his temper, which he scarcely controlled, and for his icy sarcasm. Mirabelle had once met a secretary who claimed that after three weeks in Commander Blyth's office her hands were shaking so much she could no longer take shorthand. The man was a bully, albeit a highly competent one. He had stayed in office, despite his unpleasant manner, because he had the uncanny knack of picking up just the right information at just the right time. Someone had told her once that Blyth had an incredible sense of the Zeitgeist. The German word had stuck in her mind.

"We don't have quite the word for it in English, but you know what I mean. The man's a marvel. Knows what people want and when they want it well before they do. That's a skill in itself, isn't it?"

She remembered the conversation clearly. Mirabelle wondered if Mr. Blyth ran his household in the same style as his office, because in that context the idea of an eighteen-year-old girl being given permission to visit jazz clubs was highly unlikely. If Blyth's personality was the same in peacetime as it had been during the war he'd be outraged at his daughter going against orders and, of course, with Rose's disappearance and the police involved, now he'd know what they'd been up to.

As Mirabelle crossed the Mall several horse riders were returning from a canter in the park, and she caught a whiff of horsehide as they passed. Mirabelle picked up her pace and headed toward the white stucco streets ahead. To the left was Pimlico where the façades were much more down-at-heel and to the right the upmarket addresses of Belgravia. Mirabelle took a deep breath and turned toward Eaton Square, its dark trees skeletal against the pale buildings. She struggled to remember the number of Commander Blyth's house and walked the full length of the street trying to recall its location. Upper Belgrave Street looked slightly shabby these days. Grubbier than she remembered, it was an array of pale gray and cream rather than the crisp white of its heyday. The Blyth house was one of the buildings closer to Belgrave Square, she decided, and from memory an even number. Stopping on the corner she stared back down the road. Few lights were on, though from one house a maid emerged with a wicker shopping basket over her arm.

Mirabelle took her chance. "Excuse me," she said, approaching the girl, "I'm looking for a family who lives on this street. The Blyths? I haven't been here for years and I've forgotten the exact address. I wonder if you know which house they live in."

The girl did not appear to find this request peculiar and pointed at number four. It didn't stand out, apart from the front door, which was painted a very dark navy rather than the traditional black.

"That one, miss," she said. "But they ain't there."

"Oh dear."

"Weekend," the girl said as if Mirabelle was simple. "No one's here over the weekend. Staff only. I'm sure none of the Blyths will be back till Sunday night at the earliest. None of our lot either. Everyone leaves, you see."

Of course. This part of town emptied out on Friday to house parties in the Shires. It seemed like a hundred years since she had been part of that.

"Thank you," she said.

The girl half-curtsied and scurried off in the direction of Knightsbridge.

Mirabelle surveyed the Blyths' house. There was no point in being coy. The year before, she had broken into several premises but here there would be no need for that. Still, if she wanted to find out what was what there was nothing for it but to get stuck in. She walked confidently up to the front door and rang the bell. A butler answered. He was so elderly he looked as if he had been coated in white powder. Mirabelle wondered if he shouldn't have retired.

"Madam," he greeted her in an imposing voice.

"I know Commander Blyth is away—"

The butler interrupted. "Mr. Blyth, madam. The Right Honorable Mr. Blyth."

"Yes, of course. I knew him during the war, you see. The thing is, I'm most dreadfully worried about this business with Rose Bellamy Gore. I'd very much like to have a word with Mr. Blyth's daughter. Lavinia, isn't it?"

"Madam." The butler raised his hand only very slightly but its meaning was clear. Mirabelle stopped speaking immediately. "Miss Lavinia will not be coming back to town. She is very active in the hunt this season. If you would like to leave a card I shall give it to the master when he returns."

"When will he return?" Mirabelle asked.

The butler froze, as if this question was deeply personal and asking it was an affront. "One cannot say precisely, madam."

Mirabelle thought for a moment. "Very well," she said. "I'll try again on Sunday evening if I'm still in town. I would very much like to speak to Miss Lavinia and to Commander, that is, Mr. Blyth."

The butler didn't move. "If that will be all, madam," he said.

"Well, yes, I suppose it is."

The door closed and she moved back, hovering momentarily beside a white column before stepping back onto the pavement.

Lavinia Blyth. The name was bringing back a memory. Yes, she hadn't realized before. There were two memories—both newspaper articles over the last year. Yes, she's a clever girl—that's good, she thought. Glancing back at the closed door she suddenly remembered why the name had stuck in her mind and her heart sank. This didn't make sense. The butler must be mistaken.

"No," she muttered under her breath, "that isn't right at all."

9

Difficulties are things that show a person what they are.

With disturbing facts falling into place, Mirabelle had a new direction. It was obvious, really. It had been years since she'd gone to the club and whether they'd let her in or not she couldn't be sure; however, if they did she'd certainly be able to put to rest her suspicions about Lavinia Blyth. The sun was bright as she passed the palace. A flock of pigeons flurried in her wake. Outside the underground station the early afternoon editions were hitting the newsstands. A boy was kneeling on the frozen pavement, clipping the string to get at the first copies, as a man in a cloth cap took down the morning headlines to be replaced.

"*Evening Standard!*" he shouted.

Mirabelle considered crossing the road to buy a copy but thought better of it. They had newspapers aplenty where she was going, and she had enough to think about already. It was, she decided, a measure of her recovery that she was prepared to go to the club at all. But the more she found out the more it seemed to her that several facts were amiss. She needed somewhere to sit down and think—ideally somewhere that might also provide information. If her memory served her correctly the Oxford and Cambridge

Club would certainly have plenty of that. She picked up the pace once more as a stiff breeze whisked straight through her coat, and having cut through the park she rounded the corner into Pall Mall. It had been a while, and Mirabelle was almost surprised when she saw the old place. The exterior hadn't changed, although the building was a little closer to the park than she remembered. It was as if London had shifted. Perhaps, she mused, memory always worked that way. There was no brass plaque, of course. The club was nothing if not discreet—a bolt-hole for those in the know. She mounted the entrance steps straight into the hallway, where a steward stepped forward at the bottom of the stairs. He had a broad Northern Irish accent and was wearing formal clothes.

"Good morning. I'm afraid I don't have my pass. I was at St. Hilda's," Mirabelle explained. "I used to come here when I lived in London. My name is Mirabelle Bevan."

The steward didn't move. "No card, Miss Bevan?"

"Sorry. I am a member though."

"I'll have to get someone to look it up, miss."

"Oh yes. In fact, I'd love to speak to someone who could look things up. I have an inquiry about another member. At least, I assume she's a member."

"Please wait a moment, miss."

The man disappeared through a door painted the same deep red color as the walls. Mirabelle turned and peered outside. A man was parking a car and he kept misjudging the space. As the vehicle roared back and forward clipping the curb, a small white cat rubbed itself against the railings of the building beside it. Something was niggling Mirabelle. What she needed, she thought, was a cup of tea to winkle it out. Was it some crazy sense of nostalgia that had led her here? The door in the wall opened once more.

"If you go up to the Ladies' Sitting Room, someone will come down, miss."

"Thank you," she said, but the steward had already retreated.

Mirabelle took the stairs to the first floor. She looked around. The club had been redecorated but it looked much the same. She peeled off her gloves. The Ladies' Sitting Room was off to the right and had been done out in a soft peach color that reflected a warm light into the dark burgundy hall. Inside, curled up in a comfortable armchair, was an odd-looking girl with short blond hair. She was reading a book in Russian. When Mirabelle squinted she could not make out the title, only the writer. It was by the humorist Fonvizin, although the girl did not appear to be finding the story amusing. There were so few women in the club and indeed at the universities that the atmosphere in the ladies' rooms was usually friendly. Mirabelle was glad of the peace though—it would allow the time for reflection that she needed. She removed her coat, perched on a wooden chair near the fire and stared out of the window. The little white cat was now weaving in and out between the lampposts. Mirabelle wondered to whom it belonged.

"Sweet little thing, isn't it?" a shrill voice said.

The girl reading Russian looked up, shaken by the noisy intrusion. Fonvizin must be riveting.

In front of Mirabelle, a woman in a gray pinstripe suit held out her hand. A pair of black-rimmed glasses dominated her face, which was otherwise very pretty. "I understand you're a member. St. Hilda's was it? Mirabelle Bevan? I'm the membership officer. I see you're on our register."

Mirabelle shook her hand. "Yes. I haven't been here in years. I'm only visiting London for the day and I thought . . ."

"Quite. We're always delighted when out-of-town members pop in. You know the drill? Ladies are permitted in the Dining Room but only the foremost part, and this is the Ladies' Sitting Room. Between seven and nine we're admitted to the bar but only if accompanied. The Library is open to you, of course."

"Oh yes, I remember. I'm keen to find out about one of our St. Hilda's girls. The daughter of an acquaintance. She went up to read mathematics if I'm not mistaken. A very bright spark. I wondered how she was getting on. Lavinia Blyth?"

The woman stared at her feet as she thought for a moment and then her eyes lit on the girl with the Russian book who let out a gurgling laugh and sat up.

"Gosh. What on earth do you want to know about *her* for?"

"Well, I rather admired that astonishing debate in which she took part. About the rights of animals. Quite provocative stuff. I read the report of it but I haven't heard anything about the girl since. She seemed remarkable—clever and principled but in an interesting way. And very young, of course."

The girl ran a hand over her head and plucked at her earlobe. "Really? You liked all that guff?"

"Was it guff? Didn't Lavinia mean it?"

"Just because she meant it doesn't mean it wasn't guff."

"So she hasn't taken up with the hunt then? Rescinded her ways? Started to eat meat and kill foxes?"

"Not the last time I saw her."

The membership officer stepped back. "Well, well, there we are," she said. "So you're very welcome, Miss Bevan. I'll leave you both to it, shall I?"

Mirabelle nodded and focused on the girl. She wanted to find out more. She moved to sit on an armchair next to her.

"I didn't think Lavinia would change her ways and take up hunting. She was so very impassioned. I knew her father, you see. I can't imagine the girl's views went down well at home and that made me think it was doubly brave of her."

The blonde snapped shut her book.

"Are you a vegetarian, then?"

"No."

"And you're a friend of Lavinia's father?"

"I knew him during the war. Quite a character! His office was next door to where I worked and he was a stickler. I made the connection when I saw her name. He had two daughters, I think. Lavinia must be the younger."

The girl surveyed Mirabelle carefully as if she was making a decision. "I'm starving," she said. "Let's have some sandwiches, shall we?" She reached out and rang the bell.

"Ham sandwiches and tea," the girl instructed the maid who hardly had time to enter the room. "Lots of mustard, as well," she called out. "I can't bear bland food, can you? It reminds me of everything that's lousy about institutions. What did you read when you went up?"

"Oh, that's a while ago! Classics," Mirabelle replied.

She had realized after she graduated that her degree wasn't likely to lead to much of a career and like most women, she was expected to meet a suitable husband while she was up at university and marry in her early twenties. She hadn't planned much beyond her graduation ceremony and when nothing presented itself she took a Master's in Modern Languages. Mirabelle loved college—an orphan by then it gave her something worthwhile to do. Later, after she'd graduated a second time, she'd worked for a translation agency until the war broke out. Then at least her education had proved useful. But there was no need to go into all that now.

"Classics? Crikey," the girl said.

Giving a little information always seemed to turn the tables. You gave a little and then the person you wanted to talk gave back. It came so naturally she scarcely thought about it.

"Are you still at college?" The youngster seemed no more than twenty at most, but still, it was hard to tell these days.

"I should come clean," she volunteered, reaching out her hand. "I'm Deirdre. Call me Didi. I'm Vinny's sister,

Deirdre Blyth. Paul Blyth's elder daughter. That's why the membership lady scooted. A potentially windy situation— you inquiring about my sister in front of me."

Mirabelle paled. "I'm terribly sorry . . . Oh dear, that was most indiscreet of me . . ."

Didi Blyth beamed. "Oh, no need. It was jolly watching Speccy Four Eyes squirm. You're absolutely right about my father. He's a character. In fact, he's a beast! That's why I'm here, actually. I've been staying in town over the weekends. That way I still get to spend time in London but I don't have to see him. He's down in the country most weekends, but I still don't take the risk of going home. The club's a super bolt-hole. To be frank, I try to keep away from the old chap as much as I can. My hairstyle seems to be particularly enraging at the moment."

The maid brought a tray and set it down on the table. The tang of fresh mustard wafted toward Mirabelle on a cloud of steaming Earl Grey as she poured from the pot.

"Well, it's very decent of you not to be offended. I think your hair is chic. Very short, so you're brave, too, Didi. And I wonder do you also like jazz?" She handed over a cup and saucer.

"Gosh no! So you know about Vinny's disaster this week? You mustn't think she likes jazz. Not at all. I've never known her to sneak out at night, and up till now the most controversial she's ever been musically is to say she doesn't like Maria Callas. Vinny called her Aida controlled screeching. I mean, she's usually such a daddy's girl. Wouldn't say boo to a goose. Kick a lousy dog and she'll fight as if she's at Sebastopol, but get a decent haircut or sneak out of the house? Not our Vinny."

Didi picked up a gray-looking sandwich, slathered it with bright mustard and chewed thoughtfully. "So what was Daddy like when he worked in Whitehall? Just as much of a dictator?"

Mirabelle sipped her tea and decided to skip the details.

"Well, he was Commander Blyth in those days. We weren't friends, more colleagues. He was a stickler for detail, if that's what you mean—a good officer—but very strict with his staff. He got results and that's what counted."

"What a good memory you've got to spot Vinny in the paper. . . ."

Mirabelle flirted with a smile. "I hope he doesn't punish her."

"Oh, it's practically insurrection in his eyes! Poor Vinny won't be back at college for a while. I mean, the police are involved. He'll hate that! No, he'll hole her up down in the country until it all dies down. She won't be allowed off the property, poor thing. And it's so dreary down there! Especially at this time of year."

"Did you know the other girl, Rose? The one who's missing?"

"I can't understand that either. Rose is, well, I don't know how to describe her. She's very confident and fashionable, and Vinny isn't at all her cup of tea. Of course they know each other because we all know each other. From town mostly—the Bellamy Gores are neighbors. They live in the annex of Chester House across the road. But what Rose and Vinny were doing out together I can't imagine. Vinny is a swot, really. In America they'd call her homely. She likes animals. She likes reading. That sort of thing. But the Bellamy Gores are more . . . glamorous. They're all about parties and cocktails and they just *drip* style. They're *smart*. In truth I find them slightly flash, though what's happened to Rose is terribly sad, of course. I do hope they find her."

"What do you mean Bellamy Gores? Are there more than one?"

"Oh yes! Rose is inseparable from her cousin. Harry."

"And he was at the jazz club, too?"

"You don't get one Bellamy Gore without the other. They're joined at the hip, practically."

"Except the other night. Rose was separated from him the other night, wasn't she? She left the club without him."

Didi dropped her voice. "Well, that's the odd thing. Harry was there. It was Harry who took the girls out. But for some reason none of the reports mention him. In the papers. Boys get away with everything! I mean, it's ridiculous—a girl steps out, goes dancing, gets her hair cut, decides to spend the summer in Italy and it's a scandal. A chap does it and no one bats an eyelid. The police spent five minutes asking Harry questions and then hours grilling poor Vinny."

"Really?"

"Makes me sick! We're supposed to have some kind of equality, you know. Especially since the war and everything. But it's just tripe!"

"Perhaps they felt Lavinia was a better witness. Did your sister see anything? Does she know what happened?"

Didi shrugged her shoulders. "Must do, I suppose. I haven't spoken to her. Father was in a fearful snot. Mother is so ineffective she's practically see-through and, well, it doesn't matter about my opinion. I just left them all to it. If Vinny did see anything she'll have told the police, naturally. I mean who wouldn't want Rose to be found? But what makes you so very interested, Miss Bevan?"

"Because I can't work out what happened. Rose appears to have gone missing and everyone assumes she's hurt. Meanwhile, in the papers there's nothing. As far as I can make out there's no evidence. They haven't discovered a body. The girl simply vanished."

Didi was obviously relishing the conversation. "You'd need to speak to the police to discover the ins and the outs. Of course, there are always rumors about girls like Rose, but now that there's something to actually base them on it's just taken off! So many people are gossiping about it— it's the latest craze. I was at a party yesterday and everyone had a theory about what happened. They say that some black man raped her, that she was pregnant and killed herself, that she was stabbed in an opium den, that she was some fearful tart who slept with everyone going. God knows what else. The truth is that Rose lived life to the full. She sparkled. People love tarnishing a woman who sparkles—any woman with a bit of life about her. And I'm not sure Rose didn't secretly want to tarnish herself a little, though that might be guff. She was a golden girl, you know. Everyone expected her to marry terribly well, although now that's unlikely. Not even Rose can disappear for almost two days in a storm of rumors like that and not find her currency devalued."

Mirabelle finished her tea. Didi's opinions were fascinating. "You're right, of course. And her cousin Harry?"

"Harry is fearfully good-looking. He drives one of those new green sports cars. He's the sort of chap who practically gets away with murder all the time. Strawberry blond, and honey eyes. Confident as hell. Still, not at all my type." Didi smiled. "Dishy and charming but not my type at all."

"Well, he must be frantic with worry."

"Oh, I'm sure," Didi said. "We all are."

Later that afternoon Mirabelle walked back to Duke's Hotel. She waved vaguely at the receptionist and wandered into the bar where some customers were finishing a long lunch with coffee and brandies. The Italian waiter floated to Mirabelle's side.

"Whisky sour, madam? Your usual table?"

"Actually, I'm looking for my friend. Eddie Brandon? We had drinks here last night. He's a regular. Do you have an idea where I can get hold of him?"

The waiter's eyebrows lifted slightly. "I can leave a note behind the bar."

"No. That won't do. Do you have a number? An address? It's essential I speak to Mr. Brandon before I leave town."

From behind the bar an older waiter pushed the fellow aside with a stream of Italian that Mirabelle couldn't completely follow but appeared to run along the lines of discretion being overrated when there was a beautiful woman involved.

"Come," he gesticulated, leading her up a small flight of stairs to a corridor where he knocked smartly on a black door. As it swung open Mirabelle stepped into a sumptuous room decorated in a velvety forest green. A picture of the king hung over the unused fireplace. This, Mirabelle thought, was one of the private rooms where Jack used to meet Naval Command. It smelled of luxury—cigar smoke and juiced oranges. Normally you'd have thought it would be used for poker games or private dinners. This afternoon, however, Eddie was sitting on a leather chair, reading a file marked "Information." There was a cocktail shaker before him and half a glass of something that was an astonishing blue color.

Eddie jumped to his feet. "Jesus! Mirabelle! You gave me a fright! Can I get you a drink? I can't recommend this blue thing. Not for a lady!"

Mirabelle made herself comfortable in an armchair.

"So, Eddie, you're still in the game then?"

Eddie motioned to the waiter. "Bring her some coffee and a saucer of champagne," he said. "She looks like she could use it."

The man nodded and the black padded door closed behind him with a decisive click. Mirabelle unbuttoned her coat.

"You know I can't tell you anything." Eddie put the file into a box and then closed it.

"I'm only asking because, the thing is, I need to speak to *someone*. It's about that debutante who went missing. Rose Bellamy Gore? Eddie, something is very wrong. They're holding that black kid, the sax player. I don't think he did anything but the police seem set. I have a lot of questions. I want to know if they're going to charge him. And I want to know what kind of statement Lavinia Blyth gave about her friend's disappearance. And if it *is* a disappearance or if they've confirmed any kind of harm coming to the girl. There was another kid there—Rose's cousin—a boy. They seem to be ignoring him and solely focusing on the women for some reason. Oh, and there's a guy called Barney who works at Mac's and at Feldman's—I want to know more about his record because he's as crooked as ninepence and they seem to be taking his evidence as gospel. The investigating officer is called Green—Chief Inspector. Do you know him at all?"

Eddie stared for a moment, sizing Mirabelle up. The questions had come in a flood. "Well, they won't be charging your saxophonist with anything, that much I do know."

"That's good. I don't think they should." Mirabelle hesitated as Eddie picked up a sheaf of papers from the table. He pulled out a newspaper—the early edition of the *Evening Standard*—and turned it over. It flashed through Mirabelle's mind that it was the edition they had been selling at the Tube station she had passed on her way to the club.

Eddie suddenly looked grave. "No. It's not good news, I'm afraid. They won't be charging your friend with anything, because he's dead." He held up the newspaper. The headline read JAZZ FIEND'S GUILTY CONSCIENCE. HANGED IN CELL.

10

Friendship doubles joy and divides grief.

The champagne and coffee lay untouched. Mirabelle sipped distractedly at the glass of water the waiter had hurriedly brought her. It was she who had insisted Lindon go to the police—his death was all her fault. And worse, she'd been in London, not a mile from where he killed himself, digging into the case without going to visit him in custody. Perhaps if she had bothered she might have saved him. The article in the paper said he had a guilty conscience but it seemed more likely that the boy had simply lost hope.

"I was too bloody slow," she sniffed, pulling out a handkerchief from her clutch bag. She could feel tears running down her cheeks. "Damn it! I knew something was wrong. I could have gone and visited him. There I was at those jazz clubs, just talking, asking stupid questions while all the time . . . Oh, poor Lindon. What did he go and do that for?"

It seemed as if she trailed a long line of corpses in her wake. Could she have saved Jack? Or, last year, Sandor? Poor Lindon would have been better off without her.

Eddie mumbled something about brandy and she waved him off. Instead, he had a phone brought in on a long cord and Mirabelle tried to ring Vesta's lodgings in Brighton—a bedsit she rented on the top floor of a shop near the People's Picture Palace on Lewes Road. In the shabby hallway there was a shared pay phone. It was after five o'clock on a Saturday and the bell rang out for four minutes straight. Mirabelle tried twice. No one was at home. Like Vesta, the other tenants were lively, young and single. It seemed unlikely anyone would be back before the pubs closed.

"Someone has to tell her," Mirabelle whispered. "And quickly."

The only blessing was that it wouldn't make the Brighton papers. She considered calling McGregor but dismissed that idea immediately. He wasn't the right person to break such upsetting news and in any case it was Mirabelle's responsibility. Vesta would need a hug.

"Poor Vesta. I'd better go back," she said. "I should tell her myself."

"Is there anything I can do?" Eddie was a pragmatist. "I'm afraid I don't know your Chief Inspector Green."

"If you'd ask around about the Bellamy Gore girl, that would help. Anything you can find out about the case, Eddie. It just stinks. And anything you can dig up on Green's reputation would be helpful, too. He's the one who's presided over this. I'd like to know what kind of police officer he is."

Eddie nodded curtly. "Don't worry, old girl. I'll assist all I can."

Victoria train station was bustling. Mirabelle loitered near a hot-chestnut stand on the main concourse, drawn to the warmth. She had ten minutes till boarding. A dense weight sat heavily on her chest and she felt sick as the passengers came and went around her. Lindon had come to Brighton to ask for help. He was young and out of his depth. Then within twenty-four hours he'd lost all hope and killed himself—the desperate and horrifying act of someone either racked with guilt or terrified, trapped and unable to see a way out. Mirabelle wanted to believe it was the latter. People had secrets—everyone did—but she was sure that Rose's disappearance was not down to Lindon Claremont. Surely only a madman would keep an object as incriminating as the cigarette case, or at least only a madman would carry it with him and show it to a stranger. Lindon might not have been the sharpest pencil in the box but he wasn't crazy. And by all accounts Rose had a strong personality—Didi had described her as a golden girl. Lindon was far too easygoing to be a natural leader. It seemed unlikely to Mirabelle that he would be able to get Rose to do much she didn't want to, certainly not in public. She was convinced the couple hadn't left the club together.

"I just handed him over," Mirabelle kept repeating under her breath. "I let McGregor send him to London."

She closed her eyes as the vision of Lindon hanging from a twisted bedsheet in a prison cell flickered into view. There she had been, enjoying London, flirting with the memory of Jack and drinking cocktails when all the time Lindon was vulnerable and in danger. She should have known better.

"I should have gone straight to Scotland Yard to see him," she berated herself under her breath. A vision of Lindon's nervous fingers twitching as he sat opposite McGregor made her stomach turn. She'd known how afraid he was. Why hadn't she done more to comfort him?

As Mirabelle boarded the train two women carrying shopping bags from the West End sensed her disquiet and moved on to another carriage. Still feeling wretched, Mirabelle headed to a first-class carriage, closed the door and sank onto a brushed velvet seat. The train juddered and pulled out of the station.

"You all right, miss?" a portly conductor asked.

Mirabelle jumped. She fumbled in her bag for her ticket.

"If you need anything, just call," he said kindly as he clipped it.

The door closed, and she fought back tears.

Brighton was colder, but at least the air was clear. Mirabelle paused at the station exit and steeled herself. It was almost seven o'clock. Snatches of music burst onto the pavement from the nearby pubs; already it seemed busy. Local trains arrived in a rush from out of town and the good-natured banter of nurses, shopgirls and secretaries floated on the air as they headed into Brighton for a Saturday night on the tiles. Everyone was wearing their colorful best—it felt like a carnival. Mirabelle started down the hill. Vesta had said she was going to the cinema but she hadn't said which evening. Still, the Regent would be a good place to start and it was only five minutes toward the seafront. If Vesta wasn't there she might well be in the adjacent dance hall. Outside the cinema an orderly queue snaked back from the ticket booth. Two middle-aged women wearing turban-style hats paraded along the line, selling delicate posies of flowers and chatting cheerfully to the revelers. Mirabelle approached the entrance.

"Here! You can't push in!" The man at the head of the queue put out his hand to stop her. "We've been out here twenty minutes in the cold, missus. That's not fair."

Mirabelle stepped back. "I'm sorry. I'm looking for a friend. There's been a bereavement and I think she's inside."

"Oh sorry, love." He drew back. "I thought you were queue hopping."

A man in a dinner suit and bow tie appeared at Mirabelle's side as if by magic and grasped her by the elbow. "I'm the manager," he said. "Bereavement, is it? Right. Come with me."

The hallway of the Regent glowed red, and people were bustling up and down the stairs, and milling around the kiosk. Two girls with trays of sweets and drinks stood at the doors to the cinema, handing out change and flirting with Saturday night chancers in sharp suits.

"We had a fella died inside one time. Takes all sorts," the man said inexplicably.

The smell of warm popcorn from the Butterkist stand made Mirabelle's stomach lurch. "My friend wanted to see *Scrooge*, I think. She mentioned Alastair Sim."

"That'd be right. What does she look like?"

"She's black," Mirabelle said simply.

"A darkie?"

Mirabelle bit her lip and looked at him sharply. She wished people wouldn't be so rude but she thought if she said something now she might lose her temper.

"Well, that makes it easier," he continued smoothly. "I don't think from memory we've got a darkie in the pictures tonight. Think I know the girl you mean. Plumpish. Comes with different fellas? I've not seen her with one of her own."

Mirabelle let his comments go. She felt slightly wobbly. The heat and the vibrant red of the walls, floors and ceiling were making her woozy. "Could we look in the screen, do you think? If she's not there she might be at the dance hall."

"If she'd gone in I'd have noticed, love."

"I think we should check."

The man didn't want to but Mirabelle's resolve was clear. He pushed open the door into the blacked-out screen and led her down the aisle, flashing a torch into the seating area on either side. The audience members squinted as he checked each row. He was right. Vesta wasn't there. Back in the foyer Mirabelle asked the way to the dance hall.

"It's upstairs on the roof. But it's too early. The dancing doesn't get going till later on—Syd and the band give it laldy from about eight. The best I can think is if she's here at all she might be in the restaurant or one of the cafés nearby," he suggested.

The man guided her gently outside. The cool air felt good on her clammy skin. She looked up and down. There were a lot of pubs, restaurants and cafés on Queen's Road. Which one would Vesta favor on a night out? Suddenly Mirabelle felt exhausted, as if her ankles were about to give way. She leaned against the wall and realized she was shivering.

"Bereavement can take a person that way," the manager said. "Might be best if you just left it to me. I'll send her home."

"No. You don't understand. I'm responsible," Mirabelle insisted. "We have to go back inside." She swept back toward the doors with the manager in her wake. Inside he was immediately approached by one of the usherettes. A young girl outside the café had a bleeding nose. He whipped his handkerchief from his pocket.

"Lean forward, love," he barked instructions, presenting her with the hankie to stem the flow.

Mirabelle took the opportunity to sneak off and wandered up to the cinema's restaurant alone. A dumpy waitress in a black uniform with a frilly apron plodded flat-footed toward her. "Table for one?" she sniffed.

"No thanks, just looking for someone." Mirabelle scanned the room. There was no sign of Vesta.

Downstairs the café was livelier with tables of weekend partygoers chattering animatedly. Mirabelle hesitated a moment. There she was. Vesta was at a table with friends. She looked happy and carefree, sharing a joke with one of the men. When she saw Mirabelle approaching, her face lit up and she waved, jumping to her feet. Mirabelle's heart sank.

"Mirabelle!" Vesta squealed. "This is Mikey, Gillian, Keith. Everyone, Mirabelle. She's my boss."

They said how do you do and Mikey fetched another chair. Mirabelle hovered.

"What are you doing here?" Vesta grinned. "Decided to see *Scrooge* after all? We haven't gone in yet so you can come with us if you like."

Mirabelle sank into the chair. It would be easier to speak if she didn't have to concentrate on staying upright.

"I don't know how to . . . Vesta, I'm sorry. It's Lindon."

Vesta extinguished her cigarette and looked at Mirabelle. "What happened?"

"He died in police custody."

Vesta took a moment to take this in. Her face crumpled. "Don't say they hurt him," she sobbed.

"No. I'm so sorry. He hanged himself. Oh, Vesta. It was in the evening paper in London, and I came down straightaway to tell you."

Gillian tried to put a hand on Vesta's arm, but Vesta brushed it off.

"No," she said. "I don't believe it. Oh, his mama. His poor mama. Why would he go and do a stupid thing like that? I've got to get up there. I've got to go to London tonight. Right now." Vesta fumbled for her coat.

Mirabelle nodded. "I'll come with you."

Vesta's fingers were suddenly thick as she did up the buttons. She flung her arms around Gillian who remained sitting at the table. The men cleared their throats and looked awkward.

"I'm sorry. I've spoiled your night now," Vesta apologized to her friends.

"No. No. Don't be silly," the others mumbled awkwardly as they watched the two women depart.

*   *   *

Outside, Vesta heaved deep breaths in the cold air as if she were drowning. The Saturday night buzz receded around her.

"Mirabelle, what the hell happened?" Vesta gasped.

"I thought something was wrong so I went up to town to have a look around. I should have gone to see him first, and I didn't . . . I'm sorry, Vesta."

"You were in London? You left me behind?" Vesta was incredulous. Fury flashed in her eyes. "You didn't even let me know? Mirabelle!"

Mirabelle hadn't even considered that.

"I'm sorry. It was spur of the moment, and it's the weekend . . . I didn't expect to find much."

"But you didn't even tell me!"

"I know. I didn't plan it or anything. I met McGregor for a drink after you left the office and he said they'd arrested Lindon. Before I knew it I was at the railway station."

"You said you'd keep in touch," Vesta glowered. "Well, did you find anything? At least tell me that!"

"There's a lot that doesn't tie up. I'm pretty sure that Lindon didn't leave the club with Rose, though people seem to accept that he did. And I'm also sure there's some kind of cover-up going on. Rose's friend Lavinia . . ." Here Vesta hooted with laughter though Mirabelle realized that the poor girl was in shock. "This Lavinia appears to have given a statement that Rose and Lindon left the club together. The doorman agrees. But I doubt it. We need to speak to the officer in charge—Chief Inspector Green."

"Do you think we should try to get hold of McGregor?"

Mirabelle checked her watch. It was approaching eight o'clock. "Yes, let's. That's a good idea. I think I know where he'll be."

They turned into town and headed for the Cricketers' Arms. Vesta was distracted and upset. She tripped on the curb and recovered her balance. Mirabelle held out her arm and Vesta grabbed on to it.

"Look, you can't leave me out like that." The girl's eyes were flooding. "You have to promise me you'll never do that to me again. I didn't even know they'd taken him into custody. You said you'd ring."

Mirabelle turned. "I tried," she said, "but there was no answer. You're right though. I promise I won't hold back in the future. I'm really sorry. I got so caught up that I didn't think."

Vesta shrugged.

"You're not on your own anymore and neither am I," she insisted. "I know there's some things I'm good at and others that are more up your street. That's fine. But you have to tell me."

Vesta pushed open the pub door. Inside it was packed. The noise of the crowd was deafening. As they stepped inside a drunken man ogled Vesta. "Nig nog," he burped.

"Have some manners!" Mirabelle shouted over the din as she pushed past him toward the bar. Vesta tried to follow but the crowd was too dense. "You go." She motioned and watched the top of Mirabelle's head heading farther inward.

Sure enough, McGregor was nursing a pint in a relatively quiet corner.

"There's nothing like a reliable man," Mirabelle said.

"Oh, Mirabelle. I'm so sorry. That boy, that friend of yours. I went to your flat but you weren't there. He killed himself."

"I'm not so sure he did, Detective. Vesta's with me, and we're on our way up to London. I'd like to speak to Chief Inspector Green. Can you put me in touch?"

McGregor looked at Mirabelle. The idea of her poking her nose into police business again set him on edge.

"Who told you that name?" he demanded, slightly drunk. "How on earth did you find out who was in charge of the case?"

"You said so yesterday!"

Oh Christ! McGregor cursed himself. The damn woman never overlooked a single detail.

"They'll give you short shrift at the Yard. It's one thing down here but you haven't got a hope up in London. They just won't tolerate women poking in their noses. . . . Let me buy you a drink. Whisky, isn't it?"

"No thanks." Mirabelle had got what she'd come for. She squeezed her way through the crowd, back toward Vesta. The girl was right. She'd behaved unforgivably. Now she'd have to find a way to make it up to her.

1 1

Jazz is black classical music.

The receptionist at Duke's adopted an artificially insouciant air when Mirabelle and Vesta arrived at ten o'clock. On the train they had made the decision to stay in the hotel overnight before Vesta went to the East End to visit Lindon's parents, and for that matter her own family, the following morning.

"Two single rooms? No luggage?" She sniffed as she cast her eyes quickly over Vesta. "Give me a moment, madam. I'll have to check with the manager."

"We'll be in the bar," Mirabelle said firmly, leading Vesta down the passageway.

Inside, the bar had a cozy feel. A few tables were taken with couples drinking cocktails and smoking, but it didn't feel crammed. Coming in from the cold the claret walls were warming.

"A whisky sour and your usual table, miss?" The waiter approached.

Vesta raised an eyebrow.

Mirabelle ignored her. "Is Mr. Brandon here?"

The waiter shook his head. "You've just missed him."

"Do you know where he went?"

The waiter was far too discreet to divulge this kind of

information. Of course, Mirabelle knew exactly where he would be at this time of night. For a moment she considered beating the bushes in St. James's Park, the way they do on country estates when they want game birds to break cover. Heavens alone knew how many scandals that would produce. Eddie was quite outrageous but he was so unapologetic that he always seemed to get away with it. He'd be back eventually.

"A whisky sour for me and my friend will have a martini."

The women took a seat at a corner table. When the drinks arrived Vesta sipped hers tentatively at first and then gasped, "Oh!"

"The best in London."

"I'll bet. And I'd say one might be enough. These babies are strong."

Mirabelle smiled. "A friend used to come here. Actually, Jack did. During the war. It's not the Savoy or the Ritz or anything, but I like it. It's . . . discreet."

Vesta looked around disbelieving. She'd never been to the Savoy or the Ritz but this hotel didn't seem particularly "discreet." The Italian waiter at the bar tossed a cocktail shaker in the air, and another waiter let out a cheer for show. The sound of clinking ice formed an elegant rhythm. An American couple clapped.

"So, who's this Mr. Brandon? Another secret from your 'discreet' past?" Vesta picked up a walnut from the bowl on the table.

"Oh, an old friend. I think he might be able to get hold of Chief Inspector Green for us. We'll need help. McGregor was right about one thing—the Yard isn't Brighton. Eddie Brandon is well connected."

Vesta's eyes filled with tears and she bit her lip. "Tomorrow I'm going to have to go home, aren't I? And see Lindon's parents. They're going to be devastated, Mirabelle. What am I going to say?"

Mirabelle wished Vesta didn't have to go through all this. It was important, though, to focus on the practicalities.

"Well, for one thing, see what you can find out. The police will have told Lindon's family as much as they can and we need to know what they've said."

Vesta sighed and took a restorative sip of her martini. She had gone to Brighton specifically to get away from her loving but intrusive family and their extended friends and near relations.

"I want to be there," she said, trying to convince herself. "But it's going to be awful."

Mirabelle laid a hand gently on Vesta's arm. "Goes without saying," she murmured.

The receptionist appeared at their table and coughed quietly. "That appears to be fine, Miss Bevan. Any friend of Mr. Brandon . . ." She laid two keys on the table and avoided looking at Vesta. "If your maid needs any help with luggage . . ."

"We don't have any luggage, we shan't require breakfast, and for your information Miss Churchill is not my maid. She's my friend and business partner," Mirabelle snapped. The receptionist looked bemused by this information but Mirabelle continued breezily. "Miss Churchill and I will both be leaving early, so if you could have the first editions of the Sunday papers delivered to my room it would be most appreciated, including the *News of the World*, please."

The girl nodded dutifully but clearly couldn't think of anything to say, least of all sorry. She turned sharply and marched back to the foyer.

"I apologize, Vesta," Mirabelle said, sitting bolt upright in her outrage.

Vesta shrugged. "If you worry about that stuff too much, you go crazy," she mouthed sadly. "What we're going to do is far more important than what Miss High and Mighty thinks. Though I can't say I'm not sick of it," she admitted. "'Specially today."

Mirabelle gave a sympathetic look.

"You wouldn't think that we'd fought for everyone to be allowed their freedom," she said.

"Freedom?" Vesta sounded the word as if it was somehow foreign to her. "Yes. I suppose. Well, we're here now and the main thing is to focus on finding out what happened and on clearing Lindon's name. So where are you going tomorrow?" she asked.

"Scotland Yard, of course."

Vesta regarded her cocktail misty-eyed. "He probably won't be working on Sunday. Green, that is."

"I'll take the chance."

Vesta took another sip. "Shame there aren't any black policemen. It might not have happened. . . ."

"I don't believe this happened to Lindon because he was black, Vesta. Honestly, he was just a kid who was in the wrong place at the wrong time and he got accused of something awful. I wish I'd gone to see him when I came up here. I could have helped. Do you think he just lost hope?"

"Lindon? We shouldn't have taken him to McGregor, should we? Oh God, it's going to be terrible tomorrow. His mum and my mum. All any of us wants is to have him back. It's like some horrible mistake has been made and now we can't get out of it, can we?"

Mirabelle squeezed Vesta's hand. Death was often that way, it seemed. Unjust and unnegotiable. "I know," she whispered.

They sat for a few minutes in silence watching the barmen concocting Singapore Slings and Cosmopolitans. The sadness at the table was palpable.

Eventually Vesta looked at her watch. "I don't think I'll sleep," she said, "even after one of these. Do they have a wireless in the rooms?"

Mirabelle shook her head. "There might be one in the Residents' Lounge. I tell you what, you don't fancy going along to one of the jazz clubs? Just to have a look? Things will quieten down here soon, but the clubs are just opening. At least we'd be doing something."

"All right, why not?" Vesta said bravely, managing a weak smile.

The doorman at Jermyn Street didn't appear to recognize Mirabelle from the night before. Sure-footed this time, she led Vesta down the stairs and through the door with the orange light above it, handing over the entrance money without even looking. Inside, the club was busier. It was a younger crowd tonight, women dressed in low-cut tops with heavy eye makeup, sipping champagne saucers of a drink that glowed orange in the low light. Men wore suits cut so sharply, they seemed to dance almost on their own. The band was playing full tilt and couples moved savagely to the raging beat. To one side a table was knocked and some drinks spilled. No one came to clear things up. The bar was three-deep, even with four men serving. Saturday night. Mirabelle stood on her tiptoes—thankfully the barman from yesterday wasn't on duty.

Beside her Vesta swayed to the music. "The band is great! Did Lindon play here?"

Mirabelle shook her head. "But he came here once or twice, and it's a small world. There'll be plenty of people around who knew Lindon, I'm sure of it. I'll get us a drink," she shouted.

Vesta was intrigued. She began to snake toward the dance floor. The band was an eight-piece with saxes of different sizes, bass, drums, piano, trombone and trumpet. The entire company was white and they were dressed in matching suit trousers and crisp shirts with rolled-up sleeves. Bottles of beer were perched beside the instrument stands.

As Vesta reached the dance floor she saw the black guy immediately. He was casually smoking a cigarette, and the sheen of his tan-colored suit glinted in the low light. He grinned widely and beat out the rhythm with one hand as he leaned in to speak into her ear. "Hey, sister, what you doing in a place like this?"

"I could say the same to you," Vesta shouted as she took the cigarette he was offering. She liked Chesterfields. He fired up a battered brass lighter and lit her.

"You into this sound?"

"I like saxophone."

"I play the horn."

"All good," she flirted.

"You're solid!" The horn player motioned away from the hubbub. The band was so loud it was difficult to hear and the number was getting more and more frantic. "Come with me."

Vesta looked over her shoulder. It was hot and the music was overwhelming. On the dance floor a group of three women looked as if they were possessed as they danced. One man threw back his head and laughed maniacally. Mirabelle was nowhere to be seen, the melee at the bar completely obscuring her. Vesta sized up the horn player and made her decision. There was only one way to find things out. She followed him past the stage and through a door into a back room. The acoustics changed as he closed the door and gestured toward a chair in the middle of a jumble of instrument cases, a coat stand covered in hats and a bucket with a mop propped in it. It was quieter back here, the jazz a thumping undercurrent.

"You fancy a bit of fun?"

Vesta shifted uncomfortably. She wondered why she'd followed him so readily and eyed the door.

"I'm not really in the mood. I don't want . . ."

"No, sister. Nothing like that. I ain't gonna lay a hand . . ." He drew a small cannabis joint from his inside pocket and leaned against the brick wall. "Just a little something, okay?"

Vesta drew on her cigarette. She crossed her arms. "You go ahead. Not for me."

"Awww, sister. Don't mind me. I'm only trying to keep my head together with all this white music banging on. The Irish guys ain't bad—the tenor sax is hep enough though he's a kike, of course. Them Jew boys got a different rhythm, you dig? But it's rhythm all the same. They're hipsters. But those lousy English boys on the horns, and, man, who has a white guy on *drums*? The guy's from Croydon!"

He illustrated his point by beating out a dull rhythm on the tabletop next to him. Then he took a draw on the joint and smiled at Vesta through the smoke. "You're one very hep lady."

Vesta felt her lip wobble.

"Hey," he said, "you okay?"

"My friend, he was a musician . . . He died yesterday."

"Shit. Not Lindon?"

Vesta nodded. She dropped her hip against the table just for something to lean on. "We've been friends since we were kids," she blurted. "Tomorrow I gotta go and face his mama, and I gotta face my mama, and . . . our folks knew each other a long time."

The horn player grabbed an unlabeled bottle of spirits and a couple of grubby shot glasses from a small cupboard.

"Here, have some of this."

Vesta sniffed. The reek of home-brewed alcohol assaulted her nostrils.

"Poteen," he explained. "Now that's something the Irish *can* do." He downed his shot in one.

Vesta sipped tentatively. She could feel the liquor kindling a fire in her chest. The warmth was comforting. "I just can't believe Lindon killed himself," she said quietly.

The horn player put down the bottle. "No black man ever killed himself in police custody, baby. Oh, sweetheart. I mean, you move like you know something. Those bastards . . ." He paused, methodically extinguishing the anger in his voice. "Don't think that of your friend, okay? I knew Lindon a little. From the scene, you know. He was a nice kid. Not a pukka cat on the horn but competent, you dig? He wouldn't hurt no one, and that includes himself."

Vesta tossed back the rest of the poteen and then gasped as it took her breath away. "Shit," she said.

"That's right, baby. Shit. Shit. Shit. They been treating us bad since the dawn of time, these ghosts, and now's when it has to stop."

Vesta bit her lip. It wasn't often in male company that Vesta didn't smile and laugh. Now she stood stock-still, serious and silent.

"I mean, I wasn't there, sister, but Lindon didn't leave Mac's with no white girl. That's what I heard. The whole band that night were black men. Police just picked one and framed him up good. Could've been any one of them. The missing girl talked to poor Lindon. So when the fingers was pointing, they pointed at him. Hey, where you going?"

Vesta had placed the empty glass on the table and was heading for the door.

"Thanks," she called out. "You cleared my head."

Back inside the club the beat was still frantic. She could see Mirabelle's head at the edge of the crowd at the bar scanning the club for her friend. Vesta pushed toward her.

"The barmen won't talk. It's too busy," Mirabelle shouted as she handed Vesta a shot of whisky. "We should try to speak to the musicians when they're finished. They'll have known Lindon. Someone must remember something."

Vesta downed her whisky and handed back her glass. The girl's eyes were drawn toward the stage. "They won't know anything. None of them were playing at Mac's that night."

"How do you know? Where did you go just now?" Mirabelle asked.

Vesta didn't answer. Her eyes were wide open. "We should get back to the hotel," she said. "This is a waste of time. This isn't what Lindon was into, and we need to get some sleep before tomorrow."

12

True genius resides in the capacity for evaluating uncertain, hazardous and conflicting information.

The receptionist was absorbed in a crime novel—the latest by James Hadley Chase, Mirabelle noticed—and she didn't even look up as the two women glided through the hallway at Duke's and took the stairs to the second floor. Vesta held her drink remarkably well, thought Mirabelle. Last year, Vesta would never have had the guts and strong-mindedness she had displayed this evening. The girl had learned a lot and she seemed to be coping with Lindon's death reasonably well. Mirabelle was impressed. At least the girl was being practical. She put a hand on her empty stomach. It was probably too late to order something to eat and she didn't have the energy or the inclination to walk over to Piccadilly to buy chips. Despite the ideas whizzing around her mind Mirabelle felt utterly exhausted and was looking forward to disappearing into the darkness for a few hours. "Good night," Vesta nodded as she put her key into the lock.

"Good night." Mirabelle continued down the hallway.

Mirabelle hadn't unlocked her room when a terrific crash emanated from behind Vesta's half-open door and a high-pitched squeal cut through the silence. Mirabelle rushed toward the noise, bursting through the doorway.

Two shadowy figures were discernible in the corner of the bedroom. Mirabelle snapped on the light. Vesta—armed with a wooden chair—had a man pinned against the wall.

"Eddie!"

"I'm so sorry. I think I'm in the wrong room," he apologized frantically as Vesta slowly lowered the chair. "Ah, thank heavens, Mirabelle. There you are. The girl on the desk said 212. I'm so sorry, miss. I didn't intend to alarm you."

The cigarette in his hand sent a trail of smoke in his wake as he tried to guide Vesta away.

"Vesta, this is Eddie Brandon," Mirabelle said. "Eddie, this is Vesta Churchill, my business partner and Lindon Claremont's friend."

"I'm lucky to be alive! So, you're Mirabelle's connection to this case." Eddie gave a charming smile as he offered Vesta a cigarette. "They said Mirabelle had gone out but they didn't say she was with anyone so I thought I would wait. They're too damn discreet by far round here."

"'S all right." Vesta sat down on the chair. "They think I'm the maid, is all."

Eddie looked at her quizzically. "I could order some drinks, if you like," he offered. "Some cocoa perhaps?"

Normally Vesta jumped at the offer of any kind of sustenance but tonight she shook her head solemnly.

Mirabelle couldn't resist though. "Cocoa's a good idea. And toast if it's not too late."

"They'll do it for me." Eddie lifted the telephone and ordered, adding a double brandy for himself. "Are you sure you don't want anything?" he whispered to Vesta before hanging up.

"I've lost my appetite."

Mirabelle perched on the end of Vesta's bed and crossed her legs. "Well, Eddie," she said, "you didn't come here for a midnight feast."

"I thought you'd want to know what transpired from my inquiries. I went looking for your key players. The Bel-

lamy Gore girl is still missing in action as it were. The police story is that she left the club that night with Lindon
Claremont, got into a cab, of which the police can find no
trace as yet, and she hasn't been seen since. Lavinia Blyth
panicked and phoned her father from a nearby phone box.
Paul Blyth contacted the police, and, given who he is, they
went looking immediately."

Vesta listened keenly.

"Well, that's rather odd, for a start," said Mirabelle.
"For three reasons. First of all, I heard that Blyth was furious that Lavinia had got the police involved. Lavinia's sister told me. But he can't have been if he called them
himself. Secondly, if Paul Blyth rules his house like he used
to rule his office, I'd have thought that Lavinia would have
done anything not to let him know what she was up to,
sneaking out at night and frequenting jazz clubs. She didn't
hurry home, either. It's odd. And the third thing is, well,
why on earth did he call the police? Belgravia operates
within its own circles first and foremost. If I was Paul
Blyth and I got a phone call in the middle of the night to
say Rose had got into a taxi with a man, I'd call the girl's
father before I called the authorities. The Blyths and the
Bellamy Gores know each other. They've been neighbors
for years. To get hold of the police immediately would risk
a scandal. The girl has only just turned eighteen, and she
certainly shouldn't have been out in a seedy jazz club, but
she wasn't overtly in any danger, was she?"

"Except," Eddie pointed out smoothly, "it looks like
old man Blyth was right, and so was his daughter. Rose
was missing. She's still missing. The police didn't get anything out of Lindon Claremont. They still have no idea
where the girl is. Regardless of the process, I think we can
say she was genuinely in danger. They can't rally the staff
and the villagers to search the outhouses in London, which
is what they'd do on a country estate. If he was taking it
seriously, he would have to have called the police."

Mirabelle frowned. "Still," she said, "not straightaway. He should have called the girl's family first."

"Well, that's what happened," continued Eddie. "Next up is our chap Chief Inspector Green. To describe him as young is an understatement. The chap is a shade under thirty and looks like a child. He's known as Babyface Green on the force, though that's behind his back, I should imagine. He did his duty with the Royal Pioneer Corps during the war but didn't make it out of the rank and file. He's handy with a spanner though—a first-class engineer. Started on the beat with a tour of duty in the East End where he exposed some black-market operations. Then promoted through the ranks. He got his big break for his part in the George Mitchell murder case in 1947 and that took him out of uniform. He didn't solve it, of course, but apparently his performance was highly competent. As far as I can make out he isn't previously acquainted with any of our players, which isn't that surprising—he came up the ranks after all."

There was a sharp rap on the door. A waiter appeared with a covered tray, which he laid carefully on the dressing table. Mirabelle thought she detected the shadow of a smirk on the fellow's face—a gentleman in a bedroom with two ladies after midnight was an event at Duke's, but he said nothing of course and left the room.

As Mirabelle sipped the sweet creamy cocoa and crunched the toast she began to feel more alert.

Eddie lit another cigarette to enjoy with his brandy.

"That's all very interesting, Mr. Brandon," Vesta said quietly, "but Lindon was killed in that man's custody."

Eddie caught Mirabelle's eye. "Do you know that?"

"We have to consider the possibility," Mirabelle agreed, dabbing her lips with a thick linen napkin. "But we don't know yet. You might be right, Vesta, though one imagines it would entail a very complicated conspiracy. Lindon was extremely nervous when he was taken into custody in

Brighton. He may simply have panicked and harmed himself. I'm sorry. But that's the truth."

Vesta's eyes flashed with anger but she didn't say anything.

"What I can say is that some of these details are fascinating," Mirabelle continued. "I mean, perhaps Green is the reason they questioned Lavinia Blyth so carefully. I heard they simply released Rose's cousin Harry and focused on Lavinia alone. But perhaps Green was as suspicious as I was about how this whole thing had been reported. He wanted to find out why Lavinia had rung her father. That would explain why they held her for so long and didn't keep Harry."

"Which brings me to the last jewel in my crown before bedtime," Eddie interrupted. "The aforementioned cousin, Harry Bellamy Gore. Society chap. Gentleman about town."

"Good-looking, wealthy, debonair, owner of a sports car and hardly worth questioning . . ." Mirabelle mused.

"It's too absurd. Our Harry has a record, albeit an unofficial one."

"Really?"

"It's quite sweet, actually. Harry was at Eton, and, oh, it's too marvelous. He's a pornographer!"

Mirabelle choked on her cocoa. *Harry?*

"Yes! Isn't it a wheeze! In his schoolboy days. He was almost expelled although, of course, the Belgrave set stepped in. He was distributing dirty pictures—actually not so much distributing as, well, selling them. He'd got hold of photographs somewhere up in London and took a supply back to school. Ladies in negligees and some girls playing tennis in a state of unwholesome dishabille. Apparently he made almost one hundred pounds and cleared out the annual allowances of several of his customers. He was only thirteen at the time! Quite the entrepreneur. Anyway, his parents sent him away for three months to Canada. The family have relations there. He went back to Eton a reformed character the following term and it was all hushed up."

"The police weren't called?"

"Of course not. Housemasters at Eton would rather swallow their own tongues than get the constabulary involved. However, the legend lives on. I know a couple of ex-Eton chaps. And it does say something about his nature, I suppose. From the boy groweth the man and all that. He's now at King's reading art history and expected to go on to work at the National Gallery or similar. He's especially interested in Renaissance sculpture, I hear. The human form is still his stock in trade," Eddie laughed. "All very amusing."

"Stop it!" Vesta leapt up. She strode over to the window and peered out into the darkness, arms folded. When she turned to face them again her eyes were filled with tears. "Lindon is dead. This isn't a joke! I don't believe Lindon killed himself. I won't believe it."

Eddie lowered his eyes and took a sip of the brandy. "I apologize," he said. "I didn't mean to upset you."

Mirabelle laid down her cup and saucer. She went over to Vesta and put an arm around her shoulders.

Vesta pulled away. "You didn't think it was funny last year when Sandor died," she pleaded. "Lindon has two sisters and two brothers, parents and aunts and uncles. He might have been too young to save anyone during the war or anything like that but he was a decent guy and he has people who care about him. We grew up together!"

Eddie stood up. "I apologize unreservedly. I'm sorry. It's a dreadful habit that people who work with difficult cases get into. It was a silly piece of information, it isn't relevant to the case and I'm sorry I made fun of it. Your friend shouldn't have died. It was disrespectful of me."

Vesta sat down wearily.

Mirabelle was intrigued. Eddie had made quite some

apology. Ex-SOE officers rarely apologized for anything. Their knee-jerk reaction was generally denial.

"Thank you, Eddie. You've cut out our work for us. Well, my work, anyway."

"Good. Good." Eddie stubbed out his cigarette. "I'll leave you to it. You know where to find me."

He picked up his hat and pulled on his coat. "Ladies, I bid you good night."

The door clicked shut.

"I'm sorry, Mirabelle. I know he was only trying to help."

"No need to be. Do you think you're going to be able to handle this?"

Vesta nodded. "I'll be fine."

"Good girl. Come on, I expect we both need some shut-eye. We've a lot to think about and a long day ahead of us."

13

Be ready for opportunity when it comes.

There was a note under Mirabelle's door the next morning. Vesta would meet her in the evening. Outside, London remained gray. Mirabelle heard the bells of a church up on Piccadilly chiming for Sunday service and wondered if it was St. James's. It was a long time since she had been in a church. She'd stopped going in 1940, increasingly disillusioned by the spiralling death toll. Since then she'd only ever attended funerals and memorial services, of which during the war years there were too many.

Shaking herself from those dark thoughts, she filled a basin with hot water and washed her face. It felt late, maybe ten o'clock, but her watch had stopped overnight. She pulled on her clothes and hurried downstairs.

Time was marching on, so Mirabelle settled the bill and set out toward Westminster. London felt like a ghost town. The buildings here were overbearingly gray and heavy. Down a side street round the corner from the Yard, a pub was just opening its doors. Mirabelle decided to duck in. Policemen drank in local bars and it seemed a good enough place to start. Besides, the walk had sharpened her appetite.

"A sherry, please," she ordered. "And do you have anything to eat?"

"We might manage a ploughman's," the barman offered. "There's always a roast on a Sunday but it's not ready yet. It's not so good neither, truth be told."

Mirabelle smiled. "A ploughman's would be fine. I'm heading round to the Yard. A friend of mine died there yesterday morning."

"That darkie?"

Mirabelle took a deep breath. "He was my friend."

The barman ignored the remark and headed to the kitchen. He returned with a plate of fluffy white bread and a sliver of buttery yellow Cheddar and laid a small glass of sherry in front of Mirabelle. In one corner of the plate a teaspoonful of chutney had been unexpectedly fashioned into a quenelle. The barman fished a pickled onion out of a jar with a long spoon and popped it delicately to the side of the meal, with a splash of dark vinegar.

"Do you know Chief Inspector Green, at all?" she inquired.

"Miss, the reason the police drink in here is 'cause we don't say a word."

"I've heard he looks terribly young. That's all. I wondered what he was like."

"You need to make up your mind about that yourself. I'm sorry about your mate. I always dislike it when they kill themselves. Being locked up is hard on a man. A trial is better for everyone in the long run, isn't it?"

Mirabelle sipped the sherry. "Does it happen often, do you know? People killing themselves in custody?"

The barman regarded the beer taps as if he was drawing inspiration from the metal plates. "Odd thing to ask. Whatcha getting at?"

Mirabelle tore off some bread and carefully placed a blob of chutney and a shaving of cheese on top. "It's a genuine question. I've never heard of it before—someone dying in police custody. But you have."

She popped the bread into her mouth and gave him a small smile as she chewed.

"Well, it happens all right," said the barman slowly. "Not too often, but I heard of it. They generally, you know, hang themselves," he gestured upward. "If a man's had enough, he's had enough, see. Plenty fellas would give up if they thought they was going down for a stretch quite apart from the guilt. That young darkie of yours killed a bird, didn't he? Maybe it hit him all at once, what he'd done. You want anything else, miss? It's only I've got to get down to the cellar to see to this tap."

"Gosh—everyone assumes the girl is dead. No one's even found a body. Do you think," Mirabelle continued smoothly, "you might manage a cup of tea?"

The barman looked nonplussed. "Kitchen's not open yet," he said. "I can't do nothing that involves cooking."

Outside, Mirabelle headed toward the river. The plane trees were skeletal and the opposite riverbank formed a vague misty outline through the gathering smog. She turned left along the Embankment and then paused in front of the sign mounted on the stone wall: CITY OF WESTMINSTER. METROPOLITAN POLICE. The building loomed. The door was open. Mirabelle took a deep breath. This was where Lindon died. Farther along the Embankment two police horses were making their rounds, the noise of their hooves echoing loudly along the otherwise empty road and across the water. It felt eerie. Had Lindon lost hope in this place? Vesta was convinced he had been murdered, but this morning it was easy to imagine someone giving up here. Even the entrance looked intimidating. Mirabelle braced herself and mounted the steps.

Inside, the desk sergeant was perched on a high stool. He was out of place, like a caricature of a country policeman. His cheeks were pink as summer plums, and his eyes sparkled. His uniform was immaculate, and Mirabelle reckoned he must be close to retirement. In the gray silence of the Embankment she had expected a shady ghostlike figure, one who might have presided over Lindon's death.

Mirabelle gave him her most winning smile. "May I speak with Chief Inspector Green, please?"

"No, madam. He's not available."

"A colleague perhaps? Someone involved with Rose Bellamy Gore's disappearance? I have some information."

The sergeant's sharp green eyes sized her up. "Give me a moment, madam."

He disappeared into the back and returned a minute later with a fresh-faced youngster who breezed through the swing doors. The officer was in plain clothes, his outfit a pale jumble of worn tweed—a suit and tie, but still shabby in contrast to the desk sergeant's orderly spit-and-polish appearance. The sergeant headed straight for his reception desk and the youngster stood alone. He didn't look as if he'd been through a whirlwind exactly, but he'd certainly endured a stiff breeze. His shoes, Mirabelle noticed, were scuffed. They looked as if they'd never been polished.

"Madam?"

"Are you C.I. Green?"

The boy laughed at the apparent ridiculousness of the question. "No, madam. Chief Inspector Green isn't in the station. I'm Constable Adler. May I get you a cup of tea?"

"Are you working on the Bellamy Gore case, Constable Adler?"

"Yes, madam. Come this way. There's an interview room we can use."

If anything the boy was younger than Lindon. She realized that was probably why he had seemed so eager. He couldn't be long out of training college. She was not, however, put off guard by his appearance. During the war some of the country's sharpest minds had looked as if they had been dragged through a hedge backward. It was something SOE had joked about. The Nazis were not disposed to take advantage of talent that came in unconventional packages. Jack always said Britain wouldn't have won the war without its eccentric geniuses—white, black, Gypsy and Jewish. Unlike the opposition, all talent was welcome. However, this kid might not be cut from that jib. Mirabelle considered him. He had already made a mistake. He'd invited her in without knowing what she wanted or, for that matter, who she was. It might be that he was simply inexperienced. Whatever it was, his incompetence was a stroke of luck. And it was fortunate that the more experienced desk sergeant hadn't intervened; no doubt thinking the smartly dressed woman would be no trouble and happy to let the boy get on with it.

"Have you been working all weekend?" she said.

"Yes, madam."

"So you were here yesterday?"

"Yes, madam."

"Gosh, you must be exhausted!"

Mirabelle followed the boy through several doors, down a corridor and into an office containing two desks and four chairs. A coat stand leaned in the corner with two regulation mackintoshes hanging forlornly from its pegs. She took a seat and the boy went off to make them tea. Mirabelle looked round. She wondered where Lindon's cell had been. Like most police stations, this building was a warren. Somewhere in here Lindon had given up or had been made to do so.

"Where are the holding cells?" she asked casually as Adler returned and handed her an overfull cup of milky white tea.

"Downstairs."

The tea was so weak Mirabelle wondered if he had administered actual leaves at any stage in the process. It wasn't even hot. She sipped politely.

"Is there something you'd like to report, madam? Before we start, I need to take some details from you."

Mirabelle decided on shock tactics. She sat back so she was open to him and then crossed her legs elegantly. He was expecting her to be uninvolved. She'd challenge that expectation.

"I'm the woman who accompanied Lindon Claremont to the station in Brighton. I know Detective Superintendent McGregor. I convinced Lindon that he had to give a witness statement, as he was possibly the last person to see Rose alive. Detective Superintendent McGregor handed him over to you on Friday afternoon. When I heard he'd died yesterday I wanted to come in. I felt I had to."

"What is it that you want, madam?"

"I'm here to ask some questions about how Lindon died, Constable Adler."

The boy hesitated. Mirabelle leaned forward. She did not break eye contact.

"Well," he started, "it's not usual procedure . . ."

"I'm asking you how a person for whom I feel responsible died," Mirabelle pressed.

Adler took a deep breath. His eyes hardened. "Mr. Claremont hanged himself. The case will go to the appropriate authorities on Monday and there will be an inquest. You're entitled to attend and to receive a copy of the report. It's open to the public and all aboveboard. Mr. Claremont died here in Westminster so the Coroner's Court is on Horseferry Road. It'll be held there."

"How did he hang himself? Do you know?"

"Madam, I'm not at liberty to give you details. It'll all be open at the inquest and you can raise any concerns there. They deal with these cases promptly."

Mirabelle allowed herself the merest flutter of her long lashes.

"Please, Constable Adler. I'm racked with guilt. Lindon is a close acquaintance of a friend of mine. He came to me for help and advice, and I handed him over to his death. I feel as if it's my fault. I've hardly slept since. I keep thinking about it. If I knew what had happened, it would make it far easier. Please."

Adler sighed. It was all due to come out in the inquest, anyway. The woman seemed genuine. "He tore the blanket. He was in one of the cells here. He rigged up something with the bars on the window. I'm not sure that it's appropriate, really . . ."

"Did you see his body?"

"What does that have to do with it? Listen, madam, I'm sorry, but the Metropolitan Police doesn't—"

"Had you charged him at the time of his death, Constable Adler?"

"No." Adler was searching Mirabelle's face, trying to figure her out.

Mirabelle pulled a hankie from her clutch bag. The boy had responded well to her comment about feeling responsible for Lindon's death. Playing on her femininity and making him feel uncomfortable seemed highly effective. "I just can't imagine why he did it," she sniffed.

Adler fiddled with his tie. "Guilt?" he suggested. "I'd say it was guilt."

"Perhaps. However, I'm fairly sure that Lindon Claremont wasn't guilty." Mirabelle blew her nose delicately.

"Why?" Adler sounded genuinely interested.

"Because I don't think he left Mac's with Rose on Thursday night, Constable."

"We have witnesses to that effect, Madam. That's a matter of police record."

"Did you find out where they went?"

"The investigation is still ongoing."

"So you haven't located the girl?"

"We're still looking," he said in an exasperated tone.

"If I were Chief Inspector Green, I'd be wondering why Lindon kept the cigarette case. I mean, honestly, what kind of a fool would keep something like that if he'd committed a violent crime? It links him straight to it."

"People do, madam, with all due respect. I admit it's not thinking straight but people do."

"Lindon told me he was warned. He was at Mac's and the doorman told him the police were after him. Might that have happened?"

"Word can get around London at night pretty quickly. But he wasn't there. He didn't go back after he assaulted Miss Bellamy Gore."

"How do you know he assaulted her?"

The boy bit his lip. He knew he shouldn't be answering these questions but he was finding it hard to control the situation and eject this smart and upset lady from his office. Still, the question cut to the chase. Just as he looked as if he was about to jump to his feet and insist she leave, Mirabelle realized she'd gone too far. She changed tack.

"I just wonder what made Lavinia Blyth concerned when Rose left the club, that's all. Rose was a confident young woman. She had, I'm sure, an air about her—she knew what she was doing. I don't understand it. And Lavinia didn't leave. She didn't follow her friend. She didn't go home. She went back into the club to dance. Doesn't that seem strange to you if she was so concerned about Rose? What made her report it, do you think?"

"Well it's not usual behavior, is it? A society girl like that leaving with, well, he was a Negro musician, madam. Miss Bellamy Gore was in danger. She was very young. Lavinia Blyth might have saved her friend's life."

"Constable Adler, I do hope you're not suggesting that a black musician is more inclined toward criminal behavior than a white musician. Some of us fought to defend our country against such beliefs."

Adler looked sheepish. "No. Of course not, madam."

Mirabelle pressed home. "Besides, Rose's body has not been found. We cannot assume she is dead."

The boy shifted in his chair. "We found part of her dress," he said to justify himself; then he put up his hand to try to prevent the inevitable questions. The gesture was futile.

"Where?"

"I can't tell you that, ma'am. But we have evidence. The dress was torn. A debutante with a torn dress returns home if she's alive. Miss Bellamy Gore didn't go home."

"Are you certain the material you found was from her dress?"

Momentarily Adler looked like a pleased little school-boy—he had the answer to that question. "Her maid identified it. It's an unusual fabric. All evidence points to the fact that Miss Bellamy Gore got into a cab with Lindon Claremont. They headed northeast. Her dress was ripped. About an hour later he caught an early train to Brighton in possession of her cigarette case. He spun you a line, madam. I'm sorry. Look, you shouldn't feel bad. You brought him in. You did the right thing. You might well have saved another young girl. Another victim. If he'd got away who knows what he'd have done next."

Mirabelle sighed. "St. Pancras? Finsbury?" she guessed.

Adler stood up. "What?"

"Well, if they headed northeast from Windmill Street, did you find the material from Rose's dress somewhere near Russell Square? Or, goodness me, were they heading for the open air? There aren't many big parks on that side of town. Let me see, did they go to Coram's Fields? Did you find the material there?"

Adler flinched. "Madam, this is an ongoing investigation. I've said quite enough as it is."

Mirabelle remained seated. To keep the boy's attention she fiddled with the cuff of her gloves. "All right. I'll go. Poor Lindon," she said, rising slowly. "I'm not convinced he has been given the benefit of the doubt, you know. Did you speak to him at all? I mean he seemed such a pleasant kid. He loved his music. He didn't appear to me to be violent in the slightest."

Adler moved to the door. "You can't tell by people's appearance," he said. "Most people, of course, probably are what they seem. But some people are like wolves in sheep's clothing. Those are the ones we end up dealing with."

Adler escorted her firmly into the hallway, a hand planted in the small of her back. The floor of the corridor had been buffed to a high shine and Mirabelle's heels clicked as they walked past the public information notices and procedural reminders tacked to the walls. She wanted to get every last drop of information she could. Adler now thought he was getting rid of her. Perhaps he'd drop his guard.

"It seems strange to me that he killed himself. Out of character," she mused.

Adler slowed slightly. "I don't think he planned it. I took him back to his cell on Friday, and he asked me if I thought he'd be out by Sunday. He had a booking to play somewhere in the afternoon. Some pub on Drury Lane."

"Did you reply to his question?"

"I said it didn't look likely he'd be getting out. Well, it didn't look likely, did it?"

Mirabelle paused before the final set of swing doors. "Thank you," she said, her gloved hand on the brass door handle. "Oh, there's just one more thing. That scrap of material. What color was it?"

"What do you want to know that for, madam?"

"Oh, idle curiosity."

Adler pushed the door open for her. He sighed. "Yellow. Pale yellow with silver thread through it," he said. "She was wearing a full-length dress. It must've been ripped as far as the knee."

"It was Coram's Fields, wasn't it? Where you found the material? Poor Rose."

Adler hesitated and then nodded.

"Good-bye," she said. "Thank you."

Mirabelle breezed through the lobby. She nodded smartly at the desk sergeant and headed for the exit.

Adler, as if coming suddenly to his senses, ran across to hold the door open. "Madam," he said, "I didn't catch your name."

Mirabelle smiled. She wondered if the boy had learned anything during their exchange. If he wanted to develop any kind of police career he'd need to up his game. "I didn't give it," she said with a smile and pushed her way into the smog by the river.

14

Home is birthplace ratified by memory.

Most of the houses in the area where Vesta was born were rented from the local council; the rest were owned by a few landlords with large portfolios and little inclination to effect repairs. Nothing much had changed in this part of town for a hundred years, apart from the sites cleared by the bombing. Rebuilding had started, but it was haphazard, and although one or two modern blocks of flats had been erected, the majority of the houses were soot-smudged Victorian brick two-up-two-downs with chipped doors and peeling window frames. Here in the East End the poorest families eked out a squalid existence, jammed up against each other; many of them crowded into tiny bedsits with no electricity.

Lines of residential streets clustered around the docks away from the water. The shoreline was reserved for small factories, dockyards and bonded warehouses. It felt heavy here and the lack of green space always depressed Vesta; it especially dispirited her that rather than being cultivated with vegetables or flowers the bombsites had descended into sludgy makeshift playgrounds for the local kids. Vesta couldn't remember finding the place so gray and drab when she was growing up here. Now, her return was muted by the feeling that life in the East End was drained of color—with its gray houses, muddy gap sites and the shit-brown river that ran through it all.

Yet, the same could not be said for the people. The rows of local shops teemed with life, and like all areas where people lived and worked together, everyone seemed to know each other. Children of all ages played on the pavements; at this time of year they were wearing hand-knitted sweaters in vibrant colors. A little girl with an orange cardigan reminded Vesta of a bright flower in the mud. Women did their shopping on the street where they lived. The menfolk worked in one capacity or another for a handful of employers. Or else they ran local businesses—small shops that provided foodstuffs and other necessities. The local pubs were the hub of the community as much as the churches. Messages could be left and parcels picked up in either place.

As the castellated outline of Bermondsey Library came into view Vesta automatically thought, *Eight minutes to go.* Her mother always said that when you passed Bermondsey Library that was the time to make sure your coat was done up and to take a deep breath in. Bermondsey housed Biscuit City—the Peek Freans factory—and for miles the air smelled of baking butter biscuits. Sure enough, Vesta checked her coat, breathed in deeply and eight minutes later she got off the tram. The smog was so thick she could make out the chime of the bell on the corner-shop door more clearly than she could make out the shop itself. The smell of freshly baked rolls wafted toward her, and a paperboy with a large bag slung over his shoulder trudged along the pavement weighed down by his deliveries. It was still early. If she hurried she would catch her mother before she left for church.

Vesta knew her way without having to see the street signs.

Normally, she dreaded going home. Her family loved her and the Churchills were close, but sometimes they could be smothering. Much to her parents' consternation, Vesta's older brother had returned to the West Indies. At least he wasn't gawped at in the street, he'd said. And it took a week before news of what he'd been up to could reach his mother and a week more before she could voice her objections. Vesta liked London but there had come a point where she couldn't stay at home. The preferred option for most girls was to get married, of course. Vesta told herself she'd probably do that sometime but she wasn't quite ready and, besides, she had Olympic typing speeds. They had joked during the London Games that if only there was a typing event, Vesta would get the gold.

The lights in the front room were off but the pane over the Churchills' front door glowed like a beacon. There was no need to knock. Like most houses round here, the large tarnished key sitting in the inside lock was rarely used.

"It's me!" she called.

"Lord Almighty, Vesta!" came the cry from the kitchen and all fourteen stones of Mrs. Churchill bustled down the hallway. She wrapped her arms tightly around her daughter.

Vesta couldn't help but burst into tears. Her mother's soft skin smelled of soap and coconut oil, and her arms were strong. The yellow floral housecoat was comforting in its familiarity.

Vesta sobbed, unable to restrain herself. "It's Lindon, Mama. He's dead."

"We know, we know. Daddy went to the phone box last night. He tried to ring you, child. Mrs. Claremont gonna be glad to see you today! You did right to come home."

Behind the two women crowded the stocky figure of Mr. Churchill and Vesta's younger brother, Edmund, who was eating a thin slice of toast ladled with dripping of his mother's making.

"My little swan," Mrs. Churchill said fondly, stroking Vesta's hair. "Such terrible news to bring you back."

The family moved into the kitchen. The house was shabby yet warm and cozy, and to Vesta it would always feel like home. The hallway was painted buttery cream with pictures of tropical flowers on the walls. A threadbare velvet chair with a huge cushion sat at the bottom of the stairs. Today, unusually, the hallway didn't smell of cooking. Everyone had been out, Vesta realized. Last night they would have gone to the Claremonts'. Vesta dabbed her eyes with a handkerchief before dropping onto one of the chairs. Mr. Churchill removed a boiling kettle from the stove and laid it to one side for his wife and then sat down in front of the fire, his white shirt so stiff with starch it looked as if it were holding him in place.

"Papers is full of it," he said, holding up the *News of the World*. "Poor Ella. I hope they aren't letting her read this stuff."

Mrs. Churchill made a pot of tea and brought Vesta a cup and saucer. "That boy wouldn't hurt a fly," she said. "It's not right! He was a talented kid not some drugged-up jazz fiend."

Vesta sipped her tea. Her mother handed her a slice of fresh bread. "Do you know who identified the body?"

Mrs. Churchill sucked her teeth. "His daddy went."

"And?"

"It was him. What do you think, Vesta? What kind of a question is that, child?"

"I want to know what happened to him, Ma. Lindon wouldn't kill himself. I'm sure of it."

Vesta's parents exchanged a glance. The news last year that their only daughter had been instrumental in uncovering a Nazi money-laundering ring had made them proud but also concerned. When Vesta left home she had got herself a job in an insurance office and that was one thing;

what she'd got up to subsequently sounded like it might be dangerous. They'd asked her to move back home in the autumn, feeling she would be safer in London where they could keep an eye on her. Vesta had refused. Now their friend and neighbor had lost a child. Mr. Churchill's eyes hardened. He'd be damned if he was going to lose one of his without a fight. Asking questions about Lindon's death might prove a dangerous business. Certainly, the world for which Lindon had quit the Claremonts' family home had proved fatal.

"Vesta, I don't want you getting into no trouble. You want to go digging, I could come with you," Mr. Churchill offered.

"I hope so, Daddy," Vesta smiled, "because everyone will be at church today. We need to find the musicians who knew Lindon. Anyone who played with him."

"Them boys don't go to church," said Edmund, looking up from his breakfast.

"They'll go today," said Vesta firmly. "Some of them are bound to." She reached out and opened a pot of apple jelly, spooning a generous portion onto the crust of bread she'd hollowed out.

"Ella Claremont is well-known and she's well-liked, and so was Lindon. It's a mark of respect. All the sinners will be lined up in a row. Reverend Thomas won't know what hit him. It'll be like Judgment Day, you'll see. I want to get to the bottom of this."

Mr. Churchill nodded and relaxed visibly. If his daughter was set to go digging for information, the local church was possibly the safest place she could do so.

"Vesta, child," said her mother, "I knew you had a talent all along but I had no idea it was going to be for something like this."

"Who can uncover the ways of the Lord?" Vesta lifted a manicured finger skyward.

Edmund giggled.

"Now that I won't have," Mr. Churchill cut in. "Not in my house. Show some respect."

"Sorry, Daddy." He probably had a point. "And if I'm going to do anything dangerous, I promise, you'll be the first to know. I don't want you worrying."

15

Anybody singing the blues is in a deep pit yelling for help.

Drury Lane ran from High Holborn to Aldwych. It was far too grand and wide to merit being called a lane, and between the theaters it was peppered with pubs. Mirabelle decided to take a bus northward and start at the Holborn end so she was working her way toward town. It shouldn't take too long to figure out where Lindon Claremont had been supposed to play that afternoon. The Embankment was almost deserted. The heavy chimes of Big Ben striking twelve resounded across the water. The Sunday bus service was infrequent but it would give her time to think. She stood alone at the stop and ran through the events of Thursday night, slotting in the information she'd just gathered from Adler.

Rose Bellamy Gore, in a full-length yellow evening dress, had gone to Mac's with her cousin Harry and Lavinia Blyth. They had all probably been drunk (if not when they arrived, then shortly after) and it was late. Rose had taken an interest in the band. She'd engaged Lindon in conversation. Sometime between 3 and 4 a.m. she'd given him her cigarette case on a whim and then left, either with Lindon or with someone else unknown or, now Mirabelle came to consider it, alone. Lavinia had phoned her father, concerned for Rose's safety. Why she had done this was still unclear, particularly if Rose hadn't left with Lindon. Mirabelle realized she should check the phone box Lavinia had used and establish how long it would have taken her to walk there and back from Mac's. One way or another, Lavinia must have been sure that Rose was in trouble. According to the police report she had been positive that Lindon was guilty. Indeed, why no one else in Mac's had stood up for the sax player, if he hadn't left with the girl, was another mystery. But it certainly seemed that the other musicians must have agreed with Lavinia's version of events or the police would have had no case at all to hold him. As for Barney, Mirabelle didn't trust him but she had no doubt he'd only lie if it were in his interests to do so—which appeared to be the case. In the event, like the musicians, he had agreed with Lavinia's version of what happened at Mac's that night. Chief Inspector Green had a good reputation as a competent officer. Even if the band had scarpered that night, he'd no doubt have tracked them down. So, the logical conclusion was that they must all have agreed with each other—not necessarily in the detail but in the broad outline of events.

Meanwhile, when he received Lavinia's call, Paul Blyth got in touch with the police who put out a description of Rose immediately and started the search. Unaware of this, Rose had headed northeast for Coram's Fields where her dress was somehow torn. Coram's Fields, Mirabelle knew, was surrounded by railings. She and Jack had once attended a bandstand concert there—an old-fashioned brass band on a June afternoon. It was out of the way and they had taken the chance of being seen together to grab a little freedom. Many of the flowerbeds had been given over to growing vegetables to supplement rations. They probably still were. After the concert she and Jack had eaten buttered scones in the Bloomsbury Hotel and had taken a room.

"A chap can't be expected to wait," Jack had insisted. "Not on a Sunday."

The down-at-heel area around Russell Square seemed an unlikely place for a debutante to go for thrills and spills. It was hardly the haunt of someone Didi Blyth had called "smart."

Mirabelle put out her hand and wrapped her gloved fingers round the cold bus stop. It helped her to focus. Now, if Rose was with a man (Lindon or otherwise) and they were going to the park for the usual reasons, why would they choose Coram's Fields over Inn the Park? That made no sense. From Windmill Street, Inn the Park was not much farther and there were no railings to climb. At this point in the story the girl had simply disappeared. Murder was most likely. But in that case, given she hadn't been found, her killer would have had to remove her body. Was there a car? That brought a whole series of logistical problems into the equation, or even a romantic flight of fancy should Rose prove still to be alive—elopement? The scrap of her dress was the only indication of violence. Lindon, believing the police were looking for him, fled to the south coast. Out of fear, as he'd said, or guilt? But if he was guilty, surely he would have used his time to get away somewhere other than the south coast. Or was his faith in Vesta so strong he felt she'd be able to get him off no matter what?

As her bus neared the stop, Mirabelle put out her hand. She hopped on and settled into a seat on the lower deck. Tapping her fingers on the side of the seat as she thought things through, Mirabelle had to admit that Detective Constable Adler's logic was impeccable. A woman with a torn evening dress wouldn't stay out. She would go home if she could. It was difficult to imagine what could be keeping Rose from Upper Belgrave Street if the story wasn't the way he had related it. It was a conundrum. As she mused, she could feel the cold radiating from the bus's steamed-up windows and she longed to lay her forehead on the glass. Of course, it looked as if Lindon was guilty. But Mirabelle kept returning to the picture in her mind of the boy, soaked, sitting with his saxophone case in the hallway outside McGuigan & McGuigan on Friday morning. He was no murderer and he was certainly no master criminal. His clothes might have been wet but they had been immaculate. He hadn't been scratched or bruised by someone fighting him off. There was no sign of blood. Most importantly, his demeanor had not been that of a murderer. Something about him belied the very idea.

Yet not much more than twenty-four hours later, Lindon had been taken into custody where he either had lost all hope and killed himself or had been murdered inside one of the country's most high-profile police stations. No matter what Vesta thought, the former was more likely. Killing someone inside a locked cell was a tricky business. Even in her SOE days only the most expert agent would attempt it and only then for a very good reason.

"You all right, love?" A man smoking a cigarette leaned over.

Mirabelle started. She'd been almost hammering the seat with frantic fingers, she realized.

"I'm trying to remember a tune," she said. "Got it now. 'Too Young.'"

The man laughed. "Rightio." He retreated back to his seat.

Mirabelle stilled herself. She could see why the police thought Rose was dead and Lindon had killed her. But she still wasn't convinced by either conclusion.

At High Holborn Mirabelle got off the bus and headed for Drury Lane. Somewhere here was the pub where Lindon had meant to spend Sunday afternoon. Mirabelle shrugged off the uncomfortable feeling she was traveling in the wake of his ghost.

Working methodically, she peered in each door and

walked smartly between the hostelries to keep as warm as possible. The first two bars didn't have live music. The third was a musty drinking den with a sticky carpet and an incongruous American jukebox blasting out Perry Como. The White Hart looked more promising. Its black-and-white sign creaked in the slight breeze, and from the doorway Mirabelle could hear a woman singing. She sounded like Dinah Shore. Inside, it was deserted, except for an old man sipping a pint of porter at a low table and a solitary barman, engaged in fixing something on the gantry. Mirabelle slipped onto a bar stool and caught his attention. She ordered a hot whisky. She needed to warm up.

"We've no sugar," the barman said, "but I can do one with cloves and a squeeze of lemon."

Mirabelle shuddered. The whisky would probably be of such poor quality, blended into oblivion, that it would hardly matter.

"Thanks. With cloves will be fine." Mirabelle removed her gloves and turned to listen to the music.

On a tiny stage at one end of the smoke-filled room was a thin black girl in a red dress. She was accompanied by an extraordinarily fat pianist, perched in an unstable fashion on a stool. Halfway up one wall there was a large stove pumping welcome heat into the almost empty bar area.

"I wondered about some jazz," Mirabelle confided in the barman. "I heard there was live jazz on a Sunday somewhere down here."

"That's here all right. It's usually jazz, anyway." He laid a steaming glass on a beer mat and took the shilling Mirabelle offered. "All the White Hart pubs got jazz on a Sunday. Our regular fella couldn't make it so we had to take what we could get. I prefer this, myself. It's more gentle, ain't it? They're only rehearsing now 'cause we're quiet."

"She has a lovely voice."

Mirabelle had danced to this tune, "April in Paris,"

with Jack. He always said he wanted to take her to Paris, though Mirabelle teased him that it ought to be the other way round. Mirabelle's mother came from the eighth arrondissement near the Parc Monceau. If they visited the French capital it would have been Mirabelle who'd know the city best. She'd wanted to show him the shabby streets of the Marais and the tiny dressmaker's shop where her mother had her clothes made and, farther into town, the glorious Petit Palais with its high-ceilinged splendor and astonishing art. Mirabelle sipped the hot whisky and felt the circulation return to her fingers as her heart fluttered. Jack seemed ever present in London—it was impossible to walk very far without tripping over a memory in the street, fresh as the day she'd left it behind.

The girl finished the number and leaned over to talk to the pianist who played a section again with a more staccato touch. The girl nodded. He made a note on a sheet of paper and then closed the piano lid, and they came to the bar together.

"May I buy you a drink?" Mirabelle offered.

Neither the pianist nor the singer hesitated. The fat man asked for a beer, the girl a port and lemon.

"You have a lovely voice."

"Thanks."

The barman poured the drinks.

"And some nuts, please," Mirabelle insisted, handing over a coupon from her handbag.

The barman brought a packet, which the girl opened immediately. She crammed the first handful into her mouth and swallowed almost without chewing.

"Thanks," she said.

Mirabelle watched her. Her nails were ragged and she was too thin.

"If you don't mind me asking, my dear," Mirabelle was curious, "how long is it since you ate?"

The girl's gaze fell to the floor. "We moved house, and

there ain't no proper kitchen. And I get confused with the coupons."

"It's usually jazz in here on Sunday, isn't it? But what you're playing is different."

"I hope the crowd like it." The girl crunched on.

"Late booking, was it?"

"Yeah." The pianist lifted his pint. "Cheers."

"Well, that's lucky."

"Some sax player snuffed it."

"Lindon," the girl said wistfully. "His name was Lindon."

"Yeah. Well, they needed someone fast. We usually only work Friday and Saturday. We got proper jobs, see, but it worked out all right. You're belting those down, Charlotte," the pianist pointed out. "Steady."

"Why don't you and I have some lunch, my dear? I'm hungry and I'd appreciate some company. My treat," Mirabelle smiled.

"We ain't serving yet," the barman interjected, "but there's pie and mash ready. It's kidney and all. I know 'cause I had some myself."

Charlotte beamed.

"Two pies and mash then," Mirabelle ordered.

The women settled down at a proper table which was set for lunch, while the pianist stayed at the bar chatting.

"Your friend is talented, too, of course," said Mirabelle.

"He's all right," Charlotte replied but she didn't take her eyes off the kitchen door.

"Did you know that chap? The saxophonist?"

Charlotte nodded. "Yeah. Nice bloke," she said almost automatically; then remembering what Lindon was alleged to have done, her face changed. "I didn't know him *that* well, of course."

"Have you ever sung at Mac's?"

The girl shrugged. "I drop in sometimes but mostly just to hang around. They don't need singers."

The barman plonked down two small plates piled with

food, gravy swilling around the rim. Charlotte had taken her first mouthful before the plate had even hit the table.

"That sax player—the name you mentioned is familiar. I think I know who he was," Mirabelle said, picking at her food. "I met him once. Lindon. Lindon Claremont, wasn't it?"

"How did you come across a bloke like that?"

"He played at a ball I helped to organize," Mirabelle improvised. "I book acts sometimes, you see."

Charlotte sat up very straight. This encounter might be promising.

"I heard he'd been taken into custody about that missing girl from Mac's. Shame. Were you at Mac's the night she went missing?" asked Mirabelle.

Charlotte shook her head. "I've met that girl though. A few times. She went to all the clubs. She was pretty. Fancy frocks, proper expensive. Furs and all. She used to hang around and talk to the musicians when they'd finished. Of course, she always had cigarettes and money for booze. I dunno what she got out of it. Must like the music. And the atmosphere."

"Was she ever alone?"

"Nah. Always had a bloke with her. Same age. White guy. Fancy car."

"What do you think might have happened to her?"

"I dunno. The only person who knows is, well, you know, dead. Lindon, I guess."

"You think he'd hurt her?"

"No idea. It was strange those two white kids were there at all. If I lived in some fancy house with a maid and all the money I wanted, I'd never go out. I certainly wouldn't trawl deadbeat dives for thrills. I spoke to her fella once. Called me Miss and when he looked at me, well, you know . . ." Charlotte beamed.

"I can imagine he might be a flirt."

"He's a flirt, all right! Asked to see me again. Wanted my number. I ain't got a number, love, I told him. Well, he says, you'll have to come and find me, then, won't you. Cheek of it!"

"Was Lindon a deadbeat?"

Charlotte considered this slowly. She tucked a lock of hair behind her ear.

"Ah, they're all deadbeats! Even Johnny over there! Musicians are the worst—they're charming if you're lucky but they ain't steady. I want a nice mechanic. Someone with prospects but not so flash as Mr. Smooth with the *come and find me*. Just a real nice fella I can look after and who'll look after me. Have you got one of those?"

Mirabelle savored the last of her hot whisky. "No."

"The good ones are hard to track down," Charlotte observed, scraping her plate clean.

Johnny caught her eye from the bar. He motioned that he was going upstairs.

"Look, I better go. Thanks for lunch."

Charlotte rose to her feet and smoothed her red dress. Mirabelle noticed that the hem was grubby.

"Did he tell you where to find him, Charlotte? The man with the fancy car?"

"Yeah. Some club on Pall Mall. Oxford and Cambridge, la-di-da. As if I could turn up somewhere like that. They'd send me round the servants' entrance. 'Ask for Miles,' he said. 'He'll send you up. I've got rooms.' Rooms! Cheeky sod! I got a mother, too, you know. No title or nothing but that doesn't make me a tart, even if I stay out late. I just like singing." She gave a brief laugh and walked toward the bar.

Mirabelle cocked her head and sighed. Tracking down Harry was turning out to be a lot easier than she had anticipated, and it sounded as if he was a devil-may-care kind of fellow. The police might have let him off lightly but she wouldn't.

16

People don't go to church to find trouble;
they go there to lose it.

The First Evangelical Church service had gone on for
well over an hour. The church was always well attended, but today, after what had happened to Lindon, it
was standing room only. In the aisle and at the front some
of the congregation were sitting on the floor. Small children wriggled on their parents' knees.

Lindon's family was seated at the front, and though this
wasn't a memorial service, the sermon, readings and hymns
had all been directed toward them, sympathizing with their
loss and remembering Lindon as the talented kid he'd been
when he used to come to church every Sunday. When the
minister finished everyone rushed to offer condolences.
Vesta loitered at the back and took stock of the crowd.
Most of the faces had been familiar all her life. There were
several of her old school friends who had now married
boys from the year above. One or two even had babies
hoisted on their shoulders.

"You looking for someone, girl?" said a deep voice with
an American twang.

"It's like a Holbein painting," Vesta murmured, and then
realized she was spending far too much time with Mirabelle.

"I never heard of a black Holbein but I reckon you're right."

Vesta spun round. There stood the best-looking black man she'd ever clapped eyes on. She reckoned he was in his late twenties, well over six feet tall, and he cut an impressive figure in an understated navy-blue suit. He was grinning.

"Gosh," she said. "You know who Holbein is?"

"Sure I do. I've been in Europe a while now."

"I'm Vesta Churchill." She held out her hand.

"Charlie Baker. I'm guessing you knew Lindon?"

"Is that why you're here?"

"Yeah. Seemed only right to come along. We played together a few times—me on drums. I was glad the preacher went easy on what happened. The papers are calling him a jazz fiend but he wasn't any of that. Poor guy wasn't a coward and he certainly wasn't a murderer. Your reverend here is all right."

"Were you there that night?"

"Yeah, but I left before it all happened."

"How was he?"

"Lindon? He was fine. Normal. He'd had some drink, you know. But I didn't notice anything out of place. No mad glint in his eye."

"Did you see Rose Bellamy Gore?"

"The skinny white chick? Yeah, I saw her. Any club that's open, right? I always knew she was trouble. I've seen her plenty times just sitting smoking up at the back with a real serious expression on her face, as if she's understanding the music, not feeling it. Chicks like that are way too intense."

"So that's what trouble looks like, is it?"

"Well, Miss Vesta, one thing I know is you might be up at the back of the hall, but trouble certainly doesn't look like you!"

Vesta savored the comment while outwardly ignoring it. He was flirting with her!

"Who else was at Mac's that evening?" she asked.

"Audience?"

"And band."

"Are you interrogating me?"

"I am."

"You haven't even let me buy you a drink yet!"

Vesta couldn't help grinning. "Charlie? You see that big woman down at the front in the dark green coat? Right next to Lindon's mother?"

"Yeah."

"That woman is my mama and this is her church. So, you aren't gonna buy me a drink but you might get me a cuppa."

"Ah"—Charlie's face lit up—"tea. I can do that."

They had just finished boiling the huge urns next door in the church hall and people were already moving through. A few children were chasing each other across the wooden floor, scattering like marbles as they crashed into each other. Vesta remembered being that age, after the service, when all her pent-up energy found release. She used to crash into boys deliberately and run squealing in the opposite direction. It had been exciting. Perhaps things hadn't changed much.

"So," Vesta said, after Charlie brought her tea and they found two chairs, "that night at Mac's."

Charlie ignored the remark and took a sip of his tea. "You want to have dinner with me tonight?"

"I live in Brighton."

"That's by the sea, ain't it?"

Vesta nodded. "I came home because of what happened."

"Brighton's not far, though? I mean, out of London."

"Just a train ride."

Charlie stretched his legs. "It's a gray old city, London. It could do with some light."

Vesta could have listened to Charlie's honeyed accent all day. She felt her cheeks burning and consciously had to restrain herself from putting a hand up to her face. She wondered what Mirabelle would do in this situation and then realized that Mirabelle wouldn't be in this situation. Mirabelle never flirted. What she would say was, "For heaven's sake, Vesta, stick to the point." She took a deep breath and tried to ignore the tingling feeling in her stomach. She had a job to do.

"He came down on Friday morning to find me. That was after everything had happened, of course. He thought I'd be able to help. He knew the police were after him and he didn't know how to prove he was innocent."

"No shit."

Vesta's temper stirred. "You think he's guilty?"

"Like I said, I'd left earlier. I wasn't there. And neither were you. I don't think he was no murderer. That's my hunch. But I don't know. How did he seem to you?"

"Just Lindon. He was scared about the police looking for him. Who wouldn't be? Who else was in the club that night?"

"Not much audience by the time I went, which was coming up to three in the morning. There'd been about a dozen or so earlier but by then, apart from the bright young things, there were only a couple of white guys asleep at the bar. Barney was on the door and he won't have gone for that. He'd have chucked them out as soon as they stopped buying booze. They wouldn't have lasted till four, or nothing. And then there were the musicians. Not everyone was playing that night. The smog was real bad, and Wednesday night there'd been a big party over in Chelsea. Some rich guy had invited the whole world—it was probably still going on over there. Anyways, there weren't the usual players at Mac's."

"Can you remember how many turned up?"

"Seven or eight guys, I guess."

"Don't any women play jazz?"

Charlie grinned. "You mean *sing* jazz? Yeah, there's a few. Are you one of those militant types, Miss Vesta?"

Vesta eyed him slowly and wished he wasn't so handsome. "Yeah. Can't you tell?"

"Well, there weren't any women there on Thursday." He held up his hand and counted the musicians on his fingers. "Me on drums, Lindon on sax, Dave on bass, Tombo on horn, Zak on tenor sax."

"Those all black guys?"

"Yeah."

"All five of you?"

"Five guys called Mo. Ben was there earlier, on keyboards—Mac's got an old piano. It ain't up to much. And there was another guy on guitar. Those boys were gone before I headed home. Mostly people were just drinking between jamming a tune or two. Duos, mostly. I like a band. For me it was one lame old night. Right up till the murder."

Vesta decided not to argue with Charlie's choice of words. She stuck to the point. "Where would I find all these guys—the musicians who stayed till the end?"

"Around. Just watch the listings. They play regular all of them. Zak's pretty good. They all got gigs. And Tombo's here somewhere. He came to the service."

"Did they see Lindon leave with Rose?"

"How am I supposed to know? I wasn't there."

"I thought you might have heard."

"What I heard is that he left. I dunno about the girl. Not to speak ill of the dead but Lindon wasn't up to that kind of action." Charlie checked to see if anyone was close enough to hear and lowered his voice. "Okay, Lindon liked white chicks. Well, in truth, Lindon liked chicks, period. But a girl like that? No way! She'd need to be really slumming it. No offense. Lindon ain't got the balls to pull that one off! Besides he got plenty, know what I mean? Maybe not so high up the social scale but he got what he wanted."

Vesta wanted to slap Charlie but instead she finished her tea and put the cup and saucer on the table. "You're pretty sure of yourself."

Charlie laughed. "I'm American," he said. "That's all. And what we do is help you Brits out, ain't that the truth?"

"Well, help me out, Charlie."

He looked delighted. "Really? You'll go for dinner with me?"

"Perhaps," Vesta conceded. "Put me in touch with those fellas and I'll think about it. I want to find out what happened. So, was Lindon drinking?"

"Yeah. Everyone drinks in those places. That's what you go there to do—play music, smoke a little reefer and get boozed up. It's pretty wild! I could take you to see it if you like? You name the club and I'll get us in—best seats in the house."

A smile played around Vesta's lips. He was irresistible! "So everyone was drunk?"

"Pretty much. Of course, Lindon would have stopped before everyone else. He usually did."

"Why?"

"Lindon didn't drink beer. You didn't know that? I thought you two were big childhood friends and all. No, the man only took spirits and ten times out of ten they run out first. Round about midnight, usually. After that the boys drink beer just to stop them sobering up too quickly. Beer takes off the edge so you can keep going. Not Lindon— he drank whisky, brandy, rum, and that was it. Didn't like gin. Didn't like cocktails. He was strictly straight up, strictly shorts. And that night there was only rum. Anyway, the hard booze ran out early and Lindon would have stopped drinking as soon as it did. . . . What time will I pick you up, Vesta? We're now up to dinner and a club, you know. You're gonna have to dance with me if I keep on being so helpful."

Vesta couldn't suppress her smile any longer. "First, you've got to point out Tombo," she insisted.

"Tombo?"

"You said he was here."

Charlie stood up, straining to find his friend across the sea of Sunday hats. "You stay right here. I'll fetch him."

Vesta regarded the two teacups perched on the small table. She wondered if Charlie had been a GI. She wondered if he was set to stay in England. She wondered where they might go for dinner. The idea of dancing with him was almost overwhelming. It had been a long time since Vesta felt shy, but now the sensation crept over her as she sat with her legs crossed, swinging an ankle as she waited.

She felt a wave of guilt that she was having such a nice time. Lindon's mother was crying, people around her at the front of the hall. After this gathering everyone was going to the Claremonts' house. She'd do her duty there, she promised herself—the loyal friend and neighbor pitching in for Lindon's memory. Her mother had made a tray of "fried chicken thighs" with Mrs. Claremont the night before. The thighs, she'd confessed earlier, were actually rabbit. The local butcher, Mr. Stott, had a cousin in Kent who supplemented official supplies. Mrs. Churchill disapproved of black-market goods but wild rabbit was unrationed. Perhaps, Vesta mused, she might ask Charlie to come to the wake.

The crowd began to thin. Vesta's mother joined her, sitting in Charlie's chair.

"These are great people we got around us, Vesta," she declared. "Have you spoken to the Claremonts yet? You should, before we head over there."

"Can I bring someone, Mama? A friend of Lindon's who came to the service?"

"Sure you can. We're all friends of Lindon today. Who you thinking of?"

Vesta peered through the crowd. She got up on the chair so she could get a better view. Then she went to check inside the church. When she returned she realized she was clenching her fists.

Charlie had vanished. No, not vanished, he had sneaked off. The snake.

17

*All you need is a tiny foothold
and the rest will take care of itself.*

Mirabelle hadn't loitered in the White Hart. She'd paid for the food, headed back out into the cold and with a renewed sense of purpose set off toward Aldwych. She was too impatient to wait for the bus and the walk would give her time to consider what Charlotte had told her.

A guardsman wearing a bearskin, hands in his pockets, loomed out of the smog and paused to light a cigarette. Mirabelle wondered where he was going and if he should be smoking while he was in uniform.

Jack always said that surveillance required very open-minded concentration. "It takes a certain kind of person to gather intelligence—the kind of person who is never bored. It's a different skill from taking action." Mirabelle felt as if action was now required but she was unsure what she ought to do. When it came down to it, she had formed no alternative theory to the official line that assumed Lindon Claremont's guilt. But too many doubts and questions continued to niggle her—like an itch she couldn't scratch.

As she turned into Pall Mall she sneezed. The winter weather in London was notorious, with half the city suffering from respiratory complaints from October to March. She scrambled in her handbag for a hankie just as she reached the grand entrance of the Oxford and Cambridge Club.

"I was here yesterday." She identified herself to the steward inside, blowing her nose discreetly. "Miss Bevan, if you remember? I was hoping to see Deirdre Blyth today."

"I'm afraid Miss Blyth departed early this morning, madam."

"Harry Bellamy Gore?"

"He's gone out, madam."

"In that case, is Miles around?"

"Certainly. I'll find him for you, madam."

"I'll be in the Ladies' Sitting Room."

The room was empty but the clink of cutlery from a few solitary Sunday diners emanated from the Coffee Room as she slipped by the half-open door. Mirabelle warmed herself at the fire before taking a seat by the window where she could stare at the foggy street. It helped her to think and she needed to think quickly. Even though Miles was on his way, she wasn't yet sure how best to tackle him. She reasoned that in all probability Harry's man was accustomed to ushering females of several persuasions, jazz singers included, in and out of the club on his master's behalf. Still, she'd need to think of something plausible to explain why she wanted to see the boy. She put a hand to her hair and checked her appearance in her compact. The tweed suit was holding up fine, though she looked a little tired. Perhaps she could get away with being an aunt again. She looked like one, she realized—a spinster aunt. Mirabelle straightened her jacket. Harry seemed rather removed from the events of Thursday night and she wondered if the police had questioned him sufficiently. She was still lost in thought when a sharp knock cut into her concentration and a bulky man dressed in overalls entered the room. Mirabelle sized him up. He was definitely ex-military, his bearing alone told her that. Part of what appeared to be a regimental tattoo showed at his wrist and there were smears of engine oil on his trousers. His salt-and-pepper hair was slicked back with Brylcreem. Despite his grubby overalls the man looked smart and capable.

"Ma'am, you asked to see me?"

"Are you Miles?"

"Yes, madam."

Mirabelle decided to try authority. It usually worked with military men. "I'm looking for Harry Bellamy Gore."

"Mr. Bellamy Gore isn't in the club at the moment."

"Yes. Quite. But I understand you might be able to help me find him."

Miles's eyes darted around the room as if he were looking for clues. "Have you tried him at home?" he said.

The man was nervous, a good thing. Gradually he controlled his gaze and focused steadily on the lapel of Mirabelle's jacket, avoiding her eyes. It was time, she judged, to apply some pressure.

"Please"—she held up her hand—"your loyalty is very touching, Miles, but I know you've been helping my nephew with some of his"—here she inhaled deeply—"*activities.*"

The man's shoulders tightened.

"You'll only make things worse if you prevaricate. Let's just say Harry comes from a long line of gentlemen with nefarious interests. He's an active, interesting chap, isn't he? Certainly likes the girls. A certain sort of girl especially."

"Yes, madam."

"But that doesn't concern me. I want to find him. And I am less interested in who has been aiding and abetting young Harry in his *activities* than in managing to have a word with him. Rose, as you are probably aware, is missing."

Miles opened his mouth and paused, assessing his options. "I'm sorry, madam," he said, keeping his eyes straight ahead. "I don't know the whereabouts of Mr. Bellamy Gore. I can certainly give him a message if I see him."

"I understand you look after Harry's interests here at the club. I understand that should a young lady be looking for my nephew you are the fellow to contact."

"I don't know where he is today, madam. I'm sorry." Miles was sticking to his guns.

"Is his vehicle here?"

"Pardon?"

"You've been working in the garage, I see. Is Harry's vehicle parked here?"

Miles looked down at his overalls. He ran a palm over his thigh as he realized he couldn't lie outright. "Yes. The Aston is round at the mews."

"He'll come in for that, then."

"I expect so, madam. He often parks it here when he stays."

Mirabelle wondered if it was worth pushing any further but she quickly dismissed the thought. Clearly, Miles was loyal to Harry, and when it came down to it, she wasn't really the boy's aunt.

"Where is the mews from here?" She craned to look out of the window.

"They got the whole of Russell Court, madam. Behind Spencer House. Across the road."

"Thank you, Miles," she said and waved him away.

Once the man had disappeared down the backstairs, Mirabelle strode into the hallway. She rapped on the glass of the secretary's office. From inside, a man she hadn't met before emerged.

"Excuse me," she said, "I wondered if you might know when Harry Bellamy Gore would be around?"

The fellow thought for a second before he answered. "I couldn't say, madam. He doesn't keep regular hours."

"But he was staying last night?"

"Mr. Bellamy Gore stays quite often, madam. I'm almost certain he was at the club last evening. He went out a couple of hours ago—for luncheon, I imagine. If anyone knows where he might be, it would be Miles. I can send for him if you like."

"No, no, it's fine. I had a super chat with Deirdre Blyth yesterday. Gosh, it's such a home from home for young people," she gushed. "I expect they even stay in the same rooms again and again."

"Usually," the secretary smiled. "People get attached to their favorite views and so forth. I can check you in if you like. We're quiet on Sundays. I could book you into a suite and only charge you for a single. Bit of a treat, madam."

"It's very kind of you, but I can't stay tonight."

The telephone rang, and the secretary apologized before heading back into the office. Mirabelle checked the hallway to make sure the coast was clear. Behind a desk at the foot of the stairs to the upper floor there was a board of numbered key hooks mounted on the wall—forty in all. The club had several bedrooms for the use of members. She wondered how long she would have to put the upper stories of the Oxford and Cambridge Club under surveillance in order to establish who was staying where. Though it was probably what Jack would have advocated, Mirabelle dismissed the notion immediately. Instead she carefully counted how many keys were missing. Eleven. These were people who were presumably upstairs or still in the club. She memorized the room numbers using an encryption code. Twenty-nine rooms unaccounted for. She delved behind the desk for a registration ledger but it must have been kept elsewhere. As she stood staring at the door to the administration office and wondering if the information was there, an elderly man came out of the Coffee Room and strode across the hall.

"Number twenty-five," he barked, without even looking at her.

Mirabelle didn't quibble. She reached out and handed over the key with a polite smile. People see what they expect to see, she remembered Jack saying. People assume.

She waited until the man had mounted the stairs. Twenty-eight to go. With a barely perceptible shrug she followed the gentleman upstairs. She'd work it out without a register. Stealing the keys from the board was not an option—even if she sneaked them off one by one she'd be bound to get caught. The downstairs hallway was far too public. As she reached the landing Mirabelle put up her hand and removed a hairpin. She'd start on the top floor. It was only a process of elimination. If the locks were the usual tumbler-and-bolt fittings, it really oughtn't to take that long.

18

No party is any fun unless it is seasoned with folly.

A s she left the church Vesta calculated there must be over thirty people walking over to the Claremonts' house. Most of the women were carrying huge casserole dishes with rattling lids that occasionally slid aside and released wonderful aromas. Last night had been the first of Lindon's nine nights and this afternoon would be the start of his second. It was an old tradition—a Jamaican way to say good-bye.

Outside the Claremonts' family home the group mustered and politely waited for Mr. Claremont to open the door. It wasn't locked but the custom was that a member of the family had to invite visitors inside.

"Welcome. Don't stand on ceremony. Not at a time like this, for heaven's sake," Lindon's father said as he ushered them into the narrow hallway. He ran his hand over his short, white hair. He was a tall man, but he seemed to have shrunk today, somehow.

Inside, the place was almost unbearably warm. All the fires had been set before the family left for the service and the table was laid ready for a buffet. In their grief the Claremonts had turned to organization of the practicalities for comfort. A mismatched pile of plates teetered at the edge of the kitchen table as the women put down their dishes and removed the lids. Meanwhile, Mr. Claremont opened the back door and rolled in a couple of thick glass flagons filled with home brew of an alarming yellow color.

"I didn't know you made your own, Mr. Claremont," Vesta smiled.

His eyes were bloodshot but he was trying his damnedest to keep his spirits up. "Oh yes. I'm a master brewer, young lady! Mostly beer, of course, but last year I tried cider. It was a bumper year for apples, and Ella had a friend who got us a barrel very cheap. We had apple cobbler for weeks! Baked apples. Stewed apples. There was applesauce with everything! Apple this, apple that. I got sick of it, to tell the truth. Your mother made apple jelly." He smacked his lips. "We didn't use to tell you about my brewing when you were little. We didn't want to encourage you kids," he said quietly, "and in the end that worked out. Teetotal, my lad was. That's quite something for a sax player, but Lindon stuck to his guns and never touched a drop."

Vesta bit her tongue. "Here, let me help." She picked up a glass. "If you pour, I'll serve."

"You gotta taste this," he insisted. "It's last year's. It'll revive you after a long morning. Demon drink notwithstanding, church ain't always easy, especially today. Not for none of us."

Vesta took a gulp and froze. The liquid was utterly revolting—it tasted strongly of fermenting grass. The only blessing was that it was so cold the flavor was probably inhibited.

"Well," she said, forcing herself to swallow, "that seems to have done the trick."

"I always hoped Lindon would get married, you know. Nice girl like you," Mr. Claremont said ruefully.

Everyone helped themselves to food and drink and then spread around the ground floor, perching on the arms of the Claremonts' comfortable chairs or standing plate-in-hand in the hallway. One or two of the neighbors, white folks who didn't attend the First Evangelical, came in by the back door. Everyone was wearing somber colors for the wake. Nonetheless, the new arrivals greeted their friends noisily—everyone in the neighborhood knew each other. One woman flung her arms around Lindon's mother, and the two of them stood for what seemed like several minutes, just hugging.

"We thought we'd lost all the young men we were gonna lose when the war wound up. We thought those days were gone," the woman sniffed. "It's a tragedy, Ella. He was a fine lad, your Lindon. I don't care what the papers say. I don't care about nothing. We knew him and he was a fine lad."

Vesta busied herself with serving the drinks and surreptitiously disposing of Mr. Claremont's home brew where people had put it to one side. Everyone was talking about Lindon when he was a child, telling stories of him playing football in the street or practicing loudly on his saxophone. He'd often played so late into the night that the neighbors couldn't sleep and Mr. Claremont had had to confiscate the instrument, only letting Lindon practice during daylight and sometimes not even then. Vesta remembered Lindon as a skinny ten-year-old, playing keepie-uppie on a bombsite.

"Whatcha doing?" she'd asked.

"Not playing my horn," he'd winked, and mimed holding his saxophone.

In the center of the room Lindon's mother sat as if she were in the eye of the storm. She was still wearing her hat and she seemed too delicate, somehow, to survive the huge and unexpected tragedy of losing her eldest son. Vesta could see that the reminiscences swirled around her but none of them was hitting home.

"Tea," Ella Claremont declared suddenly, clapping her

hands as she removed herself from the throng and headed into the kitchen to boil the kettle.

There was a knock at the door.

"Get that would you, Vesta, dear?" she called, her tone of voice exactly the same as when Vesta visited the house as a kid.

Peeling off her cardigan, Vesta pushed her way through the crowd into the hallway and turned the doorknob. When she saw who was there she had to struggle to suppress a whoop.

Charlie almost filled the entire doorframe. "Sorry I ran out on you," he said. "Had to catch up with Tombo. And here he is."

Vesta's heart was in her throat. "I thought you'd gone."

Charlie looked bemused. "Tombo left. And I couldn't come back without him, could I? I ran to the tram stop and he was still there. I figured you'd be with the others. I hope it's all right just to pitch up."

Tombo was staring unsmiling at Vesta. "Charlie says you're looking into things. I can't tell you much though. No more than I told the rozzers."

Vesta motioned them inside.

Tombo was as skinny as a rake and wearing a brown woolen suit with patches on the elbows. His tie was so thin that it looked as if someone had drawn a line from his chin down to the buttons of his jacket. Next to Charlie he looked like a tiny totem carved out of dark hardwood. Judging by his accent he was from out west somewhere— past Notting Hill perhaps. They squeezed their way up the hall to the entrance of the kitchen.

"If nothing else, I've figured out why Lindon only drank spirits. Don't dive into Mr. Claremont's home brew, okay?" she whispered. "Though you might have to take a glass— to be polite."

Charlie winked. "Roger that," he said.

Tombo lit a cigarette. Mr. Claremont shook both musicians by the hand and patted Charlie on the back with un-expected vigor.

"Friends of Lindon? Good to have you here," he en-thused, pushing glasses of cider their way.

Tombo didn't heed Vesta's warning and downed half his glass immediately. He seemed to quite like the stuff.

Charlie sniffed his. He put it down on the table, de-clined the offer of food from the buffet and eyed Vesta, en-joying the view. She was a fine-looking woman with skin like satin, and not too thin, like some British girls. When she smiled her eyes sparkled.

"You help yourself," Mr. Claremont insisted as he dis-appeared into the front room to top up glasses.

"So." Vesta fanned herself with her open palm. "It's hot in here! Tombo, Charlie said you were at Mac's on Thurs-day night?"

Tombo nodded and looked around. "We can't talk about that in here, can we?"

"Whisper," she said, cupping her ear. "I'm trying to fig-ure out what actually happened. Tell me, did Lindon leave with the white girl or not?"

Tombo's eyes dropped to his shiny shoes. "Yeah, he did." He leaned closer. "He left with the girl, all right. About three in the morning, after Charlie left, give or take. They went outside, and I didn't see Lindon again that night or ever."

Vesta's face betrayed her confusion. "You sure?"

"Yeah, course I am. There weren't that many of us and we all saw them going out together. I'm sorry. Charlie says you're not sure Lindon did it. I couldn't tell you whether he did or not. But he left with the girl and that's for sure. He went outside with all of them, but then the smooth guy and the fat girl came back on their own."

"Tell me about the other girl, the glamorous one," she asked. "What was she doing there?"

"I dunno. What they all do. She was hanging out for a

couple of hours with her friends, I suppose. They arrived after midnight. They were dancing some of the time, sitting up at the back, even though there was hardly anyone in. People think it's hep—keeping a distance. Too cool for school. It was kind of a mix-up. Then the girl got chatting to Lindon—all crazy about bebop and dropping names like they was going out of fashion. It didn't take him long. She left with him pretty quickly. The others just ended up dancing."

"But that's not what he said to me," she mouthed in disbelief. "He said they'd left and he'd stayed. It doesn't make sense. Do you really think he'd do anything to that girl?"

Tombo shuffled from foot to foot. "You can't ask me that, sister. Not here with Lindon's family and all . . ."

Charlie laid his hand gently on Vesta's shoulder. "The police took statements from all the guys. And they all saw him leave."

Tombo confirmed this with a nod.

"And the other people she was with? The couple?"

"Like I said, they came back in." Tombo downed the rest of the cider and sucked on his cigarette as if he needed it to breathe. "They couldn't have been outside more than a few minutes. Seeing her off, I guess. They were dancing for a while but we were slowing down by then and when we stopped playing it wound up early. Four, maybe. Round then anyways when the police arrived."

"So," Vesta put the story together, "Lindon left with three of them, two of them came back in, and you assume that Lindon and Rose ended up together? I mean, you didn't see that happen. They could have left separately."

"Yeah, well, I didn't see them get in no taxi. That was Barney. And the girl's friends, of course. I mean, one of them called the police, didn't she? That's what I heard. She'd seen everything and so had the white guy—Lindon and the posh bird leaving together."

Vesta glanced through to the front room where Mrs. Claremont was sitting on the sofa. She felt her heart sink as she took a moment to consider Tombo's story. If it was true, Lindon had lied to her—but what innocent explanation could there be for doing that?

From the other side of the room, out of Vesta's field of vision, her mother spotted the two young strangers beside her daughter. Her interest piqued, Mrs. Churchill worked her way toward them and arrived like a liner coming in to dock, proprietorially linking her arm through Vesta's.

"Well, angel, who are these two fine young men?"

Vesta bit her lip. Tombo turned away to pour himself another cider. It was awkward explaining the connections, somehow. Charlie, however, rose to the occasion with a half bow.

"Mama," Vesta found her voice, "this is Charlie. He's from America."

"Mrs. Churchill." Charlie kissed her hand. "Let me introduce you to my friend Tombo."

Tombo nodded.

"And you two boys knew Lindon?" Mrs. Churchill checked.

"We played with him, ma'am. We're both musicians."

"I'm on horn," Tombo confirmed.

"What happened is a terrible thing." Mrs. Churchill put her head to one side pensively.

In the front room someone started playing blues guitar. The rhythm spread through the crowd and one or two of the women swayed their hips and made appreciative noises. Tombo beat time on the side of the staircase.

"We came to pay our respects, Mrs. Churchill. That's all," said Charlie smoothly.

"I'm glad you fellas is here." She winked slyly at her daughter. "You're both welcome. I'm happy to meet two of Lindon's friends. We're all going to miss him."

"Mrs. Churchill," they both mumbled respectfully.

As she headed back into the sitting room a second guitar joined in.

"I shoulda brought my horn . . ." Tombo sounded wistful. "A man should never be separated from his instrument."

The words filtered through Vesta's consciousness and something clicked into place. "Did he say good-bye to you?" she asked Tombo.

"What?"

"On Thursday night did Lindon say good-bye?"

Tombo snorted with laughter. He lifted his glass and stared at it as if he might find inspiration inside.

Charlie said, "When a man like Lindon has a deb on his arm, I mean when a man gets that kind of lucky, he doesn't go back to say good-bye to his friends, Vesta. Lindon was leaving with a woman, and for him she was probably the woman of his dreams. A golden girl. He wouldn't go back to the boys. He escorted her, you know." Charlie demonstrated escorting a woman with a flourish.

Vesta ignored him. "So he didn't go back to the band?"

"No. Of course not."

The men were incredulous.

"Well," Vesta frowned, "if he didn't come over and say good-bye, then he didn't pack up properly, did he? I mean he wasn't trailing his sax about with him, was he? He wouldn't have taken it over to a group of people dancing. I'm right, aren't I? So, what happened to Lindon's instrument?"

Vesta wanted to catch Tombo's reaction. A flicker of incomprehension passed across his gaunt face and then he remembered. "Barney picked it up. Yeah. You're right. Barney sorted it all out. He had the case and everything. Said he'd keep it for Lindon."

"Thanks," said Vesta. "There. Well, when Lindon got down to me in Brighton a few hours later, he had his sax. Same old case I'd seen him with before. So, even if he left with Rose, Lindon went back to Mac's to get it. He saw Barney again. He must have."

"Can't have." Tombo shook his head. "I stayed till the end. I was there when they locked up after the cops had finished. Barney walked me as far as Piccadilly."

Vesta ignored him. The story didn't tie up. Tombo's statement was flawed. He wasn't necessarily lying—he just hadn't seen everything.

"I need to go back into town," she said, pulling her cardigan over her shoulders.

"Now?" Charlie checked his watch. "The party's only starting, sugar. Feels like it might go on all afternoon."

"You stay if you want to. But I have someone I need to see. And I'd like to have a look at Mac's. Scene of the crime and all."

Charlie loitered by the stairway as she looked for her belongings. "Hey, I'll come with you," he offered. "You owe me the pleasure of your company at dinner, remember? Perhaps we can tie it all up at once."

19

The key ... is to let go of fear.

On the top floor of the Oxford and Cambridge Club there were several double rooms and three suites. The ceilings were slightly lower up here, but it was grand nonetheless. The hallway was painted a blue tone, and a narrow Persian rug ran the length of it. Mirabelle began at the far end of the corridor, noting gratefully as she passed each door that they had all been fitted with the same kind of lock. She bent her hairpin and inserted it into the lock of the first room. Getting the hang of how to pick the lock was tricky but as soon as she got a feel for the bolt mechanism the door swung open.

The suite was vacant and enormous. The heavy cherry-wood furniture looked as if it had been in place for a hundred years, and the place smelled of beeswax and lavender as if it had been freshly cleaned. Condensation clouded the windows—it was cold outside—and the fire had not been lit. Mirabelle moved on swiftly to the room next door and the next—getting in and out fast. Each bedroom was broadly similar.

As she closed the door of the fifth room a maid appeared in the corridor, dragging a heavy suitcase. Mirabelle closed the door smartly behind her and walked confidently toward the stairs as if she had a perfect right to be there. Then she sneaked back to continue her search, clicking the locks open one by one. Apart from the room the maid had entered, only one other had a guest in residence. There were no personal effects, and the bed had not been made up. Perhaps they had checked out.

Next floor down, Mirabelle realized that her hairpin was about to break. It might be worth procuring a proper set of lockpicks, she thought. A basic set was small and would fit easily in her handbag. She would look into it. In the meantime she tentatively extracted a second hairpin from her chignon and prayed her hairdo wouldn't suffer. Only four rooms on this floor had keys left on the board— so she only needed to check those ones. The first was empty; the bedsheets were tossed back. Mirabelle wondered fleetingly if this had been Didi's room—she caught the faintest whiff of a perfume that seemed familiar from the day before. The next room was unoccupied, but the ashtray was full and none of the cigarette butts were smeared with lipstick. She deduced that the occupant had most likely been a man. A small decanter of sherry and two crystal glasses sat on a side table. In the bathroom there was a cutthroat razor. Harry Bellamy Gore struck her as a chap who'd want all the latest gadgets. Mirabelle had seen newspaper adverts for American Schick electric razors and the new safety model by Gillette. The blade on the marble washstand was hopelessly old-fashioned. She continued to the waste-paper bin, which provided two cigarette cards, an empty Dunhill packet and at the very bottom two shards of celluloid, cut from a roll of film. She picked them out carefully and held them up to the light. What could they be?

"Do you belong to Harry?" she murmured.

It was impossible to say. The plastic was definitely from a photographic negative, but the strips were too thin to be able to identify the main image. With a sigh Mirabelle turned her attention to the wardrobe. Inside hung a dinner suit. She checked the pockets: a folded handkerchief (no initials), a few coins and a book of matches from a club in the West End called The Flamingo.

She sat at the dressing table and pulled open the drawer. Inside there was a Louis MacNeice book with no dedication on the flyleaf to identify the owner. A pristine paper bookmark advertising a secondhand bookshop in Moxon Street, Marylebone, was jammed into the spine at a poem called "Bagpipe Music." Mirabelle snapped it shut. The sentiments of "Bagpipe Music" would probably appeal to someone of Harry's age and interests. That sealed it. Jazz was Harry's thing.

Checking everything was as she'd found it, Mirabelle prepared to move to the next room when the distinctive sound of a key rattling in a lock cut through the silence. The rattle stopped for a second as Mirabelle realized the unlocked door would cause confusion to the room's occupant. After a brief pause the key rattled again, turning the lock both ways, checking it was working. Mirabelle looked round frantically for somewhere to hide. Just as the door handle moved, she slipped inside the wardrobe and crouched beside the dinner suit, pulling the door closed behind her. In the dark her heart pounded and she could scarcely breathe. What if the occupant of the room had come back to change his clothes? What on earth had made her dart in here? Under the bed or behind a curtain would have been a far safer option. As her breathing steadied, she worried it was too noisy and then she forgot everything as someone entered the room. They passed the wardrobe and flung a key noisily onto the dressing table. The wardrobe was musty and cramped but it afforded one tiny shaft of light through the keyhole. Mirabelle edged silently toward it. The hole was so small she could see only three feet or so in each direction. A young man went into the bathroom opposite. He stood with his back to her and peed into the toilet. Mirabelle squinted. He was certainly of the right age to be Harry Bellamy Gore. His hair was dirty blond and as he turned she caught only a fleeting glimpse of his face, but it was enough to tell her that the occupant of the room was good-looking enough to have excited Charlotte the singer's initial interest before his behavior alerted her to the fact that he would not be a good bet as a steady boyfriend.

As he brushed past her field of vision Mirabelle heard the man light a cigarette, and then a rapid knock from the door to her left made her heart lurch.

"Yes?" the man called.

She strained to see but the visitor would have eluded her if Harry hadn't named him and in doing so confirmed everything.

"Miles," he boomed. "Is the car ready?"

"Yes, sir."

"Good. I'll need it shortly."

Mirabelle noted that the boy didn't say thank you. Her father had been a stickler for never taking anyone for granted, not even the staff. "You can tell a lot from someone's civility," he used to say. It was easy for the young to be offhand. Especially someone as privileged as Harry.

"I'll come down in a while," he said.

"I'm afraid there's something else, sir," Miles spoke evenly. "A lady was asking for you today."

"I haven't got time for that kind of thing now, Miles. Just bat them off, eh?"

"No, sir. But this was an *older* lady." Miles cleared his throat. "She said she was your aunt, sir. She asked for you by name."

"Really? Auntie Christina? Here at the club? I thought she'd be in Herefordshire."

"No, sir. If you recall I saw both your aunts when I drove the ladies to your birthday party. This was not one of those ladies. I'd never seen her before."

"What did she want?"

"She asked about your whereabouts, sir. She asked if you'd be back. Then she ascertained that your vehicle was parked on the club's premises."

"Describe her."

"In her mid-forties, I'd say."

Mirabelle suppressed a gasp. She was in her late thirties! Miles clearly had poor observational skills. Perhaps he was so much in the habit of directing teenagers to Harry's rooms that a woman closer to his own age seemed ancient.

"She had brown hair and eyes. Well dressed—green tweed. Attractive enough. She was very businesslike. Asked a lot of questions."

"Certainly not one of my aunts then. Thanks, Miles. I'll look into it."

"I thought you should know, sir. And I should also say that she mentioned Miss Rose's disappearance."

"What did she say exactly?"

"She only mentioned it in passing. As if I ought to tell her where you were because of that. She was trying to locate you. Put a bit of pressure on me. She didn't ask about anything else."

"But you didn't tell her where I was?"

"Not a peep, sir. Of course not."

Mirabelle heard the crinkle of a piece of paper being handed over. Harry, she guessed, was probably an excellent tipper.

"You did the right thing in telling me, Miles," the boy said. "We don't want anyone poking their noses into our business and ruining everything. Delicate operation."

Miles moved past the wardrobe and then Mirabelle heard the door open and close. Harry remained in the room. She could hear him pacing up and down by the window muttering to himself.

"Right. Could be bloody anyone." Here he let out a nervous giggle. "Crikey! We can't have the police." There was the clink of crystal as he poured himself a drink from the decanter and then a cough and a splutter. "I need a real drink."

He stomped across the carpet and lifted the telephone receiver to dial two digits for service. Mirabelle held her breath. How long was she going to have to stay in this wardrobe? There was a pause. She could just make out the sound of a distant ringing tone. No one answered.

"Bloody hell!" He slammed down the receiver. "Right. I'll get it myself."

Mirabelle was never so grateful as when she heard the lock turn. She heaved a sigh and pushed open the wardrobe door. Her hands were trembling. She quickly checked the room before leaving.

The Bellamy Gore cousins had been close. Everyone said that. And Rose was missing. But the young man in the room didn't appear to be in mourning or anything like it. His behavior was erratic. That wasn't the word. No, he'd been *agitated*. And he had considered that the police might be investigating him. Sometimes a person's first assumption was very telling. It revealed how they perceived the situation. Why was Harry's first thought the police? It was a sign that he felt guilty, surely. So what might Harry have to feel guilty about? Why on earth wouldn't he want to speak openly to anyone who could help—the police most of all? Mirabelle realized he was just a boy. He had the accoutrements of adulthood, but something about him was still childlike. Harry was out of his depth.

Didi had called the Bellamy Gores inseparable. Now Mirabelle wondered. Her own young life had been lonely. She was the only child of two only children. When her parents died she'd felt utterly abandoned. She'd been the same age as Harry was now. The news had come to her by telegram while she was at college. She had been called to her tutor's rooms and from there had gone back to London to arrange the funeral. It had felt like being marooned—she hadn't only been orphaned but, worse, she felt completely bereft of anyone who cared for her, anyone who mattered. The family solicitor dealt with most things, and then it was as if a silence had fallen, muffling the world. It had been inescapable. Until Jack came along she'd had no one. And since Jack's death there had been no one. Now, here was a young man whose most intimate childhood companion had apparently been abducted. In times like these one was consumed by grief and fear. One was desolate. One wanted help. Perhaps the boy wasn't as close to Rose as everyone said. Worse, Mirabelle couldn't allay the suspicion that perhaps he was involved in the girl's disappearance. Her gut turned just thinking about the betrayal. In wartime people took action because of what they believed in. In peacetime people were driven by their private concerns. Had Harry turned on his cousin? Would a child do that? He had been a pornographer, after all. But, still . . .

Downstairs, Mirabelle took off her tweed jacket and slipped unseen into the Ladies' Sitting Room where she closed the door behind her and sank into an armchair. Consciously she measured her breath, trying to recover her equilibrium, but the suspicions coursing through her mind touched a raw and painful nerve. It wasn't at all what she'd expected. Poor Rose. Looking down she realized she was gripping a cushion very tightly. Her hands felt like claws. She tried to relax but adrenaline was still pumping through her system. She'd need a few moments to let it subside before she could decide what to do next. In the meantime, the Ladies' Sitting Room would serve as the perfect refuge. Harry wouldn't find her in here.

20

Love is a game that two can play and both win.

Sitting next to Charlie on the tram was a strange experience. There was, however, not much choice if they wanted to get back into town. Of course, Vesta had a number of suitors. She was adept in the art of how to behave when she was being taken out. But the men she dated in Brighton never became part of her day-to-day life. They arrived in fancy motor cars and took her to places of their choosing—bars, restaurants, theaters and dance halls. She always flirted with them, which now she came to think about it was like slipping into a persona. She was herself in their company but a very specific version of herself. By comparison this man had just met both her parents and attended her family's church. Now, sitting on the tram with him felt curiously domestic, almost intimate. They weren't going out together, exactly—he was helping her or at the very least accompanying her, and for Vesta neither of these activities was normal. She could feel his leg next to hers and she found it difficult to meet his eye. He seemed relaxed on the other hand, and when he looked her way she blushed and felt awkward, fidgeting in her seat.

"Mac's won't be open yet," Charlie said, "but I think

there's a guy in the bar who has a key. If they're open Sundays."

"Do you live in Soho, Charlie?"

Charlie laughed. "Over the shop, you mean? No. I got a room over the back end of Pimlico. I like it there as much as anywhere else in London. It's close to everything I need to be close to."

"Are there a lot of black men in Pimlico?"

"I guess not. Does that worry you? How many black people are there where you live?"

Vesta smiled. "Sometimes feels like I'm the only one in Brighton, though that's not strictly true. There's a fellow up at the racecourse and another who works on the pier. I've seen them."

Charlie languidly slid his hand across the back of the seat, and Vesta felt a warm glow tingle up the back of her neck.

"So you've been dating white men? Have you got tastes like Lindon?"

"I get taken out!" Vesta spluttered. "I don't go 'cause they're white or black."

Charlie chuckled. "I bet you want to come home. Coming home gonna feel good, sister."

Vesta crossed her arms. "I ain't going nowhere," she sniffed.

"Not till dinner." Charlie left it at that.

It was, Vesta realized, a curious sensation to feel that the tram ride was simultaneously interminable and fleeting. Some seconds seemed to drag and yet when she looked out of the window they were at Bermondsey Library already and the next time she checked they were at London Bridge. In town they dismounted and Charlie led the way. From the stop they had to walk north and west into the warren of Soho. Now and then he took her arm to help her across the cobblestoned roads. Charlie was so tall it felt like having a statue for an escort. He was somehow immovable and yet very warm. Vesta found herself leaning into him as she walked.

"This place is deserted!" she declared.

Even the newsstands were closed, sealed with thick rope and heavy padlocks. Toward Windmill Street they passed a couple of pubs and caught the familiar whiff of cigarette smoke.

Eventually Charlie pointed at a tall building on the left-hand side of the street. "Mac's is in there. First floor."

Vesta peered. You'd never find the place if you didn't know it was there. The windows were dark, in fact they looked blacked out, and the front door was closed. There was no signage. Even if the door had been open there was no light over it. "When does it open?"

"Thursday nights and Sunday nights. That's it. Things start about ten. Apart from the jazz, a couple of the restaurants use the place for storage out of hours, if you know what I mean. A place to stash black-market ingredients. Oh, and one or two of the big theaters rent it as a rehearsal room if they need extra space."

"But Rose and her lot knew to come here? I mean, they must've been before?"

"I dunno," Charlie shrugged. "The two of them—Rose and the guy—they were all over town. They'd have heard about Mac's. I never seen them here before but that doesn't mean they hadn't been."

Vesta paced the pavement. "So, that night when Lindon leaves he comes down here with the three of them. Then a cab arrives. Probably just passing. They'd have hailed one. If not right here then up on the corner."

"And then the other girl calls her father and he calls the cops?" Charlie looked around, checking behind him. "From up there"—he pointed—"the closest phone box gotta be on Tottenham Court Road."

Vesta started in the right direction, glancing at her watch.

Sure enough, turning left at the corner of the main street there was a red phone box. She opened the door and the metallic tang of urine made her bring her hand up to cover her nose in a visceral reaction.

"Even there and back it can't be more than three or four minutes," Charlie pointed out. "And that's including whatever she had to say. And you reckon that even though she was worried about her friend, Lavinia still went back to Mac's and just carried on dancing? Drunk folks. Besides, what else could she do? I mean Rose was gone. She didn't know where. She was with a fella. Why not? It'd take her mind off it."

They made their way back to Windmill Street and stopped once more outside the door of Mac's.

"You wanna look inside?" Charlie offered.

Vesta smiled gratefully. "Could I?"

"Stay here." Charlie crossed the road and made for the St. James Tavern on the corner where the barman kept a key. Vesta shifted from foot to foot. Windmill Street seemed so ordinary it was difficult for her to accept that anything momentous had happened here, not least that this was the last place anyone had seen Rose alive. She tried to picture Lindon being given the gold cigarette case in the street and the discussion that presumably broke out when it became apparent Rose was leaving. Her friends can't have been pleased. How hard did they try to stop her? What were Harry and Lavinia like?

She walked to the door of the club and pushed open the brass letterbox so she could see inside. A narrow staircase covered with threadbare carpet led upward and downward from a tiny square hallway. On the first few steps there were boxes of tinned Spam. Vesta grimaced. She loathed Spam.

Charlie returned with the key and turned it in the lock.

"Up?" she checked.

"Yeah."

"What's down?"

"I dunno. A basement?"

"Let's see, shall we?"

Mirabelle had impressed on Vesta the importance of being methodical, not overlooking anything, so Vesta switched on the hallway light and picked her way past the Spam down to a white door at the bottom of the stairs. She knocked. No reply. She turned the handle and discovered the door was open. Inside, there was a single blacked-out window and some old tires and boxes covered in dust sheets. A tea chest and three upturned buckets served as a table and chairs. A couple of jam jars with the dregs of what looked like cold tea sat on the surface. A quick sniff told her that the liquid was brandy.

"Up?" Charlie directed.

They went back up the stairs, their bodies pushed close together by the dimensions of the staircase. Charlie produced a second key to unlock the room, which it transpired was painted black from floor to ceiling. There were a few dusty footprints, some wooden chairs and two music stands. Against the back wall there was an upright piano with its strings exposed.

"It's nothing fancy," Charlie said. "People just come here to jam. It's experimental, you know. An experience."

Vesta nodded.

She walked slowly around the space to get a feel for it. This, after all, was the last place anyone had seen Rose and, apart from Victoria, the last place in London she could say Lindon had been seen for sure that night. It sent a shiver down her spine.

Charlie crossed to the piano and played a few bars. "Heard that before? It's Bill Evans. I saw him in New York last year. Wild! I've been into music since I was a kid but the sound is changing. Everything's changing. I ain't Max Roach but it's exciting—just being part of it."

He walked over and took Vesta in his arms. "Dance with me."

"There's no music."

"We got music inside us, sister. Come on."

He turned her around the floor a couple of times, leading the way till they came to a natural halt. He didn't let go. Instead, Charlie bent over and kissed Vesta. She didn't usually condone that kind of behavior, but this time her knees felt as if they were going to buckle. Without any thought she let herself go and kissed him back, then whispered, "You're fresh."

"Can you blame me, sugar?"

Vesta struggled to recover her poise. She pulled back and smoothed her clothes, regarding Charlie carefully. Her cheeks felt hot.

"So where do you want to go now, Miss Vesta?" he smiled.

"Well, it's too early for dinner. We could walk back to St. James's. My boss is in town."

"Your boss?"

"Her name's Mirabelle. I was to meet her later at Duke's. We could wait in the bar."

"A lady boss. Cool. Let's go to Duke's then. I like the sound of that."

Charlie ushered Vesta out of Mac's. He took her hand as they made their way carefully downstairs. Her heart was still pounding.

"I've got to give the key back. Wait for me."

Vesta rested against the wall at the bottom of the stairs. It was an opportunity to steady herself.

"Charlie, is this where the bouncer was?" she asked.

"Barney? Some of the time. Other times he'd be upstairs in the doorway. He moves around, you know, checking on things. I always say they don't need a bouncer at Mac's. I mean, it ain't as if it's busy. But they always got someone just to keep an eye on the place."

"So from down here Barney would have seen what went on in the street?"

"Yeah. He did see. He told the police, remember?"

"And according to Tombo he took Lindon's sax . . ."

"Yeah. I dunno where he put it though. Coulda stashed it for him to pick up here—downstairs or something. I guess he might have left it behind the bar at the pub—they hold the key, why not a saxophone?"

"But Lindon picked it up that night. He came back for it."

"If he had it with him in the morning he must've."

Vesta couldn't concentrate. Charlie's presence was too intoxicating. She was finding it difficult to tear her eyes from him.

"Last night I had a martini in the hotel," she said. "They make the best cocktails in London. That's what I heard and it tasted that way, too."

"Well, let's get over there, baby," Charlie grinned. "It's time for some fun. Come on."

21

An ill thought leaves a trail like a serpent.

Mirabelle composed herself and formulated a plan as she powdered her nose. If Harry was somehow involved in Rose's disappearance she needed proof, but her instincts told her she should keep as far away as she could for as long as possible. She wanted to observe him until she had the measure of the boy. Potentially he was very dangerous, like a cocked gun brandished by a four-year-old.

Where had he gone to get his drink? Leaving her jacket in the Sitting Room, she checked the hallway before venturing out. Keeping out of sight, she peeked into the Coffee Room. Two elderly gentlemen sat, in silence, eating cheese and drinking port. The old duffers had probably known each other all their lives, she thought, yet they still sat at different tables. Mirabelle tiptoed farther up the hallway until she came to the Library. Without opening the door she could hear voices. She listened, and relaxed slightly as she recognized Harry's clipped tones—at least now she knew where he was. Inside, the boy was holding forth. Female laughter punctuated his anecdote of an acquaintance who had a boxing blue which had served him well out of the ring. It was a tale of bravado to make a teenage boy feel good.

"There's three of them. This might keep me a little busy," he said. "We were on the bridge and there was no one else around, so I got my jacket off and thought I'd lend a hand. Took us a couple of minutes but we got there. Landed one of them in the drink, too. Cheek of it! Saying that about Lolly's mother! Quite a giggle, really."

One of the girls clearly had a brain. "It's awfully brave of you to be amusing us like this, Harry," she said. "However are you keeping your spirits up? I mean, Rose is missing and you're just soldiering on. It must be so vexing. What do you think has happened to her? Is there absolutely no news?"

There was only a moment's hesitation.

"The police have been marvelous," Harry enthused convincingly. "They'll bring her back, I'm sure of it."

A second female voice cut in. "For heaven's sake, Lucy! Must you be so ghoulish? We all hope poor Rose is all right but best not dwell on the thing. There's nothing any of us can do and it doesn't do Harry any good at all. Does it, Harry?"

"Here, here." Glasses clinked.

"What are you planning for the break?" Harry asked.

"Harry! Hilary term has only just started!"

"Paris," said the second female voice. "We always go to France for Easter—I have an uncle there. I can't wait. Paris is so charming, *n'est-ce pas?*"

Satisfied the female company would keep Harry busy for a while—at least until he'd had another drink or two—Mirabelle decided to investigate his territory further.

Feeling more confident, she picked up her jacket from the Sitting Room, and walked back through the hallway and out of the front door onto Pall Mall, trying to work out the configuration of the buildings as she made for the end of the street. Glancing left toward Marlborough House she dismissed anything in that direction and continued on, crossing the road. To her right was a narrow passageway between two tall buildings. Mirabelle looked up to see if she might recognize the line of the roof and sure enough the back of Spencer House proved familiar as the alley opened onto a cobblestoned mews. This must be the place. However, none of the garages appeared to have a sign indicating they were in use by the Oxford and Cambridge Club. As she walked up the right-hand side she struck lucky. Through an open door she could see on the wall next to the door a sign instructing drivers to restrict their speed to 5 mph and another that read: STRICTLY PRIVATE. MEMBERS' VEHICLES ONLY. Mirabelle smiled at the correct use of the apostrophe.

The garage had a higher ceiling and was less cramped than she expected—perhaps a throwback to the days when it housed horse-drawn carriages. It was pitch-black inside. A good sign, thought Mirabelle. It meant no one was here. She felt in her clutch bag for some matches and was thankful she had picked up a book at Feldman's as a memento. She struck one and quickly located the electric switch on the side wall. Once the place was lit—albeit dimly, by a solitary grimy lightbulb—she could see the garage was large and extremely well appointed. There was a proper servicing pit and a wall-mounted toolbox. Most of the space was taken up with parking spaces, with only a quarter of them occupied. It wasn't difficult to locate the Aston Martin, which was parked right next to the servicing pit where Miles must have been working. It was green.

Her heart rate accelerated as she tentatively tried the car door. It was open. She slid into the driving seat. Inside, everything was shipshape and there was a faint, rather pleasant smell of leather and engine oil. She clicked open the glove compartment. Predictably, Harry had stowed a silver hip flask inside—brandy, Mirabelle concluded after unscrewing it. It sat on top of some papers and a half-empty packet of cigarettes. The boy was eighteen going on thirty! Mirabelle flicked through the papers: car registration documents, a handbook and some letters addressed to Harry at a house on Wilton Crescent. They predated Rose's disappearance and were purely social but they confirmed his family's address. Harry, like Rose, had been a neighbor of the Blyths in town. They certainly were a cozy bunch. The houses on Wilton Crescent, if Mirabelle remembered correctly, were very grand and only a couple of blocks from Upper Belgrave Street. Harry no doubt stayed at the club so he could indulge his predilections to the full. It would prove a lot trickier trying to sneak a black jazz singer past long-time retainers in the family home.

Mirabelle slid out of the car and tried the boot. Inside were a heavy blue waxed jacket and a torch. She checked the jacket; in the poacher's pouch there was a parcel wrapped in brown paper. The loose paper had been tied with string. Removing her gloves, she carefully unpicked the knot and put aside the crush of white tissue paper that covered the parcel's contents. What she saw made her gasp. She quickly looked over her shoulder as if someone might have seen. Hairs all over her body prickled and she felt a lurch of nausea. Rolled up tightly, but unmistakable, was a yellow evening dress with a delicate silver thread running through the fabric. She pulled it out and let the gown hang from the shoulder straps. Rose must be tiny. The dress had a waist of no more than twenty-two inches. The material at the front was grubby and smelled of cigarette smoke with an underlying vinegary tang, perhaps the trace of perfume. Mirabelle ran her hands down the seams. Sure enough, the hem was ragged. It had been torn up to the knee on the left side. No wonder Harry wanted to avoid the police.

Mirabelle's mind raced. What had the boy done to his cousin and how had he done it? His alibi for the night she had disappeared had seemed so unassailable the police had scarcely interviewed him. To accomplish that he'd need accomplices—more than one, certainly. She turned over the possibilities, her mind racing so fast that she couldn't properly analyze each thought. Was this child a murderer?

That moment, she heard feet on the cobbles outside and male voices. Mirabelle scrambled to return the dress to the package. The material kept spilling out of the paper and was making what felt like a deafening noise as she shoved it back into the jacket pocket.

She closed the car boot and frantically looked for somewhere to hide. There was no time to switch off the light but perhaps one of the other cars would conceal her. The far reaches of the garage were dark. In her panic she twisted an ankle as she tried to run toward the nearest wall where a large black Ford had been parked out of the way. In her rush, she fell headlong into the car inspection pit, managing to break her fall with an outstretched hand. She felt no pain but Mirabelle knew that was due purely to adrenaline. Her heart was racing uncontrollably. Deciding it was best to stay put as the voices came closer, she pulled herself into the corner of the pit closest to the Aston. The light was poor, and as she couldn't see the green car or any of the area around it, if the men stayed by the vehicle, they wouldn't be able to see her either.

Mirabelle froze as she recognized Harry's distinctive voice. He was playing with his car keys, flinging them into the air and catching them. Then she heard Miles open the car door so the boy could get in. Mirabelle tried to slow her breathing. Her senses were on fire and she was sure that from here, she could actually smell the men.

"I tuned her up," Miles said.

The car engine roared into life and a cloud of engine fumes sank into the inspection pit.

"That sounds much better," Harry said.

"I hope the lady . . ." Miles's voice trailed off.

"Don't you worry about that!" The boy's voice had an edge. "I'll get what I want. It's all going to work out perfectly, Miles. You'll see. And don't worry about that old aunt impersonator either, whoever she is. If you see her again give her what for. Did you leave my jacket in the boot?"

"Yes, sir."

The car pulled off slowly. Mirabelle heard Miles sighing, the light being snapped off and his footsteps receding. With some effort she pulled herself out of the pit and limped toward the pool of light at the garage exit. There was blood on her stocking—she must have bashed her ankle when she fell in—and now a long rip snaked up her calf. As she bent down to touch her leg she could see that her wrist was slightly swollen. But there was no time to attend to that now. Out of sight at the end of the alleyway she heard Harry's car turn left.

Mirabelle's mind was whizzing. Miles was an accomplice to whatever Harry had done. Had the boy really kidnapped his own cousin? It certainly seemed that way and, worse, he'd hurt her. The dress was torn. Come to think of it, worse still, the dress had been removed. Was this about money? Some kind of family feud? Surely the boy wouldn't hold his own aunt and uncle to ransom. How could he?

Mirabelle felt fury rising in her belly and then a sense of confusion. Momentarily her outrage overcame the pain. There was something else entirely going on here and poor Lindon had become caught up in it. And then it occurred to Mirabelle: the dress, the fact that Harry had kept the dress, meant that Rose must be alive. To keep it otherwise was crazy—it was too incriminating. The most logical explanation was that somehow it would be used as a lever to get something he wanted. A ransom, perhaps. And, if that was the case, the girl was safe somewhere. If she was alive she could be found. The realization spurred her on.

Mirabelle checked her watch. It was after three o'clock. She limped slowly up the alley. The main street was deserted. There was never a taxi when you wanted one. She briefly contemplated taking a car from the garage. Some people left their keys under the sun visor. Of course, stealing a car constituted a felony, but it might be worth committing a crime if in following Harry, she could rescue Rose. But it was too late now and the Aston had gone. Besides, with her ankle so badly twisted she would find it difficult to drive. Mirabelle gritted her teeth as the injury began to sting. She inhaled deeply and then coughed as the fog hit her lungs.

"Damn it," she cursed out loud.

She'd been too slow again. She should have kept hold of the parcel. If only she'd had the gumption to jump into a car the minute Miles left. Her injuries had put her into shock, she realized. She'd been in shock before. It slowed you down. In circumstances like this an agent ought to focus on fixing themselves up, she remembered. But Mirabelle felt angry. It had been her best instinct but she hadn't enjoyed hiding like a coward.

"Sorry, Jack," she whispered. "I'll do better next time."

22

Go where there is no path and leave a trail.

Vesta and Charlie were getting cozy at the corner table in Duke's bar. They were both on their second martinis and had finished a tiny bowl of crackers. Duke's bar looked the same late at night as it did in the afternoon, which, Vesta realized, made it very intimate. It was easy to lose track of time when she was with Charlie. He was telling her about his service days. He'd joined up young and she'd made the calculations—he was twenty-eight, making him, by her reckoning, the perfect age to settle down. They'd been sitting together for almost an hour, and his proximity still gave her a warm glow. It was as if they'd been there forever—in a dream world.

When Mirabelle walked in, Vesta didn't recognize her for an instant. Mirabelle seldom looked disheveled but her whole demeanor had changed. She was limping, her stockings were in tatters, and she was holding her right arm against her stomach.

"Mirabelle?" Vesta jumped to her feet. "What on earth has happened? You look dreadful!"

Mirabelle collapsed onto a seat beside the couple. She was deathly pale and looked exhausted.

"Ma'am, I think you need a drink," said Charlie.

"Water," Mirabelle mouthed.

The Italian waiter appeared. "Perhaps it would be best to help Madam into the back? We have a first aid kit."

"Do you have iodine?" Mirabelle asked.

"And we'll need ice." Charlie took charge. "Looks like your hand's taken a blow. Did you hit someone?"

Mirabelle smiled weakly. "No. I fell into a pit."

It took a few minutes to get everything organized. The barman called the receptionist who said she would try to find a replacement pair of nylons. Her tone of voice made it clear this was not an easy task on a Sunday. Of all the rationed clothes, stockings were famously the most difficult to get hold of—on or off the black market. In the meantime Mirabelle, Vesta and Charlie removed to the room where Eddie had been working on Friday night.

Charlie insisted on taking charge of the medical care after explaining that he'd had some experience during the war. He made a cold compress for Mirabelle's wrist and disinfected the leg wound with iodine.

Mirabelle eyed this new companion out of the corner of her eye and looked quizzically at Vesta.

"Charlie knew Lindon. He was there on Thursday night," said Vesta, "but he left before it all happened."

As Charlie worked, she described everything she'd found out in detail. Charlie knew Vesta was sharp but now he realized she'd taken in every word, drawn conclusions and tied together what she'd discovered. She had an uncanny eye for detail and remembered every name, time and opinion anyone had offered. He hadn't thought of the scraps of information as part of a coherent story until now. It was as if Vesta had been piecing together a jigsaw inside her head. It was impressive.

"So, Barney's the one we need to speak to next," she concluded. "I mean he kept Lindon's sax and somehow got it back to him but he didn't tell anyone that. The guy gave false evidence to the police. He was the last one out of the place on Thursday night or Friday morning—he locked up and walked Tombo as far as Piccadilly. Even more importantly, he was the bloke who told Lindon the police were after him and, basically, encouraged him to take off. Barney knows what really happened, or at least knows more than he's saying."

Mirabelle nodded. "Yes. I think he does. But I've talked to him already and I'd say we'd have a tough time cracking him. Why would he come clean? Besides, we've bigger fish to fry. I checked Harry's car. I don't think Rose is dead, Vesta. Harry has her evening gown. I don't know why."

"You mean he's got the dress she was wearing? Do you think he kidnapped her?"

"The police found a scrap of material from it up at Coram's Fields. When I saw it in the car boot I should have grabbed the parcel. It all happened too quickly. I don't know if Harry's our man, but he's involved and he knows what's going on. He's an arrogant little sod, too, but then he's eighteen, I suppose. The main thing is, Rose is probably still alive."

"What was Harry doing with the dress?" Vesta asked.

"Ransom? Either he's ransoming her or he's being held to ransom. I don't know. He's hard to read. But whatever reason he has it, at least it means she's still in the game." Mirabelle sighed.

"We should tell the police. How long ago did he leave the club?"

"No, we can't bring in the police."

"Why not? I mean, this proves Lindon was innocent, doesn't it?"

Mirabelle shook her head. "It points in that direction, and of course we could report it, but imagine what McGregor would be like if we did that in Brighton. The police up here won't be any different. Everything we've found is hearsay. There's no proof whatsoever. And we're in London, so they don't know us. The Met is convinced it was

Lindon, and he died in their custody. So they now want it to be Lindon. I'd like to have some solid evidence before we go to them. They're not going to want to arrest a boy like Harry without a concrete reason. And even if Green is a smart cookie, he's not going to be there till tomorrow. No, our best plan of action is to look for evidence. Going to the police now will hold up everything. There's a girl being held somewhere, I'm convinced of it. You know as well as I do, the police only slow you down."

Charlie looked sideways at the women. He didn't like to interrupt. He reached into the first aid kit and brought out some painkillers. "Well, Miss Bevan, you're gonna need these," he said, unscrewing the bottle and spilling a pile onto Mirabelle's palm. "Take two at a time. Every four hours or so."

She continued talking as he passed her a glass of water. "I popped into Scotland Yard this morning, and there was an incompetent toddler in charge of the case. No sign of anyone in real authority. We need to just get on with it."

"Really?" Vesta said. "Because everything I can think of winds up with Lindon being innocent. Open and closed."

"Yes. He was. But who's guilty, Vesta? There's that to consider. And where is poor Rose? We can't help Lindon today, not really, and if we clear his name one day or the next, it doesn't make much difference, with all due respect. But we could save a girl's life. That means something."

Vesta's eyes were hard, but she nodded slowly. Mirabelle had authority. Her judgment had always been good in the past. Another day wouldn't make much difference. Mirabelle was right about that. "All right. What do you want to do now?"

Mirabelle tried putting some weight on her twisted ankle. It felt a little better and her head had cleared. "Belgravia. We need to make some house calls. Ones that look social. It'll be better if I'm on my own."

"Single-handed?"

"It'll be easier, Vesta."

"No. I mean with only one hand?"

Mirabelle laughed. "Yes, single-handed."

"I hate not being able to help. Not being 'acceptable.'"
Vesta sagged in her chair. "Can't make social calls in bleeding Belgravia. Can't get a room in a hotel without some receptionist checking it's all right. It's just can't, can't, can't.
I'm fed up with it."

"Could be worse, sugar," Charlie soothed. "Where I
come from they string you up for sitting on the wrong bus.
Take it from me, England ain't so bad. The food's pretty
lousy and they stare in the street, but I like it here. We can
drink in the same bars as the white folks, not just play the
music and clean the floors."

Vesta sighed. "Hmmm, what am I supposed to do while
you're in Belgravia?"

"You said you were coming with me," Charlie objected.
"Dinner. Dancing. Jazz. I want to take you to Feldman's.
Remember?"

"Go on," Mirabelle smiled indulgently. "That's a super
idea. Work and play, Vesta! You might dig up something.
See if you can find anyone else who was at Mac's on
Thursday night. Someone saw something that will make
sense of it, they just don't realize it. And keep an eye out
for Barney. I'll meet you in Brighton tomorrow morning.
We've got the office to run as well, remember. Besides,"
the thought occurred to her, "we can hand it all over to the
police down there and let them pass it on to the Yard. That
might give whatever we find out more credibility. Tonight
I'll dig around where the toffs are and try to get something
for McGregor—as far as the Met are concerned he's the
guy who caught Lindon."

"And you don't want me to do something with a map?
Try to figure out where Rose is?"

"How can we? We have no idea where she might be. I'll

poke about at Harry's family home on Wilton Crescent. If I come up with anything, then we'll get the maps out. Now, off with you! You and Charlie deserve to have some fun."

"I bet you haven't even eaten," Vesta sulked.

"That's where you're wrong! I had pie and mash for lunch," Mirabelle said proudly. It was almost true. She'd had a whisky while she pushed the food around her plate.

23

We're all detectives in life.

It got dark a little after six and there was a nip in the air. The capital's doctors, solicitors, businessmen and bankers crowded the first-class carriages arriving from all directions into London's main stations—Victoria, Paddington, King's Cross and Euston. A row of taxicabs snaked from Victoria onto the main road, ferrying passengers home. Not everyone used the train, but petrol could be hard to come by if you were traveling very far out of town, and for many it was simply more convenient to make their way up and down by rail. Since the war more of the upper class worked for a living—everywhere from the BBC to the Bank of England—and in areas like Belgravia the traditional rhythm of the city had changed as people converged en masse on the capital ready for business the next day. There were certainly more cars on the road this evening, Mirabelle noticed, as she took a route by the palace. The neighborhood felt occupied. Occasionally she heard the strains of music or children laughing. Twice she passed footmen walking dogs.

As she headed toward Belgrave Square rooms were being prepared for their occupants' return, the first-floor windows were glowing yellow, and the chimneys were smoking.

Mirabelle glanced along the sweep of Wilton Crescent and paused for a moment in front of the lamps at the entrance to Harry's house. She thought better of ringing the doorbell. Instead she made her way to the rear, to Wilton Row, where the mews houses ran along the back of the crescent. The garage directly behind the Bellamy Gore house was marked by Harry's now-familiar green Aston Martin, parked on the cobbles. He was home. After a quick look round Mirabelle opened the boot: the jacket was gone. She stood back to survey the rear of the house at a distance. There were several lights visible on the second floor, all bedrooms—it looked as if the whole family was in residence.

Mirabelle regarded her high heels. The only way forward was to find out what Harry was up to and that meant going inside. The best way into the Bellamy Gore house was over the back wall but that could be tricky—and painful. It felt as if she had been sneaking around all day, but then sneaking around was the only way she stood a chance of uncovering what was going on. She decided that the best way to get onto the property was to scale the smallest garage in the row and make her way into the Bellamy Gores' back garden from there. Using a rubbish bin to stand on, shoes in hand, she hauled her frame onto the asphalt roof and then with surprising steadiness limped along and dropped as gently as she could onto a rhubarb patch. She put her shoes back on and crept toward the French windows that faced the lawn. The old-fashioned door catch flipped open easily.

The room was dark, and the atmosphere stuffy. The place smelled vaguely of wet dog. Squinting, Mirabelle could make out a tray on a stand with a half-finished jigsaw and beneath it a basket with knitting needles protruding. She whistled quietly—she'd broken into the day room and would be relatively safe from intrusion. The family was bound to use the drawing room upstairs before coming down to dinner. Silently, she congratulated herself on keeping her nerve. On her way up the garden and even when she entered the house her heart had scarcely stirred. She was glad she'd got over her earlier panic and grinned as it occurred to her that she was now practically a cat burglar. Being in the field was more enjoyable than she'd expected. She moved to the door, making sure the coast was clear as she slipped into the hallway and proceeded silently up the carpeted stairs. On the bedroom floor she checked through the keyholes. The smallest room to the front was empty. It housed a single bed and a desk, beside which the blue jacket lay on a chair. She entered. It was vital she work quickly. Mirabelle checked the poacher's pouch but it was empty. She eyed the fireplace. There was a pile of ash far larger than she would expect. The fires here would have been lit no later than four in readiness for the Sunday evening return of the house's occupants. She kneeled in front of the grate and peered at the detritus. The ash had retained a vague shape. It lay in stripes as far apart as the crisscross pattern of the silver threads of Rose's evening gown. He had burned it here. She was on to him!

Spurred on, Mirabelle turned her attention to Harry's desk. There was an address book, nothing notable inside, and some notepaper. A pamphlet by T. S. Eliot was this time marked at "The Rum Tum Tugger" by another bookmark from the secondhand bookshop in Marylebone. The drawer to the left contained a schoolboy jumble of pencils and geometrical tools. The one on the right contained a single brown manila envelope with an embossed crest on the flap and a red cross jotted on the rear. Her curiosity piqued, Mirabelle emptied its contents onto the desktop. Two slim celluloid negatives wafted out. She held them to the light. They were pictures of two girls dressed as nymphs next to a waterfall. Perhaps this was where the indiscernible offcuts in Harry's room in the club had come from.

The images were too small to see clearly, and it wasn't until she carefully returned them to the package that she realized the envelope also contained prints. The photographs were jammed in so tightly against the back sleeve they hadn't automatically fallen out when she turned the envelope upside down. Mirabelle pulled them out and gasped. One of the models was Didi Blyth. There was no doubt about it—right down to the blond pixie-style haircut. The girl was topless and showing a great deal of thigh. Mirabelle didn't know the other model, but she was certainly very similar to Didi, though she had mousy hair and a slightly plumper figure. The girls' eyes, however, were strikingly alike. Was the other model in the photograph Lavinia?

"Oh, Harry, you are a dog!" Mirabelle whispered.

Working in a methodical fashion and staying absolutely calm, Mirabelle opened the wardrobe and checked for hidden compartments. She looked under the bed and lifted the rugs. Obviously, she hadn't expected to find Rose here—a house full of family servants would be an impossible hiding place—but she felt disappointed. There was still no indication of Rose's whereabouts. At least she knew what he'd done with the dress even if she hadn't yet figured out why.

Checking the hallway, Mirabelle slipped back down the way she'd come, darting into an alcove as she heard a door open on the first floor. It would soon be time for the household to dress for dinner. In the downstairs hallway there was movement. She waited. A black spaniel puppy lolloped up the staircase and barked in her general direction. She kept stock-still and simply stared at the little creature.

"Come along, Pong," said a female voice. "Up you go! Up, up, up!"

Pong hesitated, sniffled and continued on his way upstairs, immediately followed by four of his siblings. One started to make its way toward Mirabelle.

"Polly! No! Go up!" the female voice insisted and a hand appeared to guide Polly upstairs.

Mirabelle held her breath. She waited until the hallway was quiet again and then smoothly slipped out of the shadows, down to the entrance hall and into the day-room. She shivered as she opened the French windows and proceeded into the garden. A cold fog was descending. She felt proud of herself. She'd spent less than ten minutes in the house—a professional job. You simply had to get into the right frame of mind for these things. She'd managed at least to gather a little more information. Mirabelle wondered momentarily what she would have done had she been spotted and assured herself that she would have thought of something. She'd made it to the garage roof when she caught a flash of movement in the lane. It would never do to be caught now! Prostrate against the asphalt she peered over to see what was going on below and was delighted to see Harry approaching his car. He flung the brown manila envelope she had just seen onto the front seat and the engine roared into life. As the car disappeared in a cloud of exhaust fumes, Mirabelle lowered herself carefully onto the cobbles. She brushed her coat with her gloved hands to remove the small leaves that were clinging to the tweed. Somehow her hat had stayed firmly in place.

Harry was in the annoying habit of disappearing just as she got close, she noted. But she was building up a picture—not an entirely pleasant one, but a picture nonetheless. She turned toward the main road with the revelation that, really, she was beginning to enjoy snooping and, better still, she was becoming accomplished at it. Relief flooded through her. She was going to find Rose!

She strode as best she could in the direction of Paul Blyth's house on Upper Belgrave Street. Surveillance work, after all, was about following one step after another. Figuring out the whole picture would simply take more information. Lavinia Blyth, now Mirabelle came to think of it, was involved in rather too many of Harry's activities. Was the girls' father aware that his daughters had posed for Harry, she wondered? If he had found Lavinia's outing to a jazz club unacceptable, heaven knows what he might do if he discovered the photographs in Harry's possession. Daughters who modeled half-naked, even in the style of a Titian painting, were not socially acceptable. There was no question that Paul Blyth couldn't hope to marry his girls well if it were discovered. The links between the Bellamy Gores and the Blyth girls seemed set to prove pivotal to what had happened to Rose. The families lived in a close-knit world, and now there were at least two major connections between them. It was unlikely that was coincidence.

Mirabelle turned onto Upper Belgrave Street and noticed that Paul Blyth's house was now occupied. The lights on the first floor were on. Still feeling confident, Mirabelle decided to check the rear. In for a penny, in for a pound, she thought. She looked at the little houses that made up the mews. There was copious wrought ironwork that appeared to have escaped melting down during the war. It would act, she decided, like a climbing frame. It made for a more difficult climb than she'd had at Harry's because here there were two stories, but still, possible. She began to scale the front of the building and then carefully and with some effort she hauled herself over the top. At this stage it almost felt routine.

From this vantage point, the house seemed busier at the back than it had at the front. Smoke poured from every chimney and there were lights blazing along the bedroom floor. Where might she gain entry though? Unfortunately, unlike the Bellamy Gores, Mr. Blyth had not installed French doors. Here, it was more like a backyard, probably used only by the staff, with a vegetable garden and a long washing line. The only door was at the bottom of a staircase that led to the basement. Through the barred windows Mirabelle could make out a bustling kitchen—a cook stood at the range, Blyth's dusty old butler was readying bottles of burgundy for dinner and a maid was peeling potatoes dejectedly at the table. There was no chance of getting in unseen by that route.

The washhouse was her only option. It would give her access to two sash-and-case windows on the ground floor. Thinking on her feet, Mirabelle dropped into the garden and climbed a small bank of earth from which she hoisted herself onto the sloping roof, edging carefully toward the main building. The first window was locked. The second, however, slid open noiselessly and she launched herself over the sill and landed as quietly as she could on a wooden floor covered with a thick Turkish carpet. Even in the dark it was clear the room was a library. It smelled of dusty paper and old leather bindings, and oak bookshelves ran from floor to ceiling. From her place on the floor Mirabelle felt momentarily as if they might topple on top of her.

She shrugged off the feeling and got up. On the desk lay a paperback—a copy of Dylan Thomas's poetry bookmarked at "All That I Owe the Fellows of the Grave." The bookmark bore the same address as those in Harry's paperbacks—Moxon Street. There was clearly an extraordinarily thriving trade in secondhand poetry. Suspicions aroused, Mirabelle tried to remember the location of Moxon Street. The bookshop now merited a visit. If she remembered correctly it was just off Marylebone High Street, near where they used to hang prisoners in the days of the old Tyburn jail. She shivered involuntarily and turned her attention back to the desk. There was nothing much else of interest. In one drawer there was a checkbook (a highly exclusive private bank, Mirabelle noted) and an address book that read like a who's who of the English upper classes, and in the other some paperclips and an India rubber. It was too dark to inspect the shelves properly, and besides she wasn't even sure what she was looking for. With the ground mapped, she decided it would be better to speak to Paul Blyth face-to-face. If she could coax him to tell her more about Lavinia and Deirdre, that would be all to the good. She may even be able to broach the subject of why he had called the police so quickly on the evening of Rose's disappearance. Putting Rose's reputation in danger before contacting her parents was mystifying. Increasingly she realized the lives of these two families were held together somehow.

Mirabelle slid silently back out the window and retraced her steps. When she reached the main road she checked her appearance as best she could in the gloomy light from the gas lamps. These kinds of maneuvers were tricky in a skirt. It was just as well she had removed her stockings at Duke's. A new pair would have been ripped to shreds by now. She powdered her face and then swallowed a painkiller with a little difficulty.

Reinvigorated, she braced her shoulders and walked toward the stucco columns of the Blyth house. It took her a second to register the car at the curbside. Harry's Aston Martin. She laid her gloved hand on the bonnet—yes, the engine was still warm. Mirabelle checked the front seat. The envelope wasn't there.

Was the boy blackmailing Blyth? Was he hell-bent on putting not only the life of his cousin into jeopardy but also the good names of Lavinia and Didi? Was he really that much of a cad? For someone so young he appeared to be wreaking an extraordinary level of havoc. Still, Mirabelle reminded herself. Jack always said that difficult people had their uses. She tried to keep an open mind.

She climbed the steps to Paul Blyth's front door. There was only one way to find out.

24

Chess is ruthless.

Mirabelle's heart was hammering as she waited for the door to be answered. How peculiar that breaking and entering hadn't fazed her, but making a social call (granted, a tricky one) set her pulse racing. It seemed to take an age before the door opened and the familiar butler peered into the gloom.

Mirabelle smiled and stepped into the light. "It's Mirabelle Bevan. I'd like to speak to Mr. Blyth, please."

The butler paused and frowned as he caught sight of Mirabelle's bandaged wrist. "May I take a card?"

"I'm sorry. I don't have one with me."

"Please wait here. I informed Mr. Blyth of your previous call," he said and closed the door.

Mirabelle peered over the railings. The shutters were closed on the servants' quarters downstairs. The room to the right of the front door was unoccupied. Paul—and presumably Harry—must be upstairs in the drawing room. She was about to step backward to see if she could catch a glimpse of what was going on up there when the butler returned.

"Please come in," he said and ushered her into the hallway. "May I take your jacket, Miss Bevan, while you wait in the library? Mr. Blyth will see you presently."

The butler clicked on the electric light as he led Mirabelle into the room she'd vacated only a few minutes before. Now at least she'd have an opportunity to examine the bookshelves properly.

She handed her jacket to the butler, thanked him and waited for him to leave. Scanning Paul Blyth's bookshelves in the light she noticed there was not a single novel or volume of poetry. The collection was composed entirely of reference material, from general encyclopedias and atlases to several medical works on anatomy and pharmacology. Mirabelle was sure Paul Blyth didn't have a medical background. She contemplated having another quick look through the address book but before she had time, the door to the room opened and in breezed Paul Blyth.

He was just as she remembered him—a handsome man with dark wide-set eyes and regular features. He seemed only slightly older than during the war—his hair had grayed and receded partially. However, anyone who worked with him would have recognized him in an instant. Although he no longer wore a uniform he might as well have. His sense of purpose and authority was tangible.

"Miss Bevan. You wanted to see me?"

"Mr. Blyth." Mirabelle held out her left hand to shake his outstretched right. "I don't know if you recall me from your service days?"

"Of course I do. You worked for Jack Duggan. I was very sorry to hear of his death. Must have been dreadful for his family. Might I offer you a drink? Don't tell me—I have an uncanny memory for drink orders—whisky, wasn't it? Single malt? Or would you prefer some tea?"

"Thank you. Whisky would be lovely."

Somewhere in this house Blyth had Harry waiting for him. His mind, no doubt, was on that meeting and on the reputation of his daughters. Yet he had decided to receive her immediately. That was interesting. She scanned his face for signs of anxiety but found none. Paul Blyth had never excelled at small talk and as he attended to their drinks it felt to Mirabelle as if each question and answer somehow had a double meaning. Or perhaps she was just imagining it. His eyes flickered toward the ceiling as he handed her the drink.

"So, please, sit down. What can I do for you? I haven't seen you for some time, Miss Bevan. The years, I see, have done little harm to your sense of style."

Mirabelle perched on a Jacobean chair upholstered in red velvet.

"Yes. It's been a while. And your daughters are at Oxford now. Such lovely bright girls."

"Is that where you wound up? Oxford? I can see that being just the thing for someone like you!" His laugh was slightly cruel. It reminded her of the things his secretarial staff used to say about him—difficult to put a finger on why he had upset them so much, but sometimes it was the small cruelties that hit home most. "I wish he'd just pester me about going out with him like the other officers," she remembered one of the secretaries complaining. This barbed politeness was more difficult to deal with than open hostility.

Blyth had taken a seat behind the writing desk rather than in the chair across from Mirabelle. *He wants to intimidate me,* she thought. She decided not to correct his assumption about where she lived.

"Yes. Oxford. And I understand we're not to have Lavinia back for Hilary term."

"No. I'm afraid not. Family duties come first."

"I heard she had witnessed something rather awful. That's why I thought I'd pop in, Mr. Blyth. First, to check the poor dear is all right and, second, to assure you that there would be a great deal of support for Lavinia if she chose to come back to college. She's so bright and very popular. A credit to you, sir, if you don't mind my saying. They both are."

"Wilson, that is, my butler, was under the impression you were working for the constabulary, Miss Bevan. Either that or for a newspaper?"

"Really? How amusing. I can't imagine what might have given him that idea."

Mr. Blyth let the comment stand. He reached into a silver cigarette box and offered Mirabelle a Dunhill before lighting his own. After a moment he decided to push the point further. "In fact, Wilson was under the impression you felt there was something underhanded about this whole business with Rose."

Mirabelle took a moment before she answered. She sipped the whisky. It was very good. "Well, yes," she admitted. "I did suggest something along those lines. Something seems wrong, don't you think? That fellow going to Brighton. Well, that makes no sense. Felons usually make for the Continent. There were so many other places he could have gone if he wanted to escape. . . . One never gets over examining the detail, does one?"

"The *detail*? Do you think the war is still on, Miss Bevan? What nonsense! There's no subterfuge here. There's no greater plan. The fellow was clearly guilty. Didn't you hear? He killed himself. We received the news by telephone. I can't say it isn't better that way, either. At least we shan't have a trial. No washing of dirty linen in public. It'll be far better for the Bellamy Gores, and Lavinia, of course, by association."

"Did you know the boy, Mr. Blyth? A musician, wasn't he?" she tried. It crossed her mind that talking to Paul Blyth was like fencing or playing a complex game of chess. At some point soon she would have to ask him something more direct about his daughters. She wasn't sure how he might react.

"The Claremont fellow? Never met him. I understand he played the saxophone. I'm strictly a classical music man, Miss Bevan. Opera by choice. Do you have a box at Covent Garden?"

"Oh, I don't run to that, I'm afraid! Not these days. Well, the Bellamy Gores must be frightfully concerned. I hope they find the girl."

"Do you know them?"

"No. Not personally. Only in passing. It all seems rather tragic. It must be awful for you, being so close to the family. And one does feel for Lavinia, being caught up in it."

"A witness. My daughter was a witness."

"Have you ever been to a jazz club, Mr. Blyth?" Mirabelle opened her eyes wide and feigned innocence.

Paul Blyth knocked back his whisky and stared at her. "Me?" he snorted, his temper rising. "Almost gave Lavinia the hiding of her life, little fool. Bloody jungle music in some sleazy dive in the middle of the night. Those Bellamy Gore children are trouble. I've known that for years. Lavinia was rather seduced, as I understand it, by their bohemian lifestyle. Young people today have it far too easy, don't you think? Values have changed. She was tempted but she won't be tempted again. Shame it took this for the girl to learn her lesson."

"And you were the one who alerted the police, I understand."

Paul Blyth stood up. "What is it that you're implying, Miss Bevan? What precisely are you doing here?"

"Me? Nothing. I was simply in London. I heard about the girls and thought I would take the opportunity to pop by. Please, don't concern yourself. Things must be worrying enough as they are. And it's just as well you called Scotland Yard. Quick thinking."

"Well, one is used to making decisions. One never forgets how to do so. It was Lavinia's voice, you see. She telephoned from a public phone box. She's just a young girl, of course, but she isn't a panicker. I knew the minute she came on the phone."

"What?"

"I knew that man had done something to Rose. Lavinia was almost in tears."

"At a time like that, a girl just wants to come straight home, doesn't she? To her family. How disturbing for Lavinia."

"Quite. Well, she's at home now. Safe."

Mirabelle paused momentarily. Lavinia had, of course, not come straight home and Mr. Blyth must know that.

"Well, I just hope the police come to a conclusion soon." Mirabelle sighed and took a final sip of whisky. She wanted to see what would happen if she sailed very close to the wind. "And if Deirdre has gone to the country as well, at least Lavinia will have her sister for comfort. I must say, I do rather admire Deirdre's wonderful haircut. She looks like some kind of magical creature—a fairy or a nymph or something—don't you think?"

Paul Blyth paused for a split second longer than would have been natural. It sounded like an innocent comment, but Mirabelle could tell he was shaken and that meant he'd seen the photographs. When he finally spoke his voice sounded calm but beneath the surface there was an air of menace.

"What makes you say that, Miss Bevan?"

"I can see her as Puck in a production of *A Midsummer Night's Dream*. Can't you? And Lavinia as Titania, now I come to think of it. Gosh, we should stage it, shouldn't we? In the Quad this summer?"

Blyth couldn't quite put his finger on whether she knew or not, but his neck had flushed a vivid shade of purple. He stared at Mirabelle, his eyes completely devoid of all expression. Then he dismissed her.

"Well, I'm glad you're at St. Hilda's, Miss Bevan. It's a comfort to think that when the girls get back you'll be there to look out for them. I shall recall you to them when I next go down to Sussex."

"Oh, are you in Sussex? I had no idea. How lovely."

"Will you be returning to Oxford tonight?"

"I expect so," Mirabelle lied. "I only hung on because I wanted to reassure you, Mr. Blyth."

Paul Blyth looked anything but reassured. He toyed with his cigarette. "Thank you, but if you don't mind I have another engagement." He stood up and rang for service.

"Ah, of course. Yes."

The butler appeared, holding her jacket, and Blyth moved toward her.

"So unfortunate about Rose. It may be she is a woman who has twisted her last smile. . . ." Mirabelle continued to babble.

"What did you say? What do you mean?"

"Dylan Thomas, Mr. Blyth. The poetry book on your desk. I couldn't help but notice it. Let us hope, of course, that Rose will smile again. I'm sure she will."

The man clearly had no idea about Thomas's poetry. Whatever was that book doing here?

"Might I take a cigarette after all?" she ventured. "It's such a cold night and smoking warms one, doesn't it?"

Paul Blyth flipped open the silver box on his desk. "Be my guest," he said curtly.

In the hallway she couldn't hear anything from upstairs. Wilson opened the front door and bid Mirabelle good night. There was a great deal to take in. Things certainly weren't what she had assumed. She moved a couple of doors up the street and lit the cigarette. Through the fog the distinctive figure of a policeman on his beat, in cape and custodian helmet, strolled toward her.

"Good evening, madam. Is everything all right?"

"Thank you, Officer. I'm just waiting for a friend."

"Cold night, madam."

"Yes, very. I hope he won't be long."

The officer continued up the street, rattling a set of railings that appeared insecure. Mirabelle managed a wry smile. As Belgravia's most active cat burglar she ought to have been carted off in handcuffs. The police really were hopeless. She took a draw on the cigarette and breathed in deeply. Things were nowhere near as cut-and-dried as she'd expected. Far from it.

25

Experience is the most brutal of teachers.

Harry emerged from the Blyth residence twenty-two minutes later. He skipped down the steps oblivious to the figure on his left, who put out an elegant and uninjured right ankle to trip him up. As Harry sprawled on the pavement Mirabelle towered over him with the streetlight behind her so he couldn't make out her face. She had used the twenty-two minutes wisely and certainly had a more coherent theory in mind than when she'd entered the Blyth residence. It had been simple, really, once she'd turned the suppositions upside down.

"At first I thought it might be you who had Rose," she said.

"What the hell?"

Mirabelle lifted a gloved finger to her lips. "Then I realized what was really going on. I misjudged you. Easily done with an arrogant young man, if you don't mind me saying. Do you think you might be able to give me a lift, Harry? It would really help. Come on, get up. I've got your attention now, haven't I?"

The boy picked himself up and inspected his trousers. "Who the blazes are you?"

Mirabelle took charge, walking round to the passenger

side of the Aston Martin. "Best not discuss that here. I'll tell you all about it on the way," she promised.

"If you think . . ."

She opened the door. "Oh yes. Thinking is my best quality. Well, you want Rose back, don't you?"

"I don't need you to get Rose back."

"Yes, you do," she insisted. "Or at least you might. I certainly advise you not to bet your cousin's life on it. Come along now. I'm chilly. Do you think we could stop somewhere to get a cup of tea?"

"Where do you want to go?" Harry regarded her warily but he swung into the driving seat and started the engine nevertheless.

"Head for Park Lane," Mirabelle directed.

They drove through Belgravia until they reached the corner of Hyde Park where there was a chip stand. Harry pulled over and bought two cups of tea, which they drank in the car. He took a slug of brandy in his and offered the hip flask to Mirabelle, who declined.

"So," she said, "you saw them take Rose, didn't you?"

"What the hell has this got to do with you anyway?"

Mirabelle sipped her tea. "I'm your best chance, Harry. Really. And my name is Miss Bevan."

"Do you work for the police?"

"No. My interest is in Lindon. You remember him? The musician the police wrongfully arrested. They did wrongfully arrest him, didn't they? And you didn't come forward."

Harry nodded. He'd tried asking questions as they'd driven but Mirabelle simply sidestepped everything. It had dawned on him that the woman appeared to know it all anyway and he had settled down to what seemed set to become a confession. It was hard to admit but it felt good to get things off his chest.

"I couldn't come forward. They had Rose. I thought we'd be able to do something about him after I got her

back. I didn't know he was going to do what he did, poor
fellow. Vinny set us up. I didn't know she had it in her. It
seemed like a perfectly normal evening, you see. We went
to the jazz club and got a bit squiffy. Then we went outside,
intending to leave, and Rose got rid of that saxophone fellow
who was a bit of a pest. And then, *wham*, these two hood-
lums came out of nowhere. Big chaps. They grabbed Rose. I
couldn't fight them off. Vinny took charge. She said her father made her do it. I expect he did, the bastard. She even
apologized afterward. Anyway, they took Rose away in a
car. Vinny calmed me down—she explained how it would
all work and that if I went to the police her father would
have Rose killed but if I did what they wanted it would all
be fine. Then she phoned Mr. Blyth to say everything was
all right. I had to go along with it. She even made me go
back into Mac's and dance with her. We both had to have
an alibi, she said. Perhaps I should have resisted more, but
Vinny said it was the only way to get Rose back . . . and I
was a bit drunk. She kept saying if I just did what her father wanted everything would be all right."

"And the guy on the door? Barney?"

"He must have been in on it. He took Lindon back into
the club before Blyth's men took Rose. Afterward he lied
to the police about seeing Lindon get into a taxi with
Rose, and so did we. We had to. The sax player was just
Blyth's fall guy. I didn't see the doorman or the musician
again. They weren't around Mac's when we got back from
the phone box."

"So it was Paul Blyth who kidnapped Rose. And he did
it because you had pictures of Lavinia and Deirdre. How
did Blyth find out you had them?"

"How the hell do . . ."

Mirabelle said nothing.

"I don't know how he found out. I think Vinny must
have given something away. It wouldn't have been Didi.
The snaps were a bit of fun but he went mad, of course.

Said it could ruin the girls for life, which it could if the photographs ever got out. They weren't for that, though—we were just messing about. I explained that to him when he asked me for them a couple of weeks ago. Demanded, really. I thought it was funny he got so wound up."

"But you didn't hand them over."

"No. I told him I had them and I wouldn't use them for anything, but I wasn't giving them to him on principle. The girls had been willing and the pictures were mine. Bloody stupid mistake. I feel shabby as hell about it now."

"But Blyth knew if he took Rose, you'd have to give him whatever he asked."

"He's ruined her reputation. I mean, Rose'll never get married now. Not married up, anyway. She could have had a title by next year—some people say she was set to be a duchess. I'll end up marrying her I suppose. Not that I mind. He tried to frame me, too, you know. Coldhearted bastard."

"Yes. He sent you her dress."

"If the police found that, there'd have been some explaining to do. He said he could have me arrested whenever he liked. I said I'd do whatever he wanted. He likes flexing his muscles, doesn't he?"

"And your behavior isn't that of an innocent. He'd have succeeded, I imagine. I thought it was you for a while myself." Harry looked hurt, but Mirabelle pressed on. "So this evening you handed over the photos and the negatives?"

"Yes."

"What's he waiting for?"

Harry stared straight ahead and drank his tea. "Bloody money, of course. He said it was to teach me a lesson. It's like he's pissing on the gatepost, really. He wants his pound of flesh. Every last drop of blood. The bank doesn't open until tomorrow. I'm to deliver to him at lunchtime. Sounds almost civilized, doesn't it?"

"How much?"

"Two thousand. It's the most I can raise. My trust fund doesn't allow for—"

"And then you get Rose?"

Harry nodded.

"You don't read poetry, do you, Harry?"

"What?"

"Just answer the question."

"No."

"The Louis MacNeice and the T. S. Eliot books came from Blyth?"

"How did you . . . Yes, they did. He has this stupid bloody obsession with code. There are . . ."

"Tiny pinpricks that spell things out. I didn't see them—I think my eyesight isn't what it used to be. It's an old trick. Has he sent you the Dylan Thomas?"

Harry shook his head.

"So that will come tomorrow with your final instructions."

"Do you think he'll set her free, Miss Bevan?"

Mirabelle considered. "He might. He didn't expect Lindon to die, you see. I think what he does will rather depend on Rose. He'll have to be certain she'll be able to lie convincingly to her family and to the police about where she's been. And she mustn't crack. Paul Blyth has excellent information sources, and judgment. Do you think Rose will be able to convince him he can trust her performance?"

"She's going to say she was drugged and doesn't remember anything after she left the club. She just woke up somewhere or other, tied up, and eventually managed to get out. She'll be set free in the street and told to make her way home. She's to be a blank canvas—that's what he called it."

"Is she capable of that? Capable of lying, I mean? Even under pressure?"

Harry nodded. A wry smile played around his mouth. "She's made of stone. She'd withstand questioning by the bloody gestapo."

Mirabelle turned sharply. "Really? Do you know what the gestapo used to do to people?"

Harry's head dropped. "No. Sorry. That was a stupid thing to say. Rose is dependable though. She's a smart dependable girl."

"Well, if you're right and Blyth believes that, he'll let her go. It's his easiest way out now Lindon is dead. The police will assume Lindon drugged her and left her somewhere, and they'll accept the witness statements as they stand. He isn't implicated in any way. As long as he believes Rose is reliable, then she'll be fine."

"And if he decides that he can't trust her?"

"He'll take your money and the negatives and he won't risk his reputation."

"You mean he'd kill her?"

"Yes. Paul Blyth is as cold as they come. I can guarantee that. And then, of course, there'd be nothing to stop you telling, so he'd come after you, Harry. Quick and sharp. He'd probably try to frame you in the process. Had you considered that?"

The boy didn't answer for a few seconds. "How do you know all this?"

"I've known Paul Blyth for years."

"Has he done this kind of thing before?" Harry's voice was incredulous.

Mirabelle shrugged. She didn't like to say that he'd done similar and worse for his country. It made her heart sink that everything seemed so much less than it had been. Blyth had never been a pleasant man but he'd worked for the greater good. Now he was reduced to bullying children over dubious photographs. Even if those photographs could ruin his family's reputation, it was a step down from fighting for right. Blyth had always been arrogant and egoistic—a natural bully—and the disgrace should the snaps come out had clearly been more than he could bear. Belgravia was unforgiving in the matter of a chap's daughters—Harry's photographs could blight Vinny and Didi for life and the rest of the family by association. She could see why Blyth would come down hard. He'd have to be sure nothing would come out. "How does Blyth know you won't double-cross him as soon as you've got Rose? You could simply go to the police and tell them everything."

"What bloody good would that do? Rose's reputation is ruined already and all I'd do is duff up mine. Enter Harry Bellamy Gore the pornographer! It'd be a terrific scandal for the press and what would we get out of it? Rose and I can't prove much—the key witness would be Vinny and she's not going to blame her father. We don't have anything that ties him to Rose's disappearance apart from her word. No, I don't want any more scandal. My parents would die. They'd blame me for what happened to Rose— they always blame me. It was bad enough getting caught with those snaps at school. There was a time, you see, when—"

"Yes, I know." Mirabelle dismissed the story. "I see what you mean."

Harry fell silent. He was beginning to think of Miss Bevan as a considerably more stylish version of his nanny. In fact, he rather liked her.

They finished their tea and Mirabelle gave him directions. They drove toward Marylebone until they turned right past Daunt's and pulled up round the corner on Moxon Street.

Harry gestured at the bookshop. "Do you think Rose might be here?" he asked plaintively.

"Come along, and bring that torch you have in the boot," said Mirabelle, to Harry's astonishment.

The pair walked toward the shop. It seemed an unlikely

prison. The lock on the door was considerably heavier than those at the Oxford and Cambridge Club. Mirabelle extracted another hairpin. I'm going to look like a fright by the end of this evening, she thought as she applied herself to the mechanism. It took a few moments but she caught the tumbler and the door clicked open. Harry looked suitably impressed. Inside, he scanned the bookshelves with the torchlight. Mirabelle made for the cash desk, which yielded only stationery, a pile of bookmarks and a ledger.

Grabbing the torch, she turned to the rear of the shop with the ledger in her hand to minimize the light visible from the street. She checked the columns of figures. Every month the shop paid eighty pounds in rent to Paul Blyth!

"Well, there you have it," Harry said. "He owns the place. That's why he got the books here."

"Yes. But why?"

"Because he's the landlord. He wouldn't buy the books elsewhere."

"No. Why does he own it? Why do they pay rent to him directly? Not a trust fund. Not a solicitor. Not a collection agency or a property agent. Not a bank. This won't be the only property Paul Blyth owns. Not by a long shot. Yet they pay him, directly, don't you see?"

Harry cast his eyes over the shadowy bookshelves, lost for words. "Why not?" he managed weakly.

Mirabelle ignored him. She worked her way around the walls from the front to the rear. She checked the toilet, the kitchen and a cupboard full of cleaning supplies. Then she started on the floor, working from back to front. About halfway down there was a square of worn carpet. She pulled it up, and sure enough there was a trapdoor.

"Here." She motioned to Harry, who turned the latch and pulled it open. A flash with the torch revealed a low-ceilinged cellar reached by a wooden staircase.

"Rose!" Harry called out hopefully.

"Oh really!" Mirabelle popped a book beside the hinge so the trapdoor couldn't close. Then she carefully made her way down the steps.

The cellar had stone walls and no windows. It didn't smell damp, but there was a faint odor of candle wax and sulfur. The otherwise empty space housed three large trunks stored off the floor on heavy wooden tables. Harry looked as if he might burst into tears. Mirabelle scanned the area behind the stairs to see if there was a key.

"We need the keys," she pointed out.

"Can't you do that thing you did before?"

"The locks are too big. I'd need a proper pick."

"I'll go and look upstairs." Harry disappeared.

Tentatively, Mirabelle tried to open one after the other, but it was no good. She could hear Harry moving overhead and then his footsteps coming down the stairs.

"I couldn't find a key," he said, "but how about this?" He thrust a half brick toward her.

"You're the brawn," Mirabelle grinned, and motioned toward the first trunk.

It took him less than a minute to smash the locks. "They'll know we've been here now," said Harry.

"They'll know *someone* has been here," Mirabelle corrected him.

Together they peered into the first trunk. It was full of books, each one individually wrapped in brown paper. Harry took one and tore open the wrapping to reveal an unmarked blue hardcover. He flipped the book open.

"*Lady Chatterley*!" he hooted. "That old thing!"

"It's banned."

"Oh, it's been banned forever. My little cousins could get a copy of this if they wanted to. Honestly! Is that all they have down here? I thought Rose was going to be locked in the bloody chest! Dead or alive. I can't tell you the relief."

Mirabelle moved on. Awkwardly, with her uninjured

hand, she opened the next lid. This time there were no books, only sheaves of papers. As she picked them up she realized they were prints that had once been bound.

"They're Victorian," Harry grinned. "Don't look, Miss Bevan! One of my more perverted uncles collects these things."

Mirabelle leafed through a series of etchings of anguished ladies in tightly laced corsets and then returned them to the chest.

"And in the third chest?" Harry whooped like a circus ringmaster. "More of the same, no doubt!"

Mirabelle sat on the stairs as Harry heaved open the third trunk. He took out several leather-bound volumes, one after the other.

"Now *these* are pretty valuable," he said, examining them carefully. "Collector's items. Specialist stuff. Erotica. And it's early in date. More of the same but better. Do you want to have a look?"

Mirabelle waved him off. There really was no need. This made sense, of course; she just had to process what they'd found. Paul Blyth had always been good at getting sensitive information that other people wanted; this was simply an extension of that skill. He was a natural pornographer—of course he was. Then when Harry had come on the scene he had reacted strongly, but now it seemed he hadn't only been defending his daughters: he was defending his trade as well. Here was a young blood, already notorious for pornography, taking pictures of his daughters. And worse, should Harry find out what Blyth was up to (for the circles must be small), Blyth would suddenly find himself vulnerable. No wonder he'd come down on the boy like a ton of bricks.

"The Zeitgeist," she murmured.

"What did you say?"

"How much is all this worth?"

Harry considered carefully. "The D. H. Lawrence? Not

much—maybe five guineas each. Though he has at least fifty copies here. The Victorian prints might make twenty or so each. But these books are worth a lot. Hundreds. Depends on the rarity of the edition. Some early Georgian drawings and engravings are worth thousands. It depends on, er, the raunchiness of the subject matter. Anyway, as I understand it, our cousins across the pond collect them, and they're known for their generosity."

Mirabelle raised an eyebrow. "You seem *remarkably* well informed, Harry."

"You can't ask me a question and then get sniffy because I know the answer, Miss Bevan."

"I'm not getting sniffy at all. You simply appear very well informed."

Harry relented. "All right. After a brief foray into something similar at Eton—on a very small scale, Miss Bevan—I became quite interested in this sort of thing. This is well out of my league though. And, I should point out, these prints do have artistic merit. Do you think old Blyth knows about all this?"

"Without question."

"What makes you so sure?"

"Well, for a start, eighty pounds' monthly rent is far too much for these premises. That's a shade off a thousand a year on a back street in Marylebone! And, to be honest, I thought he overreacted when he took Rose. It seems an overly dramatic solution to a simple problem. I mean, he could have sent a couple of heavies round to beat you up. He could have broken into your rooms and stolen the photographs if that was all he was after. But he didn't—he wanted to frighten you—to put you out of the game completely. Now I understand. He's been defending more than his daughters' honor. That kind of criminality is a small world, and Blyth's a bully. He wanted to put you off for life, Harry. He'd rather have the march on you than the other way around—at any price. And you're young, enterprising and, well, interested. Know all about him. That makes you dangerous competition. I can understand how that idea would make him jumpy. He's defending his greatest secret. He's a mastermind! An international pornographer. If anyone found out he'd be finished."

"Old Blyth!" Harry seemed delighted. "Seems like such a stuffy old duffer! Well, he might be out of my league but I've got something over him now."

"Harry, honestly. Have you no intelligence? Would you poke your hand in a wasps' nest just to teach the wasps a lesson?"

"No." Harry sounded glum. "I suppose not."

"This makes Blyth twice as deadly. God knows what else he's up to."

"What do you mean?"

"I'm not sure yet. But people in one illicit business often have links to another. Gangsters who run booze run brothels. If you wanted an illegal passport you'd start somewhere illegal—an opium den or an underground casino. If Blyth is running an international business specializing in erotica, he might well be involved in other illegal activities."

"Gosh." Harry seemed genuinely taken aback. "Do you know exactly what the old fellow did during the war?"

"Information." Mirabelle sidestepped the question reflexively and then wondered if by chance she'd hit the nail on the head. Paul Blyth had contacts and access to intelligence. He knew the system backward and forward. Mind you, he was dyed-in-the-wool Establishment. He'd never sell information to the enemy—whoever that was these days. She dismissed the thought.

"If he's hurt Rose . . ."

"I think we should try to find Rose tonight," Mirabelle decided.

"Do you know where she is?"

"Not yet." Mirabelle checked her watch. It was getting

on. "But I think I might know a man who can help us. Find me an *A to Z*, would you? I think we may need one. I'll put everything back here."

On the way to the car Mirabelle scanned the flat above the bookshop. It appeared to be occupied by a lone woman with young children. The door to the communal hallway was open, and a bashed-up pram was parked alongside two pairs of small Wellington boots at the bottom of the stairs. It seemed unlikely that Rose would be up there.

"He might have owned it." She pointed at the flat. "Wouldn't that have been easy?"

Harry started the engine and Mirabelle opened the street guide. Further up the pavement the figure of a caped policeman peered down Moxon Street from Marylebone High Street. Mirabelle could have sworn he looked too short to be taken on by the constabulary but it was difficult to tell with the custodian helmet and at such a distance. The policeman earlier hadn't exactly been a giant. Perhaps the force's recruitment criteria had changed.

26

Expectation is the root of all heartache.

Charlie laughed at her crestfallen expression. "Trust me, sugar."

Vesta had been disappointed at first with Charlie's choice of dinner venue. When they left Duke's they had trailed arm in arm across town toward Charing Cross and up beyond Leicester Square. It felt dreamy. She'd expected a candlelit bistro at the very least, so when Charlie stopped in front of a harshly lit greasy spoon on the edge of Chinatown she'd dropped his arm in dismay. The air smelled stale here—of soy sauce and musty spices. Inside the café, the menu boasted bacon butties and pots of tea. This was not what she had expected.

"Charlie Baker!" a voice shouted from the back of the café. A fat man with a beaming smile emerged from the kitchen and flung his arms around Charlie's frame. One or two of the other diners turned to witness the commotion—mostly solitary men lingering over plates of chips.

"Max, this is Vesta," Charlie introduced her. "We've come for dinner."

"Romantic?"

"Only the best for us."

Max disappeared into the back. Vesta lowered herself

primly onto a plastic chair that squeaked as she maneuvered it nearer the table. If there were things she had intended to do with Charlie later that evening she now mentally retracted the possibility. As a sign of her disapproval she refused to take off her coat.

Charlie didn't seem concerned. "You'll never be bored with me, baby," he grinned. "Cocktails in Duke's and dinner at Max's."

"Do you bring your jazz friends here?" she asked pointedly.

"Only the black guys," he said.

After a rather uncomfortable atmosphere Max returned to the table with a huge platter of what turned out to be the best jerk chicken Vesta had ever tasted, outside the Caribbean. As they tucked into the steaming chicken pieces and a mound of rice and peas Vesta could feel the spices awakening her taste buds. Damn, this was good! She felt as if she was floating.

"You see?" said Charlie, watching her face intently. "You forgive me now, right? It beats the hell out of my mama's. I bet it beats yours, too."

Vesta smiled. "We can *never* bring her here," she said. "That's the deal."

"Our secret," Charlie promised.

After the dishes were cleared and greasy fingers cleaned on paper napkins Max removed the plates. "You wanna make the lady your special dessert, Charlie? Get into the kitchen, man. You're not gonna believe this, Vesta."

Vesta was astounded. "What's this, Charlie?"

Charlie looked sheepish. "Dessert is what I do, sugar," he said. "That and the drumming."

"You didn't know about Charlie Baker? Makes the best, but *the best* cakes, pastries and puddings to the gentry."

Charlie explained: "When I'm not drumming I work a kitchen across town."

Max wasn't going to let Charlie get away with the understatement. "Charlie works in the Dorchester Hotel. He didn't tell you? Charlie, you mustn't hide your light like that!"

Charlie looked at his shoes. "I hope it's all right, Vesta. I mean, I know working in a kitchen isn't cool. I play the drums on my nights off. Making a living out of the music though, man, that's hard."

"Just make me pudding," Vesta mouthed and followed him into the kitchen.

Charlie put on a grubby apron and started to whisk eggs, flour and milk. Max brought a flask of orange liqueur. Somewhere he found a lemon.

"Crêpes Suzette," Charlie announced.

Watching him cook, Vesta felt herself relax. How could she possibly have wanted to go to a snobbish French bistro or a pub dining room when she could be here, in a cramped kitchen on the edge of Chinatown watching Charlie make pancakes? It fascinated her. His movements were so precise and quick. He knew *exactly* what he was doing. As the pan heated, Vesta smelled the sweet scent of pancakes wafting around them.

"It's a shame we can't do coffee," Max remarked. "Not proper coffee. We got chicory, of course, but it just ain't the same. Weekdays I can send out to the Italian round the corner on Leicester Square but Sunday night they're closed."

Charlie set the pancakes alight and then doused the flame. He positioned the crêpes on a serving plate and bowed, offering Vesta a fork and setting the plate on the low sideboard. Max brought her a chair. The men hovered. Vesta took a bite. The crêpes tasted like sweet clouds with a tang of orange that lingered in her mouth. It was without question the most delicious thing she'd ever eaten. She helped herself to another spoonful.

"*Amazing*," she declared. "Charlie, can you make pies?"

"Anything with flour, baby. Bread, cakes, pies, you name it. I spent most of my service days cooking. Officers' Mess. If you can get me the chocolate I can make you a mousse that'll have you singing, I swear."

"I thought you were in the medical corps."

"Everyone gets training with the bandages, sugar. This is what I really do. You okay with this? I mean, you thought I was a mean jazz dude and now . . ."

Vesta giggled. "Are you kidding? Charlie, I think I'm in love!"

The cold air was refreshing as they walked to Feldman's. Inside, they found a table and Charlie ordered house cocktails. It was busy but not overcrowded and the band was playing old-style classics and blues. Everyone seemed very relaxed.

"I don't know if Mac's will open tonight, after everything," Charlie said as they danced, "but we could go round later if you want to see it in action."

Vesta swayed to the rhythm. The band sounded good, she was full of delicious food, and, best of all, she was with this gorgeous man. She'd almost forgotten about Mac's and what had happened. A needle of guilt twisted in her gut as she became aware of the space left by Lindon. Suddenly it seemed as if she was having too good a time. She needed to sit down.

She was checking her lipstick and resolving to have a look for that Barney character when she saw Mirabelle enter the club. It was an unexpected surprise. Perhaps she'd found something! Vesta stood up and waved, trying to attract her attention, and then she saw Mirabelle wasn't alone. A smartly dressed youngster was bobbing in her wake.

"Is that kid with Mirabelle?" she asked Charlie. "Do you think it's Harry? The one who was at Mac's on Thursday?"

"Yeah. That's the same boy all right, honey."

Before Vesta had time to pass comment Mirabelle and Harry had moved through the crowd and were at the table. Mirabelle introduced everyone. "I'm glad you're here," she said. "You mentioned this is where you'd head for." Harry lit a cigarette and offered the pack around. Both Vesta and Charlie refused.

"Have we time for a drink?" Harry asked. "I could go to the bar."

"Fetch me a whisky, please," Mirabelle directed.

Vesta waited until Harry was on his way. "What the hell are you doing with him?" she hissed. "You thought he might be the kidnapper!"

Mirabelle sat down. "It's a long story, and it's all my fault. I got it wrong. Harry is the one being blackmailed. He's high-spirited, but there's nothing wrong with that when you're eighteen. He's not a kidnapper and, to be honest, he's not so bright, all in all. But he's willing, if slightly arrogant, and it seems we'll have to work with that. It's Lavinia Blyth's father who has Rose. It's a long story. Charlie, do you know where Lindon lived? He said he had a place north of the city somewhere near London Spa. Have you been there? Do you know where it is?"

Charlie sipped his cocktail. "Yeah. More Finsbury, really. Or Clerkenwell. Chadwell Street."

"Do you know the number?"

"No, but I know which it is. It's a brick building—an old house. He had a bedsit on the top floor."

"The girl won't be there," said Vesta. "If the police think Lindon took her, then they'll have checked his place. They'd be crazy not to. First place they'd go."

"Yes." Mirabelle was thinking things through.

Harry returned with the drinks. Mirabelle savored her whisky and ate a solitary potato crisp from a small plate on the table. The band changed key and played a mournful blues number.

"The thing is, Paul Blyth wants to fix Lindon in the police's minds. If he's holding her it'll be somewhere associated with Lindon. He's going to set her free tomorrow. Blyth will want to lay the blame on Lindon if he can. So, if I were him I'd want to make it look as if Lindon tied her up, panicked and then ran away. Tomorrow the story will be that it's just taken her this time to escape. He can't leave her in Lindon's flat—I mean, you're right—they'll have checked there. But he can leave her somewhere that will be associated with Lindon—somewhere nearby. Somewhere it can be assumed Lindon had access."

"But Rose wouldn't go along with that, would she? I mean, if he frees her she'll be able to clear Lindon. If this Blyth fellow kidnapped her then she'll say it was him, won't she?"

"She may not. Harry thinks she'll go along with whatever Blyth says. Actually it suits Harry if she goes along with it some of the way—at least not dragging Paul Blyth into her story. She's going to say she can't remember anything. Though if we get to her first we can alter the script. The story can be that she got into the taxi with Lindon and dropped him off. That'll clear his name. She can say the taxi driver kidnapped her. Of course, there wasn't a taxi driver but they'll never find out."

"Why would she do that? Shouldn't she tell the police the truth?" Vesta insisted. "Shouldn't she tell them about this Paul Blyth character? He ought to be arrested, surely?"

"No. That implicates Harry for a start. And Blyth's dangerous. And there are a couple of other things I haven't quite worked out yet. . . . Anyway, the important thing is to get to Rose. Once we've found her she can clear Lindon's name, even if she doesn't name Blyth. She'd do that, wouldn't she, Harry?"

Harry nodded. "Definitely. But you think he's holding Rose near Lindon's rooms? Not at the Blyth place down in Sussex? It's a big property. There are outhouses and stables."

"Don't be ridiculous! With his own girls there? Lavinia's already as good as apologized to you, for heaven's sake. He'd never be able to trust them, and if it came out there'd be no denying his involvement. No. From his perspective things have got out of hand. He needs to be able to tie things up easily. It's safer in London. If things go wrong he's not so connected to it, and he has more control. Besides, the minute Rose is set free she'll be conspicuous wherever she is. The police will make assumptions based on that. If it's near Lindon's flat, then it's just further proof. That's the only address—he couldn't arrange something near Lindon's parents or anything like that. It would only complicate matters. No, near the boy's flat is the best idea and he'll want to tie her to Lindon, I'm sure of it."

"Is that why he left a piece of her dress at Coram's Fields?"

"We used to do it all the time," Mirabelle said distractedly.

"What *did* you do?" Harry leaned in.

Mirabelle pulled back. "If you want someone to swallow a story you have to know how to make it look. Nothing heavy-handed. You never plant one big clue where you can use a series of small ones. You build a picture. That's how people process information—it's a balance. If most things point to one conclusion, then that's the conclusion they'll draw. They'll fill in the gaps. Paul Blyth knows that."

Charlie caught Vesta's eye.

"It's okay," she said. "You'll get used to it."

"So Rose is north?" Harry checked.

"Somewhere near Chadwell Street. We'll start there," Mirabelle confirmed, drawing the street guide from her pocket. "We've got all night," she said as she flipped the book open at the right page and finished her drink. "We can look within half a mile or so of Lindon's flat in all directions. That's our best chance."

"I was going to speak to Barney," Vesta said.

"Oh, no need for that," Mirabelle insisted. "I think I know what happened there. They simply paid him off. He might not even know everything that was going on. He just got Lindon out of the way and made sure no one in the club could give him an alibi after Rose had left. They probably had a drink together—that would keep Lindon busy long enough to allow Barney to nip up and get the sax. Then Barney told Lindon the rumor about the police looking for him. Lindon leaves and Barney goes back to the club before the police arrive. Barney doesn't matter. Not really."

Vesta's eyes lit up. "In the basement at Mac's there are jam jars used as glasses. They had brandy in them. But, Mirabelle, that's still illegal. I mean, he framed Lindon."

"The main thing now is to find Rose, Vesta. Then we can clear Lindon. That's what we need to focus on. Barney's just a sideshow. We're on the hunt now."

"Tally ho!" said Harry, attempting to lighten the mood. "Horse to hounds and all that!"

"What did you say?" Mirabelle said sharply.

"I didn't mean . . ."

"No. What did you say?"

"You know, when you're hunting. It might not be my greatest analogy. I was only trying to keep spirits up, you know."

"Your mother keeps spaniels, doesn't she? Black ones?"

"How on earth did you know . . . Eh, yes."

"Does Rose have a dog?"

Harry grinned broadly. "Rose *loathes* animals. Vinny used to argue with her about it because, well, she's a vegetarian—bloody invert. But Rose always says animals only have two uses: to be eaten and to be worn. So, no, she doesn't have a dog. Strangely though, dogs love her. Especially Pooch. Follows her around. Makes quite a nuisance of herself. Rose couldn't care less."

"And spaniels are gun dogs, aren't they?"

"Well, of a sort. Ours are only pets, really."

"We need to fetch the dog who loves Rose, Harry. We'll take her for a walk around London Spa. Perhaps she can help us to find your cousin. Where's the dog kept?"

Charlie whispered in Vesta's ear, "Your boss is something else."

Harry downed his drink. "She's back at Wilton Crescent. Had pups a couple of months ago. My mother is obsessed with them. The day room smells revolting and the staff hate them."

"Perfect," said Mirabelle. "Let's get going."

27

The team with the best players wins.

At midnight on the dot they parked a few blocks away from Chadwell Street as Vesta and Charlie emerged from a taxi.

From the start Pooch seemed set to slow them down. She was on the plump side, but she seemed good-natured and delighted to be out. She wanted to sniff everything.

"We should start at Lindon's place," Mirabelle said.

Charlie led them to Chadwell Street and pointed out number fifteen.

"It's pretty close to Claremont Square. That tickled Lindon," Charlie said as he stopped at a front door with a dull brass knob and a hand-painted numeral on it. "Claremont is probably the name of the family who owned Lindon's people. It was just strange it was nearby. He thought it might be lucky. Coincidences always seem lucky, don't they?"

Like the rest of the buildings on Chadwell Street, number fifteen was a dirty three-story Georgian house that had been divided into bedsits. The fanlight was smashed and the window frames had seen better days. The panes were so filthy there was little need for curtains, but a few ragged ill-fitting nets were visible. Most of the premises nearby were in similar states of disrepair.

"We'll have to get his mama to come and clear it out, I guess," Vesta said sadly. "Or I could do it for her. That might be best."

It occurred to Mirabelle that the tenants on Chadwell Street, Lindon included, probably had very little of their own behind the shabby walls. The whole area was a slum, despite its faded grandeur. As if she was reading Mirabelle's mind, Vesta piped up. "I'm sure he's got sheet music and maybe a couple of suits."

The street was deserted. Harry pushed the door and it opened onto a damp-smelling communal hallway. The lock on the front door might have been broken but every room had its own padlock. The only light came from a cupola in the roof and a long window halfway up the staircase. Bathed in moonlight, the hallway was striped with eerie shadows cast by the banister. It was as if some strange black vine had a stranglehold on the place.

"Lindon's room was upstairs. Top floor," said Charlie.

The smell of cats was overpowering. Pooch gave a half-hearted bark as they climbed upward. At the top of the stairs, the combed ceiling made it difficult for Charlie and Harry to stand upright. The wallpaper hung in tattered strips. There were three doors, side by side.

Charlie indicated the one at the end. "It had two windows because it was on the corner. Lindon liked that."

He jimmied the lock with the aid of one of Mirabelle's few remaining hairpins. The door swung open to reveal a room so tiny that the four of them could only just fit in together. On the floor was a bare mattress. Some sheet music was laid neatly on a makeshift table and beside that a cracked washstand. Next to the fireplace there was a coin-operated electricity meter and a rickety chair serving as a clotheshorse. A few pairs of Lindon's socks were hung over it to dry. A couple of morning rolls had grown stale on the mantelpiece, beside a small glass bottle of lumpy milk. Vesta put her hand to her mouth. Pooch settled on the floorboards and rested her head on her paws. They all waited as Charlie crouched down to fiddle with the meter and a harsh yellow light snapped on.

"That's better." Mirabelle stood directly under the bulb and examined the street guide. "Are you all right, Vesta?" she asked.

Charlie laid a comforting hand on Vesta's shoulder.

"I'm fine," she said.

"We'll do our best for Lindon, I promise. So this is our starting point. We work outward from here. What time is it?"

Harry moved under the light and held up his watch.

"Is that a Rolex?" Charlie asked.

"Yes."

"Time! What's the time?" Mirabelle insisted.

"Almost ten past midnight," Harry confirmed.

"Good. We need to cover about half a mile in each direction, thoroughly. From here, east as far as London Spa at least. Going north, about half a mile beyond The Angel. To King's Cross going south—which is more than half a mile, but there are a lot of potential buildings down there, garages, small warehouses and such like. I think we should go the extra ten minutes." She held the map up so everyone could see. "We'll make our way along each street, fan out as we go and check whatever we can."

"I don't know this area at all," Harry admitted.

"It's pretty rough," Charlie confirmed. "A few of the boys live in this neighborhood. I heard some stories. We better be careful."

"Do you think we'll be safe?" Vesta asked.

"We'll be fine, sugar. Don't worry. I just don't think we should split up, is all."

"Agreed," said Mirabelle. "It'll take us longer but it'll be safer, and Pooch might pick up something we can't."

* * *

The streets were so quiet that on occasion they could make out owls hooting in the nearby squares. This had once been a beautiful, rather grand area, Mirabelle realized, and felt a pang of sadness. They decided to start toward the south and made for King's Cross Road, checking the byways to either side one after the other. There were numerous dead ends. Outside a grimy tenement on Lloyd Baker Street, Pooch stopped and barked, but it soon transpired that there was a fox lurking around some rubbish bins.

On Farringdon Street, closer to the station, they passed a brothel in the doorway of which a couple of morose-looking girls leaned. Occasionally a line of garages or commercial premises ran off the main road and there was a flurry of excitement in the group. These kinds of properties were the most likely hiding place.

"Really," Harry said in an exasperated tone, "she could be anywhere."

Mirabelle said, "I know, but we have to try."

"I don't understand what we're trying though," Harry hissed. "We're just wandering about. Rose could be in this building or that one or that one over there. We can't check people's houses. All these flats and bedsits—there are thousands of them."

"Yes, she could be anywhere. You're right. We might even have passed her by. We might never find her. We're just hoping to get lucky, Harry. If we get lucky and we find Rose, we lower the risk of Blyth killing her tomorrow rather than handing her back. That's what you want, isn't it—to lower the risk? I mean, for the time it's taking, I'd say it's worth it."

"Of course," Harry mumbled. "Sorry."

Close to King's Cross the streets grew busier. The group excited a few "Good evening's" from passersby now and then. At the station they bought cups of tea and bacon rolls from an all-night stand. Pooch perked up when Harry flung two sausages her way and the men smoked cigarettes to warm up, waiting for Vesta and Mirabelle to use the station's lavatories. Then they decided to turn back and make their way to Lindon's bedsit from the west.

"Clerk-en-well." Charlie sounded out the word phonetically.

"Clerkenwell." Vesta corrected his pronunciation with her clipped vowels.

Sometime after two, sustained only by the rapidly decreasing contents of Harry's hip flask, they came across a makeshift shed on a bombsite near Cruikshank Street. It was their most promising find so far. Harry sneaked across the rough ground and peered through the small window.

"There's someone inside," he hissed. "Rose," he called gently. "God, it's freezing here. She could die of hypothermia. Rose."

Charlie opened the door, which was unlocked. Inside, he put his hand on the shoulder of the sleeping figure who snapped upward instantly, growling, with a makeshift knife in his hand.

"Whoa! Take it easy, brother," Charlie insisted as the old man lashed out weakly without fully rising from his bed. "We're looking for a girl," he explained. "Do you know of any girls around here? Kept somewhere?"

"You sick or something? The whores down by the station not good enough for you, nigger?" the tramp spat.

"This girl is missing, man. Take it easy. She's a white girl being held somewhere. You know anything about that?"

The tramp focused on the figures crowding the doorway to his shed. "What the hell are you doing here in the middle of the night?" He began to laugh. "Are you vigilantes? D'you want to kill me, do you? I've got nothing now. Not nothing. I was a soldier. I fought for this bloody country! I don't care anymore. I don't care what you do!"

They moved on to The Angel where they spent a fruitless hour checking premises alongside the canal. Sleek water rats scuttled out of cracks in the brickwork and slipped into the dark water, and Pooch had to be restrained from diving after them.

By half past three they were heading east. The dog was exhausted. She kept stopping, and Vesta had to haul her along on a taut lead until at last Pooch simply sat down on Rawstorne Street and refused to move.

Harry gathered her into his arms. "She's bloody heavy!" he complained. "I can't believe I bought you sausages, you fatty. Mirabelle, do you think we should jump ship?"

"We haven't finished yet, so no, I don't," Mirabelle replied abruptly.

Charlie curled an arm around Vesta's shoulder. She was starting to flag, too. He was impressed by how methodical she'd been all night. It was Vesta who checked in the corners, Vesta who consulted Mirabelle at the perimeters of the search to figure out if it was worth extending another street or two. They hadn't missed a square inch of the territory.

"Perhaps," Vesta said, "we should go back and leave Pooch in the car."

As they wandered toward the car they could see signs of life. The day started early on this side of town. Near London Spa on Tysoe Street a market was setting up. Harry put Pooch down on the ground, grateful for a rest. The dog sniffed with renewed interest. The marketplace was a haphazard affair, as if entirely by chance people had brought boxes and baskets of random bric-a-brac and home produce. Shadowy figures were unloading goods from vans parked on side streets, and as the men passed Harry's Aston they stopped and stared, not quite believing their eyes.

A couple of younger fellows were peering through the driver's window as Harry strode toward the car. One of them kicked a tire.

"Hey!" Harry shouted. The men moved on reluctantly.

"All this stuff is nicked, isn't it?" Vesta grinned.

It was still well before dawn. Gradually, as if some tide had washed it all up, the pavement was covered with radio parts and old candlesticks, leather belts, nylon stockings and tins of biscuits. A black-and-white television took pride of place next to a rusty bicycle. Two young boys laid out a selection of watches on a thick piece of sacking. A woman sat on a bollard on the street corner with two baskets of jam jars—gin on one side and old-fashioned moonshine on the other. From her pocket a sheaf of ration books protruded. Slowly but surely people appeared from nowhere on bikes, on foot and by car, dressed in shabby coats and scuffed shoes. They perused the stalls with hushed voices, exchanging money for goods almost by sleight of hand. There were over a hundred people now thronging the square, but, unlike most markets where the stallholders shouted about their wares, here the transactions took place in near-silence.

"What d'you want, darkie?" An old man squared up to Charlie.

"He's with me," Harry stepped in. "We're looking for someone."

"You won't find none of your mates round here," the old man sneered. "This is a respectable neighborhood!"

The men were distracted by the sound of Pooch barking farther up the road. Vesta and Mirabelle were at the far end of the square where tinned goods and butcher's meat wrapped in paper parcels were being sold from the back of a van.

"Shush, Pooch," said Vesta.

The parcels, she supposed, must contain black-market cuts. Pooch yelped as Vesta tried to drag her away.

"Let's go for a walk around the square," Mirabelle suggested. "At least it'll distract her."

"She can't be hungry," Vesta said.

Pooch resisted and strained at the leash, trying desperately to get back to the butcher's van, but Vesta tutted loudly and left no slack on the lead.

"You need to be strict with dogs, don't you? I think this one might have had it too easy. I thought the upper classes trained their animals! Looks like we're going to have no luck tonight," she sighed. "And tomorrow, gosh, not even tomorrow, *today* we have to get back to work. Brighton seems a long way away."

"Rose has to be around here somewhere." Mirabelle looked upward. The windows around the square were dark. Pooch continued to bark loudly.

"Oh, for heaven's sake," said Vesta.

Harry and Charlie caught them up.

"There's a guy with three big copper pans back there. Good ones, too. He can only have got them from a proper kitchen," announced Charlie. "I asked him the price but he said to make an offer."

"Do you want copper pans?" said Vesta.

"Hell, I might as well get something after being up all night."

A pale yellow light seeped through the fanlight at number seventeen. Harry lit a cigarette and offered the last of his packet to the others as a man opened the front door. Pooch jumped up, almost knocking the lighter out of Harry's hand.

"Pooch! Get down!" Vesta snapped. "What's wrong with you?"

Harry took a deep reflective draw on his cigarette and began to walk toward the black door as the fanlight darkened again.

"Jesus," he whispered. "Do you think she's in there? Bring Pooch! Come on, girl! Is this what you're excited about?"

But as he turned he saw Mirabelle heading in the opposite direction toward the market. She had fallen into step behind the man who'd just walked out of number seventeen. He was on the pavement farthest away from the stalls. He didn't so much as cast a glance at the market.

"He's not scruffy enough," Vesta murmured as it dawned on her. "Look at his shoes. They're expensive."

The man drew keys from his pocket and unlocked a small van with blacked-out windows. It was parked directly opposite the butcher's van. He fired the ignition and as the headlamps came on, the two stallholders at the end of the street put their hands to their eyes.

"Oy, mate! We can't see!" one of them shouted.

Vesta gave Pooch her head and the spaniel, suddenly all muscular energy, tore off in Mirabelle's wake.

"Excuse me?" Mirabelle peered in the driver's window and knocked.

The man ignored her. Pooch launched herself at the rear doors as the van pulled into the street. Mirabelle tried to catch the handles as they passed but Pooch jumped up once more and knocked away her hand. Pooch was now racing alongside the vehicle as it headed for Merlin Street.

"Harry!" Mirabelle called as she ran toward the Aston. "The keys!"

Harry fumbled in his pocket. "Oh God," he cursed as Mirabelle opened the passenger door and jumped into the car.

He threw himself into the driver's seat and the Aston's engine roared to life.

In the rearview mirror Mirabelle could see Pooch barking on the pavement and Vesta and Charlie trying to catch her as Harry's car screeched off, tires smoking. Harry was chewing his lip, focused completely on the road. At the end of Merlin Street they looked frantically left and right. In the darkness they caught a glimmer of light on the road heading toward Skinner Street.

Harry accelerated toward it. The Aston's engine was more than a match for the commercial van and they made ground as it turned up St. John Street, in the direction of Lindon's flat. The van tried to speed up but in only a minute Harry and Mirabelle were right on its tail.

"What will I do now?" Harry shouted.

"Get him to stop!"

The van suddenly veered left toward Sadler's Wells and Harry went for the kill. He smashed into the rear and forced the vehicle straight into a lamppost. The Aston jolted to a halt.

"There! I'll get him!" Harry yelled, springing from the car.

Mirabelle fumbled for the door and scrambled onto the pavement. Harry was hauling the driver into a pool of lamplight. He was a big fellow but he seemed to be in shock. Still, in a split second he landed Harry an upper cut which sent the boy reeling.

Mirabelle made for the van doors. The Aston was in the way. The left door was ajar but only slightly. It was enough.

"Rose?" Mirabelle called. "Are you in there, Rose?"

There was an incoherent mumbling and some small movement. Mirabelle squeezed into the back of the van and crawled quickly toward the noise, ignoring the shooting pain in her wrist as it took her weight. "Rose?"

The girl was there all right, tied up so she could scarcely move, blindfolded and gagged. Mirabelle ripped off the blindfold and helped Rose to sit up. She was wearing a stained white shirt and a pair of what looked like men's trousers. Mirabelle worked the knot of the rope around Rose's ankles. She was barefoot and her skin was icy.

Mirabelle could hear the grunts of the men outside. Rose began to kick and twist, and the rope loosened.

"Come on!" Mirabelle dragged the girl to the van doors. "We've got to get out of here."

Rose's knees buckled, and Mirabelle put an arm around her. Together they climbed gingerly out of the van, Rose scrunching up her eyes in the yellow streetlight. Mirabelle removed the gag. The poor girl was filthy. Lines of mascara encrusted her cheeks and her hair was matted, but she managed a brief smile. She caught sight of her cousin and shouted, "Harry!"

Harry looked up and the van driver took his chance with a powerful left hook that felled the boy. Rose moaned and began struggling with the ropes that were still around her wrists. There was no time for that. Mirabelle pushed the girl into the Aston and made for the driver's seat, clambering over the bonnet as the van driver wiped blood from his face and looked round seemingly recalling something. He ran to the front seat of the van and emerged with a determined expression.

Mirabelle started the Aston and backed it up about three feet before the engine cut out. The van driver raised his hand, and she realized with horror that he was holding a revolver. Time slowed. She tried the engine again. He moved his arm to the right, aiming, Mirabelle realized all too slowly, for Rose. I haven't been up all bloody night just to get this poor girl shot, she thought. In a split second, without thinking, she was back out on the pavement. She threw herself at the gunman with such force that he lost his footing, tried to steady himself and tripped over Harry's legs. The gun went off. Mirabelle felt a stinging sensation, but she somehow kept her balance and kicked him hard. Someone had told her once that her legs were the strongest part of her body. That made sense now. She hauled up her skirt and kicked the man again with all her might, then stamped on his wrist until he dropped the weapon. After what had happened last year she wasn't going to pick it up. She kicked the revolver away and collapsed on the pavement, gasping for breath. Her shoulder exploded with pain, and she tried not to look down. She could feel warm liquid dripping down her skin inside the tweed jacket. She couldn't faint now. She was aware of Rose running past her toward Harry . . . followed by a pair of expensive shiny shoes tearing down the street into the distance . . .

Mirabelle closed her eyes, allowing herself a single moment of relief, before there was the sound of running and Charlie and Vesta rushed to her side. She looked up gratefully. They were both out of breath.

Across the street Harry got to his feet, spitting out blood-flecked phlegm and swearing profusely. Pooch jumped up on Rose, delighted.

"Vesta!" Mirabelle said urgently. She pushed Charlie away and pulled Vesta close. "Listen to me very carefully. You need to take charge. Right now. We don't have long. Harry has to take Rose back home, do you hear? And he mustn't stay with her. He's to drop her off. She's to say she escaped under her own steam from somewhere else—*not up here*—and she's to clear Lindon, like we discussed. *She mustn't mention Paul Blyth.* Not a word. That's really important. Tell Harry the car has to go to the club—Miles can fix it up and hide it for a while."

"But, Mirabelle, you're hurt. Seriously hurt."

Mirabelle took a deep agonizing breath. She was worried she was going to pass out. "Vesta, no questions. You have to do what I tell you. You have to trust me. Do you understand?"

Vesta looked at Charlie, who gave her a nod.

"Whatever you say," she promised.

"We haven't long. Someone will have heard the gunshot. The police'll be here any moment and we don't want a bloody inquest like last year. Charlie has to disappear now. It's too risky for him. If they place us all together it puts everyone in more danger. Get me to the hospital and say that we went to the market looking for something or other—just you and me. Something for the office. Make it all as true as you can, whatever you say. That way there'll be less to remember."

"A typewriter?" Vesta tried. "That green typewriter I wanted."

"That'll have to do. We got into a fight with some ex-serviceman over what he was charging. We bought it off him, then walked away, and he followed us in his van. He crashed it in a fury and took the typewriter back. I tried to fight. Nothing about Charlie, and nothing about Harry and Rose. We don't know them. They don't know us. Not from here, anyway. They mustn't be able to tie it together."

"But why . . ." Vesta's voice trailed off. She was close to tears.

Mirabelle was shaking violently now. She couldn't feel her legs. Intense heat pulsed through her followed by a wave of icy cold. She grabbed Vesta's hand. "I've realized what it was about the policeman . . . You have to get everyone out of here *now*."

"The policeman?" Vesta sounded as if she was speaking to a child. "Do you think the police are after us? Do you think they did for Lindon?"

Mirabelle shook her head. The pain was excruciating. She laid her hand on Vesta's forearm to reassure her. "Wrong policeman," she mouthed.

Then it all went black.

28

Every normal person is only normal on the average.

4:50 a.m.

Vesta tried to make out the notes the matron had taken about Mirabelle's injuries but the angle of the clipboard made it difficult. The woman's appearance was terrifying—not a scraped-back hair out of place and a graying complexion made more severe by the harsh lighting in the corridor. The uniform made her look unreal, like part of the hospital itself—as if she'd been installed with the Victorian plumbing. Squinting, Vesta checked the time on the watch that rested upside down on the matron's flat chest. It was almost an hour since they had arrived.

"It's family only, I'm afraid," the nurse said firmly. There was a hint of Yorkshire in her accent. "You can't go in."

"Mirabelle doesn't have any family. I'm her family. I'm the only one who really knows her." Vesta felt this was an overstatement the minute she said it. Mirabelle remained very much a mystery. "I'm the only one who cares about her, you see," she persisted.

The matron's brown eyes remained expressionless. Her

air of cold efficiency was frustrating. "Doesn't she have someone else? Anyone else? A blood relation?"

Vesta shook her head. "I'm it," she said.

The matron took a moment to consider the plea. It was a difficult situation but it wasn't the first time someone unrelated to a patient appeared to be their only friend. Not by a long shot. "Look, I can't let you in if you're not family. Sometimes, well, people pretend. But we can't have that, can we? Miss Bevan and you are clearly not related. Couldn't be." Vesta crossed her arms and suppressed a flare of anger. "In any case, visiting isn't until the late afternoon. And Miss Bevan will only receive visitors then if she wakes in time. You won't be able to go in for hours."

Vesta felt suddenly tearful. Her lip quivered. "What do you mean, if she wakes in time? She was fine until she passed out. She's all right, isn't she? I mean, I know she was shot but she'll be all right."

The matron sighed. "It may take her a while. She's had a terrible shock. Sometimes the body simply cuts out. We don't know when she'll wake up. The doctor has seen her and we've dressed her wound and made her comfortable. Now she needs to rest. It may be later today or it might take longer."

"I'll wait," Vesta said. "I don't want her to open her eyes and there's nobody here." She turned away and slumped into a seat beside the wall.

"We don't allow . . ." Matron started but the look on Vesta's face stopped her. "Look, let me see if I can find out any more. I can't promise anything. We can't just let you sit here once we've started our rounds. But you can wait until I come back."

"Thank you," Vesta nodded. She wasn't such a bad old stick, after all.

After no more than five minutes the matron appeared again at the end of the corridor. She's a fast worker, thought Vesta, until a policeman in uniform came through the swing doors behind her. The woman was still holding the clip-board. Vesta tried to breathe evenly. Mirabelle's instructions had been clear but they ran contrary to everything Vesta believed—to lie to an officer of the law. Despite her brush with Hove's uniformed division the year before, there was something about the dark wool suit and chrome buttons that made Vesta want to go into awkward details and spill every last bean.

"This is Constable Brewer," the matron said. "This is Vesta Churchill who was with the lady who was shot." She turned tail and walked smartly back up the corridor.

"You were with Miss Bevan?" the officer asked, reaching for his notebook and taking down Vesta's name. "V-E-S-T-A?"

"Yes, that's right," Vesta replied. "And Churchill as in Winston." So far, so good.

"Just the two of you?"

"Yes. And the fellow with the gun."

"What happened exactly, Miss Churchill?"

"Well, we went up there for some office supplies." Vesta kept her voice even.

"To Clerkenwell at four in the morning? Two women on their own?"

She'd just have to make it sound as plausible as she could. "Mirabelle and I work together in Brighton. McGuigan & McGuigan. It's a debt recovery office. We'd tried to find what we wanted in the shops, of course. We'd been trying for weeks. We were up in London seeing friends. We stayed at Duke's Hotel on Saturday night. But we still couldn't get hold of some of the items. We wanted a particular make of typewriter. It's American. We couldn't find one anywhere. Then someone mentioned this market, up by London Spa on Sunday night."

"Who?"

"Sorry?"

"Who mentioned the market?"

Vesta thought for a second. "I don't know," she said. "Someone Mirabelle knew. Maybe someone at the hotel."

"So"—the policeman noted down her reply—"it was a black-market item you were buying, Miss Churchill? The market up there is all off the ration and stolen goods, you see."

"We hadn't exactly realized, Officer. I mean, it was apparent there was black-market stuff up there once we arrived, but we were just after some office supplies—a new typewriter specifically. No such thing as a black-market typewriter, is there? It was stupid of us to go up there, I know. It started as a lark."

"London Spa is no place for ladies at that time of night. Tysoe Street especially," the officer commented.

"We realized that when we arrived but, well, he had what we wanted."

"Who did?"

"I don't know his name. He was on one of the stalls. Quite tall. Brown hair, I'd say. It was difficult to see properly in the dark. He was ordinary-looking—not particularly handsome or anything. I think he was from London. He sounded as if he was anyway."

The officer reviewed his notes. "This fellow was tall with brown hair, and not particularly handsome, speaking with a London accent."

"Yes. He was wearing a demob suit." Vesta felt inspired. It was easier to be vague than she anticipated. She fluttered her lashes. "It was so dark. It was difficult to tell his hair color, too, with the hat. I'm sorry. I think it just got out of hand. He took offense. I don't really know why but he just lost his rag. We left with the typewriter and we were walking back into town and he obviously had second thoughts and followed us in his van. Then it turned out he had a service revolver."

The policeman sighed heavily. "Yes. A service revolver," he repeated. "We've retrieved that. And the van, which appears to have been run off the road by another vehicle. There's a large dent in the rear of the vehicle. But you were walking, you say?"

"Yes. That's how we got up there and that's how we were going to get back. There wasn't another car or van or anything. It's very quiet up there at that time of night. I think he was trying to scare us. He screeched down the street as if he was going to run us over. He might have been drinking, I suppose. Then he ran off the road and got out shouting and waving his gun. He grabbed the typewriter from us. You know, perhaps the van already had a dent in the back . . ."

"What was he shouting about?"

"'Bloody women,' that's what he kept saying." Vesta thought it was going rather well.

"I see. So he took the typewriter back, Miss Churchill?"

"Yes. He said it was worth more because it was the new model. Mad as a hatter—he'd already sold it. Anyway, Mirabelle shouted at him, they got into a tussle and he shot her."

"Over a typewriter?" The officer's voice was laden with sarcasm. "In the early hours? Can you recall the make of this foreign typewriter?"

"It's an IBM Model A," Vesta quoted from memory. "Green casing. They're supposed to be awfully good. I wish we hadn't gone now." Vesta heaved what she hoped was a sigh of remorse and kept her eyes wide. "Do you think you'll catch him?"

The officer didn't reply. It was patently unlikely. "I'll need your contact details, Miss Churchill."

Vesta reeled off the office number and address.

The constable narrowed his eyes as he took down the number. "Brighton. And you couldn't get this typewriter anywhere closer to hand?"

"No," said Vesta. "They're in short supply and our old one was dicky." That really was true.

The constable closed his notebook and replaced the elastic band. "Van was stolen," he commented, slipping the pencil into its slot. "We'll come back when Miss Bevan wakes up and see what she remembers. They'll ring us as soon as she's compos mentis. In the meantime, we'll ask around. It's not much to go on, really."

"I'm sorry," Vesta said. She sounded as if she really meant it! "That guy is dangerous. He must be crazy."

"Sounds like it, Miss Churchill." She didn't seem like the wayward type, this girl, albeit she wasn't very observant. And from what he could make out the other woman was perfectly respectable. What on earth had induced the two of them to head toward Clerkenwell in the middle of the night for a typewriter was a mystery. Occasionally nice, normal people did something stupid. He'd check with the Brighton station to see if these women were what they seemed. The unconscious one wasn't going anywhere. Not for a while.

"Might I ask if there was drink taken?" the constable tried. "On your part?"

"Mirabelle and I?"

"Yes."

"We'd had a couple of cocktails with our dinner. Just a normal amount."

"In town?"

"Feldman's. The jazz club."

"And the man with the gun?"

"Well, of course he may have been sozzled. It was hard to tell, really, what with all the shouting and commotion. It would explain a lot though, wouldn't it?"

"And you hadn't seen him before?"

"Never."

"Right, Miss Churchill." There was nothing else to ask. "We'll be in touch. We may have to talk to you again. I've never known the like. Over a *typewriter*."

The girl didn't flinch. "It is a mystery, isn't it? A bit like a thriller," she said.

As the officer walked back up the corridor Vesta watched him carefully, half expecting him to turn around and ask something utterly impossible or to slap on the handcuffs and take her to Scotland Yard. But he ambled through the doors at a steady pace. She waited. She grinned. Mirabelle would have been proud of her, and if he checked them out with Brighton (which no doubt he would) he'd find they were clean—squeaky clean, in fact.

Vesta rested the back of her head on the cold wall and closed her eyes for a few moments. It was difficult to sleep upright, but she wondered if she might manage it today, when no more than a minute later, one of the doors swung open. It was Harry. He was carrying a basket. He looked much younger under the neon lights, about twelve years old, actually. The truth was, Vesta was glad to see him, but she shooed him away as he approached.

"What are you doing here?" she whispered. "You've just missed the police."

"I wanted to check how Mirabelle was," Harry whispered back. "And to give you two this to say thank you." He handed over the basket. A puppy's face peeked over the edge beside a bunch of flowers wrapped in newspaper. "The puppy's name is Pong. You and Mirabelle were just terrific. I didn't think we'd get Rose back. But we did, and it's because of you. Is Mirabelle recovering?"

"You shouldn't be here," Vesta scolded, although her heart wasn't really in it. "Mirabelle doesn't want us all tied together. The police have gone now but you'd better leave. The nurses might mention something if they see you. Mirabelle has figured something out, you see."

Harry didn't move. Pong whimpered and settled down in the basket.

Vesta couldn't help smiling. The puppy was adorable. "Is Rose all right?" she asked.

Harry's face broke into a grin. "She kept asking for gin!

'Course we couldn't go out for a gin—she'd have been recognized. We had to make do with some brandy I had in the car. She'll be fine. We've got it all worked out. I dropped her near her place. She's going to say she was held somewhere near Victoria by a taxi driver. She's going to be in shock and give a general description. That's the plan. She won't be able to identify where she was held. She'll say she just ran off blindly and didn't notice anything until she got to the station. She said the main thing was that she had to have a bath. She was in a frightful mess. She thinks you and Mirabelle are the most glamorous people she ever met. When I got home I went to my room but I was too jumpy," he admitted. "I just couldn't sleep."

"If you're out you'll miss the news though."

"The news?"

"That Rose has been found."

"Oh, yes. Don't worry. I can feign surprise. Joy, even." Harry gave a convincing grin. "I'll be back before breakfast. Where's Charlie?"

"He went to work as usual." Harry seemed mildly bemused at the idea of going to work at all. He might be in shock, Vesta realized, as she waved him off.

For what seemed like ages Vesta perched on the uncomfortable chair, her head resting on the wall. The sense of isolation was overwhelming. It was after six when the matron returned. Vesta handed over the flowers to be arranged in a vase by Mirabelle's bed. They still wouldn't let her in.

"She needs rest now," the matron insisted. "You can ring, if you like, later on. I'm sure Miss Bevan wouldn't want you sitting here exhausted for hours. That's no good to anyone. And you can't have an animal in the hospital. Where did that come from?"

Vesta said nothing, and the matron did not press the point. The nurses changed shifts and the wards sprang to life. The puppy dozed in the basket. By seven Vesta shrugged.

There was nothing for it, she realized, as she got up, tucked the basket under her arm and quietly left the building.

Outside, the sun was rising and a fog-softened light illuminated the busy street. The air was full of early-morning baking aromas, which Vesta, unusually, had no appetite to investigate. A small black nose protruded from the basket as she bobbed down the steps and hailed a taxi.

"Victoria, please," she said to the driver.

"No dogs," he insisted.

"Oh, for heaven's sake! It's only a five-minute ride and he's just a puppy."

The cab driver looked unconvinced.

"I'll pay an extra shilling."

"All right then, but there better be no mess."

In the cab Vesta felt as if time had telescoped. Had it really only been a weekend? Lindon had died two days ago, on Saturday. She had met Charlie only yesterday. Since Friday she'd passed the longest and the shortest days of her life, and most definitely the strangest. Vesta put a hand on the puppy's head and stroked him gently as she gazed in the direction of Belgravia and wondered if Rose would be able to keep her side of the bargain.

As she alighted at Brighton station just before nine Vesta felt removed from the world. Monday morning usually entailed tea and toast, a catch-up with Mirabelle and a long day of paperwork. She walked straight to the office. Pong had fallen asleep on the train and now, as she lifted him gently out of the basket, he woke, wriggled out of her hands and scampered around the floor with enthusiasm. Vesta filled a saucer with water and wondered what puppies liked to eat. She had just decided to nip to the butcher's to investigate when the office door opened and a man's face, pink from the cold, peered in.

"Is Miss Bevan around?"

"I'm afraid not. Can I help you?"

"Name's Bill Turpin." The man held out his hand. He

was wearing an ill-fitting suit—navy with a moss green tie—but Vesta liked him on sight, or rather she would have if she hadn't been so distracted. "I'm to start today," Bill announced. "I'm the new collector."

"Oh yes. Of course. Mirabelle mentioned you. Miss Bevan has had . . . an accident, I'm afraid," Vesta said. "I don't expect to see her this week, Mr. Turpin."

"Nothing serious, I hope?"

"She damaged her collarbone while she was in London."

"I did that once when I was a kid. Fell out of a tree. Takes a while to heal. Hey, who's this little fella?"

The puppy was sniffing Bill's shoes.

"Pong."

"Spaniel, isn't he? Cor, that's not a kind name. Pong. Who lumbered him with that?"

"That was his name when he arrived. Perhaps we should call him something else."

"I'd say so. Lovely animal, he is." Bill squatted on the floor and picked up the puppy. "Aren't you, little fella?"

"Mr. Turpin," Vesta seized the moment, "I wonder if you might like to help with, er, Pong. Do you know what puppies like to eat, perhaps?"

Bill regarded Vesta as if she was an idiot. "Eat? Well, you need to get some dog biscuits, something for him to chew and the odd bit of meat. Nothing fancy. The butcher will do scraps. He only looks about three or four months old. Probably needs a bit of training."

Vesta reached into the petty cash box and drew out some coins. It felt good to be in charge again or at least to be efficient. "Well, how would you like the job? Why don't you take him with you? I'm sure he could use a walk. Here's your call sheet. There are fifteen addresses on there to get you started. The amounts owed are in this column. Take whatever payments you can and arrange to call back if need be. You know to note down everything?" Vesta handed over a pencil.

Bill looked at the sheet. "I'll bring the money back when I'm done," he said.

"If you want to rename him, please do," Vesta said. "I think it's family tradition that it starts with a P. His mother's called Pooch, you see."

"Is he the office dog?"

"I suppose he is."

Pong licked Bill's shoes and chewed on the laces. The man's eyes shone with delight. "Beautiful color. Silky coat. I reckon you're a Panther, boy, aren't you? A black panther. You're a tough one underneath it all, I'll bet."

Pong looked up, his brown eyes wide and his bottom wriggling from side to side.

"I had thought of getting a proper dog—maybe a Doberman pinscher," Bill said with a twinge of regret as he scooped the puppy into his arms. "But we'll see how you do. Miss Bevan didn't say nothing about an office dog. You just need to grow a bit, don't you, fella? Time will see to that. They're loyal, they are, spaniels, and that's the main thing. Do you have a lead?"

Vesta shook her head.

"Leave it with me. I'll look after it."

"Thanks, Mr. Turpin." She smiled and gave him a key to the office. "So you can let yourself in and out."

"Oh, of course," he said. "Thanks."

After Bill departed Vesta slipped off her shoes. I could just lay my head down for a moment, she thought. I should probably try to eat something and then ring the hospital to check on Mirabelle. The desktop felt solid and reassuring against her cheek. The office was quiet. The puppy was gone. The money would come in later. She wondered what the papers would say about Rose. There would be nothing until the afternoon editions and perhaps not even then. Vesta's eyes slowly closed, her breathing evened and before she knew it she let out an unladylike snore and passed into a very deep, much-needed sleep.

29

We dance round in a ring and suppose,
but the secret sits in the middle and knows.

Mirabelle opened her eyes and had no memory of who she was or where she was for what felt like several minutes. The room smelled of bleach and the walls were painted pale blue. The bedsheet was starched and turned down so tightly she could scarcely move. For a second or two she wondered if Jack was here. Had they been in a bombing raid? Had the flat come down? Then she remembered all at once that it was 1952, the war was over and Jack had been dead for almost three years. Her heart sank and she let out a cry. Then, out of what seemed like blue sky, an older lady in a nurse's uniform leaned over the bed.

"Miss Bevan," she said, "you're awake. I'm Sister Dalby."

Mirabelle tried to speak but her mouth was too dry. The nurse lifted a glass of water to her lips. As Mirabelle moved the pain kicked in. It surged across her upper chest and down one arm. When she looked down she could see she was bandaged to the wrist and there was something binding her chest and holding her head in place. It all ached.

"Has anyone been to see me?" she asked.

Sister Dalby nodded, a twinkle in her eye. "Missing

your fancy man?" she said. "He'll be waiting for you, I'm sure. And there's been the police, of course, and a colored girl. She phoned last night and again this morning."

"Vesta?"

"Yes. She's very concerned. You have a good friend there. We need to get some food into you, Miss Bevan. Before anything else. You've had a nasty shock."

"Could I see the newspaper? I'd like to keep up with what's going on."

"Well, that's ambitious, I must say. Newspapers, indeed, with a shattered collarbone! I'll fetch some milk pudding to start with and then we'll see."

The pudding tasted good. The sweetness melted in Mirabelle's mouth, an unaccustomed pleasure as she usually didn't enjoy sugary food. Sitting upright, the details of everything that had happened came into focus.

"How's your memory?" Sister Dalby asked.

"Hazy," Mirabelle lied. "I don't remember getting here. Or much about being in London. I remember leaving the office on Friday. And seeing Vesta on Saturday."

"The police want to ask you about what happened on Sunday night. They've checked a few times."

"How long have I been here?" Mirabelle asked.

The nurse took Mirabelle's pulse and checked the pace against her watch. "Well, you seem quite excited to be up," she commented. "You came in early on Monday morning and now it's Tuesday."

"What time is it?"

"One. You can have a cup of tea and then nothing until you eat with the rest of the ward at five. I've informed the doctor and he'll examine you on his evening rounds."

"Did you get the bullet out?"

"It went straight through."

"Clean?"

"Very."

"And the pain?"

"I can give you something for that. Medicine round is at two. How bad is it?"

Mirabelle didn't reply. She didn't want to take anything that would make her drowsy. She had to keep on her toes. Her eyes wandered to the cupboard beside the bed.

"We've all your things, don't worry. The jacket and blouse have been laundered. You'll be able to patch them, I imagine."

"Thank you."

When the sister left the room Mirabelle pulled back the covers and swung her legs over the edge of the bed. She wobbled slightly as she went to the cupboard. She was already anticipating the pain in putting on her jacket. At least she hadn't worn a pullover—getting anything over her head would be impossible. She slipped on the tweed skirt and her shoes. Somehow, the heels helped her concentrate. She took off the hospital smock and, deciding to abandon her blouse, slowly got her arms into the jacket and did up the buttons. The bandaging was almost completely hidden. Across the room there was a tiny mirror fixed to the wall. By tortuous degrees she fixed her hair and pinned on her hat. With her handbag over her least painful arm Mirabelle crept to the door. The hospital corridor was populated with nurses and the occasional patient, the latter mostly wheelchair-bound. She drew herself up as tall as she could and stepped out, closing the door behind her as if she had been visiting a patient. The smell of cottage pie and the clink of plates being cleared came from the wards. A burst of laughter sounded as two nurses rounded the corner, gossiping. Mirabelle followed the exit signs. Approaching the front door, she saw a policeman heading toward her. She paused and turned aside, pretending to rummage in her handbag.

Outside, it was sunny and cold. The fog had lifted and it felt like spring, the air as clear as gin. Mirabelle felt like skipping down the steps. She was in the East End. Of course, she would have been sent to St. Bartholomew's.

She quickly realized walking into town was out of the question. The pain was sharp now and she had too far to go. She gingerly raised a hand to hail a cab.

"Duke's Hotel, St. James's," she instructed the driver.

As Mirabelle alighted at Duke's she realized how little money she had left. Still, she tipped the driver before making her way gingerly up the steps and through the hallway to the bar. At least she could sort it all out now—she'd find out what had really been going on.

"Is he in?" she checked with the barman. He nodded in the direction of the back room.

Mirabelle knocked sharply on the black door. Eddie opened it.

"I thought you chaps were caught up in Eastern Europe," she said smoothly. "The Russian Menace and all that. What the hell are you doing with this little domestic drama in Belgravia?"

Eddie ushered her in. "Actually, I was stationed in East Berlin for a while but then it turned out we had trouble closer to home. How did you know we were involved, Mirabelle?"

"The policeman . . ." she admitted. "The policeman. The one outside Blyth's house and the one over in Marylebone. Same man, I think. He was on the short side, you see, so I couldn't help but notice. And, looking back on it, the fact that you came to my room and buttered me up with all those details about Harry. And you apologized to Vesta for being thoughtless about Lindon. There was that, too. You've been tied up with this all along, haven't you? Lindon's death is the department's fault."

"You noticed the policeman?"

"I didn't realize at first, to be honest, but then it dawned on me. You better have a bloody good reason for killing that boy, Eddie."

"Lindon?" Eddie sank into his seat. "Yes. Frightful mess."

"So we aren't strangling young men in police custody now? Is that what you're saying? It wasn't deliberate?"

"No. We do. We strangle people in police custody. You know we do. It's only that this time we didn't mean it. It wasn't properly authorized. A bloody shambles. We weren't sure how to deal with Blyth, you see. The kidnapping of Rose caught us on the back foot. We were gearing up, batting around some options of what to do with him, and then, *wham*, suddenly Blyth had snatched her and we didn't know the parameters anymore. With Lindon it was only supposed to be a scenario, but the wires got crossed and the agent took it on as a job. A bloody eager beaver and damned bad luck. Of course, then I had that on my plate, as well. As soon as you turned up I realized you'd uncover what was going on more effectively than anyone I could bring in. You were practically on the inside already. I knew you'd track down the girl if it killed you. Then we'd be able to deal with Blyth, which is what we were really after. If it's any consolation, the man responsible for Lindon Claremont's death has been punished. . . ."

"Oh, don't tell me. Rapped his knuckles, have you? But he won't face charges, of course. It was murder, Eddie."

Eddie lifted a glass to his lips. It looked disconcertingly as if he was drinking water. "He was a rogue agent, Mirabelle. He exceeded his orders. It happens sometimes. Very regrettable, of course, but do I have to remind you we're not the bad guys? We're the British Secret Service and we made a mistake in the course of our operation. It's regrettable, but there you are. You were a tremendous help. I'm sure that's what you'd want, of course. We're very grateful. Forgive me, I'm forgetting my manners. Would you like a drink? May I get you something?"

Mirabelle didn't reply. She wasn't finished yet. "What the hell did Paul Blyth do anyway? From your perspective you should be giving him a medal, surely, not putting him away?"

"Oh, it was all over the papers this morning. Once we knew Rose was safe we got on with it. He's a pornographer. He'll never live it down. His wife has already booked tickets for herself and the girls. New York, I believe. They're going to have to go farther west than that to get away from it though. The trial will be sensational. Some of the books he was selling were national treasures. He nicked them from the library at the British Museum among other places. Absolutely shocking. And national treasures are our department, to some degree."

Eddie turned over a couple of newspapers. The front pages showed photographs of Paul Blyth being taken into custody.

Mirabelle scarcely looked. "Yes, but what was Blyth actually up to? The Secret Service doesn't put pornographers under surveillance, Eddie. That's a police investigation in the normal run of things. I've never known us to mobilize over a book, for Christ's sake. You just found something to put him out of operation in terms of whatever he was really up to. Like prosecuting Al Capone for tax evasion. Paul Blyth is a pornographer, but that's the least of it. Is he a spy?"

"You know I can't tell you. It's classified. Let's just say that there are some forthcoming events that are of national importance and Paul Blyth was endangering those events."

"Selling information? That was always his field."

"I don't think he was selling it, actually. He was more of a security leak. He's not a traitor. Well, not exactly. You have to trust me, Mirabelle, it's a serious matter and we had to deal with it. I was glad when you walked into Duke's on Friday. I knew you'd help and you have."

Mirabelle stared at Eddie coldly. She was thinking: what was the best she could get?

"I think you owe Lindon's family something," she said. "His parents have lost their son. Actually, I think you owe me something, too. I got Rose out and I didn't blow your cover. You'll be damned lucky if I don't blow it now. I've been shot, you know."

"Oh, Mirabelle, you're a patriot. You wouldn't blow anything. You and I know that perfectly well."

"Or perhaps you'll strangle me in a police cell somewhere and make it look as if I killed myself?"

"Don't be ridiculous."

"I want death by misadventure," she snapped.

"Pardon?"

"At Lindon's inquest. It hasn't happened yet, has it?"

"It's tomorrow morning."

"I don't want a verdict of suicide. It's not fair to his family. I want a verdict of death by misadventure."

Eddie shook his head. "Well, that's not going to look very good, is it?"

"It's the best offer I'm going to give you."

"What? From a washed-up secretary turned debt collector? Come on, Mirabelle. The department is grateful, I'm sure, but . . ."

"I'm a washed-up secretary turned debt collector who just got you out of a fix."

"Is this your idea of revenge?"

"No. But it's the nearest Lindon's going to get to justice, isn't it? My friend lost one of her closest people. We can't bring him back—that's what she wants. That's what the boy's family will want. Look, I know the truth can't come out, Eddie, but you have to do something. Something to allay their loss, just a little."

Eddie thought for a moment. "And if I organize the verdict you'll keep everything quiet?"

Mirabelle nodded. "I'll go back down to Brighton this afternoon." She held out her hand and adopted a distressed tone. "I'll give a statement to the police before I go.

About the shooting. It's so difficult to see on a dark night, and the lampposts on the north side of town are in a state of terrible disrepair. I can't remember much, of course. Because of the shock."

The police would accept that; Mirabelle could be trusted to be convincing. Eddie held out his hand. "Good girl," he said. "Death by misadventure it is, if it makes things tidier for you. As a favor, a one-off. I might remind you that you've signed the Official Secrets Act and I don't have to do this. I'll organize your interview at Scotland Yard. And if it's any consolation I'll make sure His Majesty is made aware, Mirabelle."

Eddie picked up the phone.

Mirabelle studied Brandon carefully as he organized a car and a driver. Generally, as far as she recalled, people said the department would be grateful or perhaps the country would be grateful. As far as she could remember she'd never heard anyone say the king himself would be informed. The person to whom Paul Blyth had been supplying information was clearly someone special. But who was it? Often these things were about asking the right questions. She wondered momentarily why Eddie was stationed within spitting distance of Buckingham Palace. Then she remembered something about Eddie's expertise—he spoke French like a native. During the war he had run several resistance cells in Normandy. Although these days, of course, France was less important, politically speaking. Her eyes scanned the room. She noticed a Paris street guide and a map of New York on a side table below the obligatory portrait of the king. Paul Blyth hadn't been selling information, Eddie said. He wasn't a traitor *exactly*.

At that moment Mirabelle knew why Eddie was stationed here. By the palace. With guidebooks for Paris and maps of New York.

"Oh my, I don't envy you dealing with that," she said in a low voice.

"Pardon?" Eddie hung up.

"The Duke of Windsor, Eddie. That's what this is all about, isn't it? Our abdicated king. Paul Blyth has been passing information to the Duke of Windsor, hasn't he? Keeping him in the loop. News of home after his exile. Not just news, but the inner workings. He and the duchess are living in Paris mostly and visiting New York. But never London, of course. And Blyth has been sending His Grace information. That's what Blyth's good at. He probably saw it as his duty, if the duke inquired. You must have been frantic. Paul Blyth has some of the best inside contacts in the world—he could find out anything. That's why you're stationed at Duke's—it's palace business. You couldn't get much closer without being inside Buckingham Palace itself, and that would never do—it'd be as good as an admission. You're on secondment of a kind and you had to stop him any way you could."

"Nonsense, Mirabelle! Don't be silly. What an imagination you have." Eddie downed the last of his drink.

Mirabelle smiled. "We secretaries have little else to which to turn our minds," she said. "I can see why you can't have a leak of that nature. Gosh, how dreadfully embarrassing." She let the statement hang in the air. "Still, I understand why the duke might have encouraged Blyth. It's not exactly treason, is it? Tricky. There's life in the old dog yet, eh? You chaps must have been walking on eggshells. Windsor feels he's a right to know—family business. But you couldn't have that, could you? Blyth's not a traitor. Not exactly. That's what you said. And he told you to piss off, didn't he, when you asked him to stop? So you had to do something. I'm right, aren't I?"

She knew Eddie had two options. Either he had to shoot her or he had to up the game. Jack had always respected Eddie. It takes a lot to fly crooked, he had said. She mustn't underestimate him. Still, she wasn't entirely sure which way he would go, so she felt a huge weight lifting from her pain-racked body when Eddie didn't smile and nodded slowly.

"Mirabelle, I think we ought to do something better for Mr. Claremont and his family. It's only fair. And if you don't mind I think it would be best if we put you up here, at our expense, until things are sorted out. I'll arrange a room upstairs and a nurse, shall I? You're injured, after all."

"What a good idea," Mirabelle said. Checkmate. "Why don't I go and give my statement to the police and you see what you can come up with for the Claremonts? And I'll need something to wear, Eddie. This jacket has a bullet hole."

30

From infancy on we are all spies.

Vesta had tidied the office. It had been a frantic couple of days and she didn't know what she would have done without Bill. Each day he'd come back with his calls fully completed. He even dropped off the money at the bank on the way. He'd posted her letters to Charlie and looked after Panther. She had simply kept the office ticking over, filling up the daily ledger and trying to avoid looking at Lindon's battered sax case. It's worse than a corpse, she thought, stomach lurching. A constant reminder. Seeing Mirabelle shot had shocked her. The revelations in the newspapers had given plenty of food for thought. The inquest was coming up and she had no idea what was going to happen. The only good thing was that she was in love.

It was Charlie she was thinking about when the telephone cut through the tranquillity. She'd been thinking about him a lot and had turned down a date with one of her gentleman callers the day before. He'd been most put out. She checked the clock on the wall—half past four—and considered leaving the phone to ring. It was almost time to close after all, but the shrill tone was annoying so she picked up the receiver.

"McGuigan & McGuigan Debt Recovery."

"Vesta, you're there. Is anyone else with you?"

"Mirabelle! You're awake! Are you allowed visitors? How are you feeling?"

"I'm fine. I've left the hospital, actually. I've got a room at Duke's—a suite, in fact. Are you coming to the inquest tomorrow?"

"Yeah, of course."

"Well, get the train as soon as you can and stay here. There are two bedrooms and it's all been paid for. Shame to waste it, eh? How's the office?"

"Mr. Turpin is marvelous. He's sorting everything out wonderfully. I've given him a key. Mirabelle, you know they've arrested Paul Blyth on indecency charges?"

"I know. The police interviewed me this afternoon. They haven't joined the dots, though, so well done, Vesta. You managed it perfectly."

Vesta glowed with pride. "Thanks," she said, chucking the files on her desktop into the cabinet and grabbing her coat. "I'll get the train."

The suite at Duke's was beautiful. The door to the bathroom opened onto an enormous tub with a shower over it—a feature that made the hotel popular with Americans.

Mirabelle was sitting on the sofa when Vesta arrived. The nurse had just finished changing her dressing and was giving her some painkillers before she left for the evening. Instruments lay disinfecting in an enamel bowl.

Vesta smiled and closed the door. It was raining outside and her coat was drenched. "Wow," she said. "I've never stayed anywhere as swanky as this before. It's much nicer than the last room I had."

She noticed that Mirabelle looked thinner. Her face looked drawn, but she wasn't too pale.

"You need to sleep tonight, Miss Bevan," the nurse scolded

as she packed up her things and made to leave. "Rest is very important. Good night."

"Yes, I think I shall. I'm very tired now. Good night."

Vesta wanted to fling her arms around Mirabelle, but she knew it would be too painful.

Mirabelle's eyes sparkled as she gestured toward a decanter on a side table. "Would you?" she asked. "A whisky with a little water?"

Vesta grinned. She took off her coat and hung it up to dry. Then she got to work. "How does it feel?" she asked as she handed over the tumbler.

"Well, I'm exhausted, to be honest," Mirabelle said flatly. "And my shoulder's painful. But the tablets will help."

"Will you come to the inquest tomorrow?"

"Yes, of course. I'd like to be there." She paused a moment and then said what she had to say, or at least as much as she could. "I've taken some advice, Vesta. On what's likely to happen."

Vesta considered a whisky but poured herself a brandy and soda instead and flopped into a chair. "What do you mean?"

"The inquest. I dug around to see what we can expect."

"Well, they can't say anything other than he's innocent, can they? I mean, Rose has cleared his name."

"Yes. And they'll rule death by misadventure. There's a case for suicide but his innocence will call that into question."

Vesta looked serious. "Lindon wouldn't have killed himself. You know he didn't."

"No. And death by misadventure means there was no negligence or crime. They simply don't know what happened, Vesta. There can be no blame. I wanted to warn you. I thought you'd be relieved that they're unlikely to say it's suicide."

Vesta nodded. "I see. But who killed him, Mirabelle? I assumed you knew."

Mirabelle had been dreading this question all afternoon. She told herself it was better if Vesta didn't know what had happened quite apart from the information being embargoed under the Official Secrets Act. She had got the best she could negotiate and this was the price. Still, she'd promised the girl not to hold anything back and now she had to.

"I don't know who did it. I don't think we'll ever know." She let the statement sink in. "Sometimes there just isn't anything to go on. I'm sorry. We don't get back the people we lose, Vesta. And the truth isn't a jigsaw—sometimes too many pieces are missing and there's no way to find out what actually happened. But this afternoon I heard something wonderful—good news, really. People have been terribly shocked by Lindon's death and there's a foundation which wants to commemorate him."

"What do you mean?"

"They're going to endow music scholarships for kids from the East End."

Vesta looked at her questioningly.

"It'll be called the Lindon Claremont Trust. For music lessons. Not only jazz. Any kind of music. It's for disadvantaged children—any kid with talent will be eligible. They're going to set up practice rooms in a primary school in Bermondsey. They'll teach from there and the kids can put on concerts."

"In Southwark? Near us?"

"Yes. Just off Jamaica Road. In memoriam."

An image of Lindon flitted across Vesta's mind—a skinny kid, on a sunny summer evening, kicking around a bombsite because he wasn't allowed to practice his sax at home.

"He'd love that," she said, and her eyes filled with tears. "Oh, and his mama will love that, too."

"They haven't told her yet. They're going to announce it tomorrow after the inquest."

Vesta took a handkerchief from her bag. "But I wish none of this had happened."

"I know. But life goes on, Vesta. Truly, that's the main thing. Life goes on."

The women ordered dinner in the room, and after they'd eaten Vesta helped Mirabelle into bed. It wasn't even nine o'clock, but the pain was exhausting. Alone, Vesta sat on the sofa. There were some books and magazines on a table. It was dark outside. There was nothing much to see. Mirabelle was such a mystery, but she trusted her. Life had to go on. Vesta slowly picked up the phone and dialed.

"Is Charlie there, please?" She waited. "Charlie? Is that you? . . . I'm over at Duke's . . ."

31

You can do a lot if you're properly trained.

Wednesday, February 6, 1952

At least it wasn't raining. Vesta and Mirabelle had taken a cab to the Coroner's Court on Horseferry Road. The ornate Victorian brick building stood out on the street—one of the few unaffected by bomb damage. The hearing was due to start at nine in a gloomy meeting room overlooking a yard. Mirabelle shooed Vesta to sit with Mr. and Mrs. Claremont at the front. She wondered if the other woman Vesta kissed on the cheek was Mrs. Churchill. It seemed likely. For herself, Mirabelle took a place at the back. When you sit at the back of a room you can keep a check on everything. Eddie slipped into the end of the row at the last minute and whispered in Mirabelle's ear, "Sorry. It's been a busy morning."

Mirabelle pretended to ignore the comment but kept an eye on him. She was pleased he'd agreed to the idea of the Lindon Claremont Trust. Granted, he'd had little choice.

The judge didn't take long. Two policemen and a pathologist gave evidence, and the minister from the First Evangelical Church delivered a character reference. Then

Detective Inspector Green took the stand. He confirmed Lindon's innocence in the Bellamy Gore abduction and said that since this had become apparent his team had made an arrest for the submission of false evidence that had led to Lindon's being taken into custody. Barney, Mirabelle thought.

"It's most regrettable that we didn't realize Mr. Claremont's innocence earlier. Had we done so, this tragedy might have been avoided. The police were grievously and maliciously misled," he said, "which is not to belittle our duty of care."

The verdict a foregone conclusion, Mirabelle watched the reactions in the courtroom as it was read out. There were no journalists, she noticed. Eddie must have seen to that. The Bellamy Gores were also absent, though that was definitely for the best. The judge pronounced death by misadventure. There was a murmur. Mrs. Claremont burst into tears and Mrs. Churchill put an arm around her friend's shoulders. Then the judge announced the news about the Lindon Claremont Trust. There was a smattering of applause and more crying. Several people in the front rows hugged each other. Eddie nodded at Mirabelle. She nodded back. He placed a small brown paper package on her lap, and then, without saying a word, got up and slipped out of the courtroom. It was, Mirabelle thought, the best to be made out of a bad lot.

Outside, Mirabelle lingered as the crowd dispersed. Vesta introduced her mother and Mrs. Claremont.

Mirabelle extended her condolences, gazing straight into Mrs. Claremont's eyes. At least, she thought, she got something good out of this terrible mess.

In the silence Vesta's mother regarded Mirabelle. This well-dressed lady was not what she had had in mind after all the trouble Vesta had landed in last year. She'd envisaged someone far more racy.

"Come back with us," Vesta insisted.

Mirabelle shook her head. "I need to lie down. Why

don't you stay on for the weekend, Vesta? I'll look after the office tomorrow. You take some time off."

Vesta managed a smile. She looked a little tired, Mirabelle thought. Perhaps she hadn't slept well.

"Yes, stay, Vesta," Mrs. Churchill boomed, liking Mirabelle more every second.

"Perhaps just for the weekend," Vesta agreed. "I'd like to hang out with some of Lindon's friends."

Mirabelle gave the girl a hug. "It was lovely to meet you all," she said.

As she walked up Horseferry Road, Mirabelle took Eddie's package from her handbag and tore a corner of the brown paper. Inside, there was a set of lock picks. Cheeky bugger. She slipped them into her bag.

"Mirabelle!" a voice called.

She turned. Detective Superintendent McGregor was jogging toward her.

"Oh, were you inside? I didn't see you." Mirabelle realized suddenly that she was glad he'd been there.

"I stayed at the door, but I wanted to see everything," he admitted. "Nasty business. Wanted to come and pay my respects, I suppose. We turned him over, after all, and I knew it would mean a lot to you, and to Vesta, of course. Are you all right, Mirabelle?"

"I got into a scrape and injured my collarbone," she said.

"Yes, Green told me. You really ought to be more careful. Clerkenwell in the middle of the night! What were you thinking? Are you going back down to Brighton?"

Mirabelle felt her heart sink. She didn't have anywhere else to go. "Yes. Later."

"I don't suppose you fancy some lunch? We could catch the train together afterward. It's a treat to be up in the big city. We could make a day of it—somewhere swanky—if you're up for it."

Mirabelle smiled and McGregor put out his hand to hail

a cab. It was only as they set off that they saw the news boards. THE KING IS DEAD. Mirabelle felt suddenly as if she was a very small speck on a huge map.

McGregor asked the driver to stop and spoke to a news vendor. The morning editions had missed the announcement but the afternoon editions were on their way. McGregor returned to the taxi and removed his hat. "Poor Princess Elizabeth," he said.

"Queen Elizabeth," Mirabelle corrected him.

McGregor was taken aback. "A girl? And at her age? That's a lot to take on."

Mirabelle looked back down the street. The fog was clearing. The Claremonts and the Churchills were heading in the opposite direction—she could just make out the outline of Mrs. Churchill's dark coat. She could have asked for more, she realized, much, much more. But it was too late now.

"I'm sure Her Majesty will be fine," she said. "She has good people looking after her." It was over. There would be no more inquests and no more inquiries. It was time to get back to normal, whatever normal was. Mirabelle took a deep breath. Sometimes it was difficult to let go. "So, Detective Superintendent," she smiled, "shall we push the boat out? Lunch is it? Why don't we treat ourselves and go to the Savoy."

AUTHOR'S NOTE

Writers of novels live in a strange world where what's made up is as important as what's real. It's not always easy for the people around us! Thanks are due to my husband, Alan, and my daughter, Molly, and the rest of my lovely family and friends who indulge my hare-brained ideas, administering strong coffee and encouragement by turns. On top of that, I have a sterling professional team from Jenny Brown Associates and from Polygon—realists with notions, every one. A special thanks to my editor, Alison Rae, with whom I giggle a lot, and to Jenny Brown, my intrepid agent, who deals! Thanks are also due to the many, online and off, who've taken an interest in what Mirabelle and I get up to. I hope you enjoy this one as much as, if not more than, the last.

Follow Sara@sarasheridan and Mirabelle @mirabellebevan
Like Sara on Facebook: facebook.com/sarasheridanwriter
www.sarasheridan.com

The quotations and misquotations used to open each chapter are taken from the following sources: "Society has the teenagers it deserves" is from "Like its politicians and its war, society has the teenagers it deserves" (Joseph B. Priestley); "A scout is never taken by surprise" is from "A scout is never taken by surprise; he knows exactly what to do when anything unexpected happens" (Robert Baden-Powell); "I'm not against the police; I'm just afraid of

them" (attributed to Alfred Hitchcock); "Dogs are my favorite people" (Richard Dean Anderson); "Manners are
love in a cool climate" (Quentin Crisp); "Sometimes I
miss the spirit of London but it's a very gray place"
(Claire Forlani); "The best thing for a case of nerves is a
case of Scotch" (W. C. Fields); "It's not always the cold
girls who get the mink coats" (source: me, Sara Sheridan,
from *The Pleasure Express*, said to me once in conversation by Professor Neil MacCormick); "Be careful going in
search of adventure—it's ridiculously easy to find" (William
Least Heat-Moon); "Difficulties are things that show a person what they are" (Epictetus); "Friendship doubles joy
and divides grief" (from "Friendship doubles our joy and
divides our grief," Swedish proverb); "Jazz is black classical music" (Wynton Marsalis, but also Roland Kirk—no
one seems sure who said it first . . .); "True genius resides
in the capacity for evaluating uncertain, hazardous and
conflicting information" (from "True genius resides in the
capacity for evaluation of uncertain, hazardous and conflicting information," Winston Churchill); "Be ready for
opportunity when it comes" has been said in different
ways by many people, but I like "The secret of success in
life is for a man to be ready for his opportunity when it
comes" (Benjamin Disraeli); "Home is birthplace ratified
by memory" (from "Home is one's birthplace, ratified by
memory," Henry Anatole Grunwald); "Anybody singing
the blues is in a deep pit yelling for help" (Mahalia Jack-
son); "People don't go to church to find trouble; they go
there to lose it" (James Brown); "All you need is a tiny
foothold and the rest will take care of itself" (Branford
Marsalis); "No party is any fun unless it is seasoned with
folly" (Erasmus); "The key is to let go of fear" (Rosanne
Cash); "Love is a game that two can play and both win"
(Eva Gabor); "An ill thought leaves a trail like a serpent"
(from "An arrow may fly through the air and leave no
trace; but an ill thought leaves a trail like a serpent,"

Charles Mackay); "Go where there is no path and leave a trail" (from "Do not go where the path may lead, go instead where there is no path and leave a trail," Ralph Waldo Emerson); "We're all detectives in life" (from "You're right on the money with that. We're all like detectives in life. There's something at the end of the trail that we're all looking for," David Lynch); "Chess is ruthless" (from "Chess is ruthless: you've got to be prepared to kill people," Nigel Short); "Experience is the most brutal of teachers" (from "Experience: that most brutal of teachers. But you learn, my God do you learn," C. S. Lewis); "Expectation is the root of all heartache" (attributed to William Shakespeare); "The team with the best players wins" (Jack Welch); "Every normal person is only normal on the average" (from "Every normal person is, in fact, only normal on the average," Sigmund Freud); "We dance round in a ring and suppose, but the secret sits in the middle and knows" (Robert Frost); "From infancy on we are all spies" (from "From infancy on we are all spies; the shame is not this but that the secrets to be discovered are so paltry and few," John Updike); "You can do a lot if you're properly trained" (from "It's all to do with the training: you can do a lot if you're properly trained," Queen Elizabeth II).

QUESTIONS FOR READERS' GROUPS

1. Was Vesta's family what you might have expected?

2. What is the modern equivalent of a Soho jazz club?

3. Should Mirabelle have settled with Eddie Brandon on the Claremonts' behalf? Would Vesta have?

4. What makes Mirabelle and Vesta good friends and good partners?

5. Do you have a favorite character in *London Calling*? What attracts you to that character?

6. What details in *London Calling* did you find especially evocative of the book's period?

7. Is patriotism an effective motivation for the characters' choices and actions?

8. Can any man live up to Jack Duggan's memory?

Don't miss the next intriguing MIRABELLE BEVAN MYSTERY
by Sara Sheridan

ENGLAND EXPECTS

Coming soon from Kensington Publishing Corp.

Keep reading to enjoy a preview excerpt . . .

PROLOGUE

Murder is always a mistake.

8 a.m., Monday, 22 June 1953, Brighton

Joey Gillingham got off the train and checked his watch. He had a little time before the meeting. Walking out of the station, he angled his hat to keep the sun out of his eyes. It was another scorcher. The paving stones were radiating heat already and Brighton felt summertime sleepy compared to the buzz of Fleet Street. Joey tucked his newspaper under his arm and headed toward Cooper's. It was on his way. Then he remembered the new place and changed direction. Three schoolgirls walked lazily down the road in front of him sharing an illicit Kula Fruta on their way to school and squinting into the sunshine. Sticky red liquid dripped off their fingers and left stains like blood smears on the pristine cotton of their summer blouses as they jostled to make sure the division was fair. Joey smiled. Oxford Street was quiet. A new sign glinted in the sunshine. Seymour's Barber. He'd heard this new place was good. The glare obscured the interior of the shop from easy view as Joey poked his head through the open door. Three black leather chairs with chrome trim faced three square mirrors. The only nod to the old butcher's shop that used to be there was the heavy block at the back, now displaying an array of Brylcreem advertisements. *For the clean smart look.* The air smelled of carbolic soap.

Joey shrugged his shoulders and entered. Why carry on to Cooper's when this new place looked all right? The shop was cool—a relief already. It took his eyes a moment to adjust.

"Morning, sir."

"A shave and a trim?" Joey inquired. "I ain't got long."

"Certainly, sir." The barber was dapper in a white jacket. The man looked like he could land a decent right hook. He had the shoulders for it, but his eyes were too kind to make him any sort of fighter. Joey always said it was a pitiless profession.

The barber motioned him toward the first chair. "Some tea?"

You never got that at Cooper's. It was a smart move. Not long off the ration, tea still felt like a luxury. "All right, yeah, thanks." Joey hung up his hat, took the newspaper from under his arm, and settled down. "Short back and sides. None of your Teddy Boy nonsense," he instructed.

The barber grinned. "You heard about that, then?"

"A mate told me."

"I can do you a military cut if you'd prefer, sir."

"That's it."

Joey checked his byline. When he saw his name in print it always reminded him of his English teacher at primary school. The bitch had said he'd no facility for words. "I don't know what will become of you, Joey Gillingham. All you care about is sport," she had sniffed disapprovingly. Joey smiled. Well, he'd done all right, thank you very much, Miss Prentice. More than all right. Joey Gillingham boasted several thousand readers, or at least the *Express* did. And he was about to up his game. In an hour he'd be onto the story of his life, and if he cracked it he'd be able to screw a bonus out of the paper.

Joey liked the money but he liked the recognition just as

much. He'd been lucky to stumble across something big. Something out of his usual field. Brighton was like that—small and friendly. A bloke with his eyes open could pick up a lot. Joey reflected that "investigative journalist" sounded better than plain old "journalist" or "sports reporter." An investigative journalist wasn't a hack.

The barber swept a spotless napkin around Joey's shoulders and fastened it in place. Then he combed Joey's hair. Every customer was important to a new business. That was why he opened early—he always caught one or two blokes on their way into work or on their way home from the night shift. It was worth getting up sharp.

"Right. Tea," he said and disappeared into the back room to boil the kettle.

"Milk and one, if you've got it," Joey called and turned his attention back to the paper as the sound of heels on paving stones, squabbling children, and distant traffic on the main road floated through the open door.

Joey didn't see the man. He paused for only a second at the doorway, checking right and left up Oxford Street. There was nothing distinctive about him—just a regular fellow sporting a shabby demob suit like thousands of others, with a worn brown hat cocked at an angle. No one noticed as he slipped inside out of the sun. As the man walked swiftly to the chair, Joey licked his finger and turned a page. This inattention was a particular irony because Gillingham was known to be unforgiving when a boxer didn't see a knockout punch. "You gotta be on your guard all the time. Gloves up," he always said. "It takes less than a second if your opponent's on his game."

The man was a professional. He moved silently, pulling a flick knife from his pocket and smoothly slicing the journalist's jugular without hesitation. There was no time for Joey to call out as his blood spurted onto the mirror. His body stayed upright in the chair. It always went too quickly, the assassin thought, as he calmly took off his jacket—a crimson spot had marked the sleeve. Coolly he folded it over his arm, dipped the knife into a glass of blue fluid on the old butcher's block to clean it, and, checking the corpse's inside pockets, took what he wanted. Then, glancing in the mirror to alter the angle of his hat, he sauntered into the sunshine toward the station as if nothing untoward had taken place.

1

It takes an unusual mind to analyze the normal.

Mirabelle Bevan swept into the office of McGuigan & McGuigan Debt Recovery at nine on the dot. She removed her jacket and popped the gold aviator sunglasses she'd been wearing into her handbag, which she closed with a decisive click. The musky scent of expensive perfume spiced the air—the kind that only a sleek middle-aged woman could hope to carry off.

Bill Turpin arrived in her wake. Like Mirabelle, Bill was always punctual. He was a sandy-haired, reliable kind of fellow. At his heel was the black spaniel the office had acquired the year before. Panther nuzzled Mirabelle's knees, his tail wagging. Mirabelle patted him absentmindedly.

"Glorious day, isn't it?" she said. "Who'd have thought it after all the rain? It feels like a proper summer now."

"Nasty business on Oxford Street," Bill commented, picking up a list of the day's calls from his in-tray and casting an eye down the addresses. "That new barber's."

"Tea, Bill?" Mirabelle offered without looking up.

"Nah. Always puts me off, does a murder." His voice was matter-of-fact. An ex-copper, he was used to dealing with crime of all stripes. As a result, Bill Turpin never panicked handling the ticklish situations that he encountered at McGuigan & McGuigan. Debt collection was a tricky business but it wasn't as bad as policing Brighton.

"A murder?" Mirabelle glanced over.

"Yeah. A slasher. First thing—just after eight. The fellow went in for a trim and got more than he bargained for. Poor blighter had his throat cut. I met the beat bobby on my way in. A murder right on the edge of Kemptown. It's five minutes from Wellington Road, nick and a spit from Bartholomew Square. There were coppers everywhere. They think the victim's from London—some hack."

"Did the barber do it?"

"Nah. Poor fella was in the back. Just about had a fit when he found his customer dead in the chair. Must've only taken seconds. In and out while the bloke was reading his newspaper. They reckon it's got to be a professional job."

"Did they find the weapon?" Mirabelle inquired out of habit.

"Well, it was a barber's shop, wasn't it? There were razors everywhere, though the murderer might have brought his own. Bit early to say. Where's the girl?" Bill looked around as if he'd only just realized that the third member of the office staff was not at her desk.

Mirabelle leaned over to peer out of the window. There was no sign of Vesta Churchill on the street below. "Oh, she'll be on her way," she said indulgently. Vesta was habitually late but she was a hard worker. Efficient to a fault, especially with paperwork, so what was ten minutes here or there?

"Well, I suppose it's nothing to do with us," Bill said, his mind still on the murder.

Over the last two years several murders had been personal to the employees of McGuigan & McGuigan. The day-to-day business of the firm was humdrum, but now and again Mirabelle had found herself embroiled in what Bill referred to as "police business." It was the upshot of being curious, she thought, and all three of them were certainly that. Bill was the most recently recruited to the firm and he had fitted in so well precisely because he was nosey. Nosey in a nice way, but still it was true—they were all curious about the world. More than that. McGuigan & McGuigan's little team was a tremendous minder of other people's business. Bill still acted like a policeman a lot of the time. He was slower to make assumptions than Vesta, and that, Mirabelle told herself, provided balance.

"They reckon the fella was down to see the boxing," Bill said as he slid the day's paperwork into his inside pocket. "Poor sod wrote a sports column for one of the red tops." He shrugged and then whistled for Panther. "Sounds like he got on the wrong side of someone serious, doesn't it? Well, see you later." He tipped his hat and sauntered out.

Mirabelle looked at the kettle. There was no point in making tea for one. When Vesta arrived they'd brew a nice pot and chat about the weather. She lifted the first paper off the pile in front of her, sighed, and wondered what kind of person followed a man into a barber's shop to slit his throat.

2

Most men's greatest achievement is
persuading their wife to marry them.

Vesta Churchill walked down Lewes Road hand in hand with Charlie. She tried not to speak. People stared enough as it was without the pair of them arguing in public. Still, she hadn't finished what she wanted to get out, and now her dark eyes flashed dangerously.

Charlie lifted his free hand and flicked a flake of pastry from his collar. He'd made croissants for breakfast in an attempt to seduce her. Unexpectedly Vesta was not to be won over by pastry—not in this matter. Initially he'd tried chocolate éclairs brought home from the kitchens of the hotel where he worked. After that there had been a Victoria sponge. Vesta, after all, was English. But no dice. She'd turned him down flat. Not only that but she seemed furious.

"Don't you see?" she hissed. "We can't get married, Charlie. Think what would happen."

Charlie had been thinking about exactly that. He'd looked at houses all over Brighton's suburbs and calculated that with the savings he'd put by, they'd have enough for a good deposit somewhere really nice, or, if Vesta insisted, they could keep living in the bedsit and save up till they could buy a place outright. The acquisition of a mortgage, after all, might be too American.

"I want to make it official, baby," he said. "I love you."

"It's a big change," Vesta started. "If we get married, everyone will expect things."

"It doesn't have to be different," Charlie cajoled her. "We live together as it is. You'd just be Mrs. Charles Lewis, is all. Your mama would be happy if we got married, wouldn't she? And so would mine. We're living in sin, baby."

"But I like living in sin." Vesta kissed him on the cheek. "Can't we leave it at that?"

It turned out Charlie couldn't. He'd done his best to move things on as far as possible. He'd relocated from London to Brighton, leaving his well-paid job at the Dorchester for a worse-paid one at the Grand, and he'd found a bar where he could play now and then—a dive in the Lanes that had jazz nights on Tuesdays and Thursdays. They weren't a bad bunch of guys. At first he'd taken a room near Queen's Park, but then a bedsit had come up on the same floor as Vesta's in the lodging house where she stayed on Lewes Road. It was closer to town and there was a connecting door that they could unlock to double their space and effectively live together.

He still hadn't got over having to negotiate his tenancy. Vesta, uncharacteristically, had let him do the talking though she'd stood beside him while he made the arrangements with her recently widowed landlady, Mrs. Agora. He railed against asking the old lady for permission but there was no other way. Vesta hadn't been prepared to lie.

"Is this how you people do things?" Mrs. Agora had grumbled. Her hair was set in such a permanent wave that it appeared to be made of sheet steel riveted to her head.

"Do you mean Americans?" Charlie inquired.

Mrs. Agora didn't flinch. "You coloreds, is this how you do it? Because it ain't entirely respectable. Not here."

Charlie swallowed the words that initially sprang to his lips. "Well, ma'am," he drawled, affecting his most charming accent, "I've asked Vesta to tie the knot and she won't have me. So I guess living together will have to do. If you'll let me move in."

Mrs. Agora sucked furiously on a Capstan with her Revlon-red lips, all the while regarding the young couple as if they were a fairground curiosity. "You sure about this, dearie?"

Charlie held his breath and felt a wave of relief as Vesta nodded curtly. He couldn't be entirely sure of her when it came to this—something was going on with Vesta and he couldn't figure out what it was.

Mrs. Agora stubbed out her cigarette. She folded her arms. Vesta was a regular payer and never any trouble. This fellow had been hanging around for months. He'd fixed the wiring at Christmas when it had gone on the fritz. "You'll do odd jobs now and then?"

"With pleasure." Charlie grinned. "And, lady, if we're still here next Christmas I'll bake you a cake."

"I suppose you can't say fairer than that." The old girl felt herself relenting. Lewes Road wasn't that respectable, after all, and the fellow was certainly handy. "Any trouble and you're out, mind. I can't stand a ding-dong. Not since Mr. Agora passed."

Charlie gave the widow his solemn word and only later inquired of Vesta what on earth a ding-dong was.